Stormy Valley
Ruthie Ambrose

JUKEBOX
& BELMONT
PRESS

Jukebox & Belmont Press

Published by Jukebox & Belmont Press
Pittsburgh, PA

ISBN: 979-8-9994576-0-8

Printed in the United States of America

First Edition

Contents

To the ones who carried the weight, even when no one else could see it.

1

Sheriff's Demons

The fog curls around my cruiser like ghostly fingers, shrouding the winding roads of Stormy Valley. I grip the steering wheel, knuckles white, eyes scanning left and right. The streets lie deserted, but something waits just beyond sight.

I take a sip of coffee, wincing at its bitterness. It reminds me of darker days, a haunting echo of past sins. The acrid taste stirs memories of nights spent in alleys, chasing a high that always left me lower than before.

"Pull yourself together, Johnny," I mutter, shaking off echoes I thought I'd buried.

But they cling like cobwebs, impossible to fully brush away. One slip, one moment of weakness, and I could tumble back into that abyss. The thought chills me more than the morning mist.

The radio crackles, jolting me from my reverie. "10-32 at the old Thompson property. Possible break-in."

My pulse quickens. The Thompson family's ancestral home stands as a symbol of explosive emotions and turbulent histories woven into the very fabric of our town for generations.

"Copy that," I respond, my voice steadier than I feel. "En route."

The cruiser lurches forward as I press the accelerator. The fog parts reluctantly, revealing glimpses of Stormy Valley's familiar landmarks, a patchwork of memories and regrets. The general store where I once shoplifted to feed my habit. The alley where I passed out, lost in a haze of my own making. Old Man Wilson's barbershop, its striped pole a ghostly sentinel. The abandoned movie theater, its blank marquee staring, accusing.

As I approach the Thompson property, a familiar silhouette emerges through the haze. Mike Langley, his stout frame unmistakable even in the murk. Our eyes meet, and a simple nod passes between us, carrying years of shared history—triumphs and failures distilled into that fleeting gesture.

"Headed to Thompson's?" Mike's voice carries, gruff yet laced with concern.

"Yeah," I reply, my throat suddenly dry. "Got a call. Disturbance."

"Johnny," He says, his voice cutting through the quiet hum of the cruiser, "you ready for this?" His words linger, a silent acknowledgment of the looming darkness awaiting us at Thompson's.

As we set off, gravel crunches beneath my tires. The old farmhouse looms in my mind, a specter of past sins and unresolved tensions. My thoughts race, each scenario grimmer than the last.

The landscape shifts around us, trees whispering ancient secrets as we draw closer to our destination. The air thickens with the scent of damp earth and decaying leaves, evoking hidden graves and buried secrets.

I can't shake the feeling that I'm driving toward something I'm not ready to face. But when have I ever been ready? Life doesn't wait for you to steel yourself—it comes at you, relentless and unforgiving.

Gravel shifts beneath my boots as I step from the cruiser, the sound echoing in the eerie stillness. Fog hangs thick, a suffocating blanket over the Thompson property. The silhouette of the old farmhouse looms faintly against the gray backdrop. Tires grind behind me as Mike's cruiser pulls up. He steps out, his face etched with concern.

We approach the house, its weathered facade a patchwork of peeling paint and rotting wood. The porch boards sag visibly with age, brittle underfoot, their creak reverberating through the fog.

We move forward in tandem, years of partnership guiding our steps. No words are needed—a glance, a nod, and we're in sync. The fog swirls around us, playing tricks on my eyes. For a moment, I swear I see a figure in the mist, but it vanishes as quickly as it appeared.

"You take the barn," I mutter, gesturing toward the dilapidated structure on our right. "I'll check the house."

Mike nods, his hand instinctively drifting to his holster. As he moves off, I fear that I'm sending him into danger. The thought feels like an icy warning, chilling the air around us.

I approach the farmhouse, each step measured and cautious. The porch groans under my weight, its creak echoing through the air. My hand hovers over my gun, ready for anything.

"Sheriff's Department," I call, my voice sounding hollow in the oppressive silence. "Anyone home?"

The only response is the creaking of the old house settling into its foundations—or is it? As I reach for the doorknob, I swear I hear a faint whisper, the echo of a long-buried secret.

I step inside, floorboards murmuring beneath my feet. The air is thick with dust and neglect, each breath a reminder of abandoned dreams. My eyes scan the dim interior, searching for signs of life or disturbance.

In the living room, an empty whiskey bottle catches my eye from the corner. My mouth goes dry, a phantom burn searing my throat. The urge to drink, to numb the fear and doubt, surges like a tidal wave.

I force myself to look away, focusing on the task at hand. But the temptation lingers, a persistent whisper in the back of my mind.

"Show yourself," I mutter, more to shatter the silence than anything else.

A sudden crash from upstairs jolts me back to the present. My hand flies to my gun, heart pounding.

"This is Sheriff McCallister," I call, my voice steadier than I feel. "Come down slowly, hands where I can see them."

The house holds its breath, waiting. So do I, caught between past and present, duty and doubt.

Michael's familiar footsteps echo behind me, a steady rhythm in the unsettling silence. We move in tandem, a well-oiled machine forged by years of partnership. No words are needed—a subtle nod, a quick hand gesture, and we're in sync.

We ascend the creaking stairs, our movements cautious and deliberate. I take the stairs two at a time, adrenaline surging through my veins. At the landing, a floorboard creaks behind me.

"Johnny," Michael whispers, his bushy mustache twitching, "you take left, I'll go right."

I nod, swallowing hard. The hallway stretches before us, a dark maw threatening to engulf us. As we part, an unnatural chill fills the air. The walls seem to pulse, to breathe.

"Clear," he calls from the other room, his voice muffled and distant.

I press forward, gun raised. The master bedroom door looms, slightly ajar. As I ease it open, the hinges wail like damned souls.

For a fleeting moment, I see her—sprawled on the bed, needle still in her arm. My greatest failure, my deepest shame.

I blink, and she's gone. Only rumpled sheets and dust motes dancing in the wan light remain.

"Johnny?" Mike's voice, laced with concern, cuts through the mental static. "You alright?"

I nod, my voice untrustworthy. The line between reality and memory blurs, leaving me adrift in a sea of doubt and creeping dread.

The floorboards creak beneath my feet as I step into the room. A glint of metal catches my eye, peeking from under the bed.

"Hey!" I call, my voice hoarse. "Get in here."

I crouch, ignoring my aging knees' protest. With trembling fingers, I reach for the object, half-expecting it to vanish like a mirage. But it's solid, real.

A silver locket, tarnished and cold.

Michael's heavy footsteps draw near, deliberate and unhurried, as if he already knows what I've found. "What've you got there, Johnny?"

I hold it up, the chain dangling. "Recognize this?"

His sharp intake of breath answers my question.

"Christ," he mutters without hesitation. "Sarah Lawson, Sam's girlfriend from that cold case?"

The name hits like a gut punch. Images flash through my mind—a young girl's smile, a grieving mother, endless dead ends.

"Lawson, yeah," I say, my throat tight. "How the hell did it end up here?"

Michael shakes his head, his face grim. "Nothing good, that's for sure."

I pocket the locket, its weight a cold knot in my palm. Shadows stretch in the corners, too dark for the afternoon light filtering through grimy glass.

"We need to call this in," I say, fighting to keep my voice calm. "Get forensics out here."

"Yeah," he says, his agreement quiet but certain, as if we're both already picturing the same dark conclusion.

I know this is just the beginning. Whatever darkness lurks in Stormy Valley is about to rear its ugly head.

"Johnny," Michael says softly, his hand on my shoulder. "You okay to handle this?"

I meet his gaze, seeing the concern etched there. He knows my history, my demons.

"I have to be," I reply, squaring my shoulders. "This town needs me."

As we leave the room, an uneasy prickle trails down my spine, like unseen eyes tracking our every move. The house seems to breathe, guarding secrets I'm not sure I'm ready to uncover.

The cruiser's engine chatters. I've been sitting, parked at the station for—Christ, I don't know. The sky's gone dark and the sodium lights on Main grind holes in the windshield grime, bulb-lit insects smearing the glass. Inside the car it's cold, a wet cold that rides up the sleeves and settles in the joints. My fingers grip the steering wheel for what feels like hours before I convince them to let go.

Inside, the station is nearly empty, eerily quiet, except for the faint clack of the clock above the dispatch window. The desk is dark. The phone's red message light blinks slow, like a warning.

The air inside my office smells of dust. The flag in the corner sags limp. My desk sits where I left it: coffee ring, gray monitor, badge sticker peeling from the side. A Post-it on the keyboard reads: "Johnny: update from Langley. See you 7AM. – Sally." The letters tilt, half asleep.

I drop into the chair, bones protesting, and fire up the computer. The screen glows black for a moment—my reflection staring back, haggard like someone with too much to do and little time. I blink, and the desktop snaps awake.

First order of business: incident report on the Thompson farm disturbance. I open the file. My own words stare back at me—fragmented, clinical, bloodless. There's a line at the bottom, half-finished: "Evidence bag #0176: contents—"

Contents.

I reach for the desk drawer. The motion is automatic: top right, key taped to underside. Twist, pull, open. Inside: pens, a torn packet of aspirin, one evidence bag with the label pre-printed: Thompson, S. – 10/3/23 – Chain of Custody. The bag is flat, uncreased, never opened.

I stare at it.

I remember—no, I know—I placed the locket in here myself. Silver oval, blue enamel, hinge worn near-burst. I found it under the bed in that house, where it shouldn't have been. I remember weighing the bag in my hand, the locket's shape pressing through the plastic like a tiny frozen heart.

Now: nothing. The bag is empty, adhesive strip never peeled.

I check the drawer again, the other drawers, slap them open and closed. I check my coat, crumpled over the back of the chair. I run my hands through every pocket—shirt, pants, even the goddamn change pouch on the inside of my boot, where I kept a razor blade during the bad years.

Nothing.

Heat builds in my chest. I slide the drawer shut, press the bag flat, and peel the sticker. I write "empty" in the contents section and sign my initials. Behind me, the side door yawns, hinges squealing. I jerk halfway to standing, heart lurching, and watch as Mike Langley steps in from the dark. He closes the door carefully, like he's sneaking up on something fragile.

"Johnny," he says, low. "Didn't know you were here. "

His uniform is wrinkled, badge half-unclipped. Eyes red and puffy, like he's been up too late with the bottle—or a memory.

"Report's not gonna write itself," I say, but my voice sounds hollow even to me.

Mike approaches, glances at the evidence bag, then back at me. His lips pinch, then relax.

"You want the barn details for this? "

I nod. My hands rest flat on the keyboard, unable to move.

He shifts his weight. "Barn was clear. Couple floodlights, some marker tape, gravel bags in the corner. Looked like the septic crew left their gear behind. No tire marks, no prints, no sign anyone broke in." He shrugs. "Cleaner than a hospital."

I start typing. The keys sound too loud.

Mike watches me. "Everything okay, Johnny?"

"Yeah," I say. "Just tired." The keys clatter again.

He drops into the guest chair, voice soft. "You look like shit."

I try to smile. It barely happens. "Thanks for the pep talk."

He half-laughs. "You're fading. When's the last time you slept?"

"Don't remember."

He nods toward the evidence bag. "You lose something?"

The urge to explain—about the locket, the gaps, the static in my brain—flares, then fizzles.

"Misfiled. I'll check in the morning."

He grunts, unconvinced, but lets it go.

We sit in the hum of the fluorescents. The building creaks. I watch his hands—thumb worrying his badge. A nervous habit I've never seen before.

For a second, I imagine he's here to confront me. That he'll slide a gun from under his vest and put me down like a sick animal.

Instead, he just waits.

"Did you ever—" I start. "Did you ever feel like someone was watching you, even when you were alone?"

Mike blinks. "You mean, like, ghosts?"

I shake my head. "Not that. More like—" The room tilts, tiles jittering. "Like your own shadow's got an agenda."

He considers me—no judgment now.

"Yeah," he says. "After Becky left. I used to wake up and see her in the doorway. Never spoke. Just watched." His voice tightens. "Wasn't her, though. Just the shape left behind."

For a moment, the room fills with ghosts.

I finish the report. Lock the drawer. Pocket the key.

Mike stands. "I'm calling it a night. You need anything, you call."

"Thanks."

He hesitates at the door. "You were always the best man for this job. No matter what people say."

"I appreciate that," I say—and I mean it.

He leaves. The glass swings shut. Seals me in.

I lean back in the chair and let the static of the lights eat the minutes.

The drive from Thompson's flickers in the corner of my mind, but when I reach for it—

Nothing.

2

A Body Unearthed

The crunch of gravel under my boots echoes like breaking bones. I approach the huddle of workers, their faces ashen in the fading light. The stench hits me first—decay and damp earth blending into a sickly perfume.

"Sheriff McCallister," one of them nods, stepping aside.

The grave yawns before me, a maw of disturbed soil and shattered secrets. I steel myself, willing professional detachment to smother the dread clawing at my insides. But some horrors refuse to stay buried.

"How long?" I ask, my voice rough.

"Found it this mornin', Sheriff. Diggin' for the new septic line when Tommy's shovel hit somethin' soft."

I nod, kneeling beside the shallow pit. My fingers brush away loose dirt, revealing tatters of faded fabric. Recognition blooms, cold and insidious.

"Christ," I mutter, a chill seeping into my bones.

The flannel pattern, though faded by time and earth, is unmistakable. Sarah Lawson's favorite shirt. Missing since '95, presumed a runaway. How wrong we were.

My mind races, memories surging like a tide of whiskey-soaked regrets. The frantic search parties, the accusations, the hope that faded into bitter resignation. And through it all, the nagging sense that we missed something vital.

"Gonna need lights," I call out, my voice steadier than I feel. "And cordon off the area. Nobody leaves until I say so."

As the workers scramble to comply, I remain crouched by the grave, unable to look away from Sarah's earthen shroud. But I can't falter now. There are truths to be unearthed, no matter how ugly.

"I'm sorry, Sarah," I whisper, the words tasting of ash and broken promises. "We'll make this right."

But even as I vow to bring her justice, a treacherous voice whispers from the recesses of my mind. Some secrets are better left buried, it hisses. Some sins can never be absolved.

I shake my head, trying to silence the doubts. But they linger, phantoms at the edge of my vision, as night descends on Stormy Valley. The floodlights flicker to life, casting long shadows across the once-peaceful Thompson property.

Boots scraping gravel pulls me from my brooding. I turn, squinting against the harsh floodlights, to see Ashley Kowalski hurrying toward me. Her red curls bounce with each step, her eyes wide with a mix of excitement and apprehension.

"Sheriff McCallister," she calls, slightly breathless. "I came as soon as I heard. What do you need me to do?"

I stand, my knees protesting. "Easy there, Deputy. This ain't a rodeo."

Ashley's cheeks flush, but her gaze doesn't waver. "I know, sir. I just... I want to help. Whatever you need."

Her eagerness contrasts sharply with the grim scene before us. For a moment, I see myself in her—young, idealistic, untouched by the darkness that seeps into a lawman's soul. It's both heartening and terrifying.

"Alright," I say, gesturing to the growing crowd of onlookers. "I need you on crowd control. Keep 'em back, take names if anyone seems too curious. And Ashley?"

She looks up, expectant. "Yes, sir?"

"Watch yourself. Small towns have long memories and sharp tongues. Don't let 'em rattle you."

She nods, squaring her shoulders. "I won't let you down."

As Ashley moves toward the perimeter, her voice firm but kind as she directs the curious townsfolk, I can't shake a gnawing worry. She's capable, sure, but green as spring grass. And Stormy Valley has a way of wearing down even the toughest souls.

I watch her for a moment, pride mingling with an uneasy sense of foreboding. This case could make her career—or break her spirit. In this town, with its secrets and sins, I'm not sure which is more likely.

I turn away from Ashley, my fingers fumbling for my phone. Calling her again feels like lighting a match in a room full of gas. But I tap her name anyway. Liz Montgomery. Her name alone stirs a mix of respect and unease.

The line rings, each trill echoing my pulse. When she answers, her voice is crisp, professional.

"Montgomery."

"Liz, it's Johnny. We've got a situation in Stormy Valley. Remains. Old case, maybe."

I hear her sharp intake of breath. "How old?"

"'90s, I reckon. Clothing matches a missing persons case from back then."

A pause. I can almost see her mind working, piecing together fragments.

"I'll be there in thirty," she says.

As I hang up, a chill creeps up my spine. Liz is good—damn good. But she's an outsider, and Stormy Valley doesn't take kindly to outsiders poking into its skeletons.

True to her word, Liz's sedan pulls up exactly thirty minutes later. She steps out, all business in her dark suit, her eyes already scanning the scene.

"Johnny," she nods, approaching.

"Liz," I return, gesturing toward the grave. "Welcome to our little slice of hell."

She crouches by the remains, her movements precise, analytical. I can practically see the gears turning behind those sharp eyes.

"Soil composition suggests long-term burial," she murmurs. "Fabric degradation consistent with…"

I cut her off, my gut twisting. "It's Sarah Lawson. Has to be."

Liz looks up, one eyebrow raised. "You can't know that for certain."

"I don't need a lab to tell me what my gut already knows," I growl.

Her lips thin. "Intuition has its place, Johnny, but so does hard evidence."

We lock eyes, a silent battle of wills. I feel the old frustration bubbling up—the clash between her by-the-book approach and my years of small-town policing.

"This isn't just another case file, Liz," I say, my voice low. "This is Stormy Valley's darkest secret come to light."

She stands, brushing dirt from her knees. "Then let's make sure we do right by her."

I nod, a reluctant truce formed. As we turn back to the grave, I get the feeling that we're standing at the edge of a reckoning—and when it breaks, nothing will be spared. God help us when it does.

The murmurs of the gathered crowd seep into my consciousness like a rising tide. I turn, scanning the faces behind the hastily erected police tape. Familiar eyes meet mine—old Bill Thompson, wringing his weathered hands; Sarah from the diner, her usual smile replaced by a tight-lipped frown; even young Bobby Miller, who should be in bed at this hour.

"Quite the turnout," I mutter to Liz. "Small town. Big gossip."

She nods, her eyes scanning with sharp intent. "Their reactions could be telling. Who looks nervous? Who's too curious?"

I grunt, unwilling to voice my unease at treating neighbors like suspects. Instead, I focus on Michael, who's setting up floodlights as darkness creeps in.

"How're we looking?" I call out.

He gives a thumbs-up and flicks a switch. Harsh light floods the scene, and I wince at the sudden glare. Familiar landmarks blur under the intensity, the field transformed into a nightmare I don't recognize.

"Christ," I whisper, the sight hitting me anew. The skeleton, half-exposed, seems to grin in macabre welcome.

"You alright, Johnny?" Liz asks, her usual coolness softened by concern.

I shake my head, trying to dislodge memories threatening to surface. "Fine. It's just... been a while since I've seen her."

"Her?" Liz's eyebrow arches. "I thought we hadn't confirmed identification."

I bite my tongue, cursing my slip. "Figure of speech," I mutter, but Liz's eyes narrow. She doesn't buy it. Hell, I barely believe myself.

As night fully settles, the floodlights cast everything in stark relief. The landscape warps beneath the glare, familiar shapes rendered uncanny. The crowd's whispers swell, a backdrop of unease that makes my skin crawl.

"We should wrap this up soon," I say, more to myself than Liz. "Nothing good happens after dark in Stormy Valley."

She nods, her face half in shadow. "Agreed. But Johnny... this is just the beginning, isn't it?"

I look at her, at the grave, at the watchful eyes of my town. A chill runs through me, colder than the night air.

"Yeah," I whisper. "God help us, I think it is."

The stark white of bone catches the floodlight, glowing with an unholy luminescence. I kneel beside it, the damp earth soaking through my jeans. Liz crouches opposite, her eyes scanning the remains with clinical precision.

"Female, late teens to early twenties," she murmurs, her pen scratching against a notepad. "Signs of blunt force trauma to the skull."

I nod, my gaze fixed on a scrap of faded fabric clinging to a rib. "That dress... I remember it. Blue with little white flowers."

Liz's head snaps up. "You've seen it before?"

"Yeah," I say, my throat tight. "Sarah Lawson. Missing person case from '95. Never solved."

The pen stops. Liz's voice is careful, probing. "You worked that case?"

I shake my head. "I was just a rookie then. But I remember... God, I remember everything."

Liz leans in, her analytical facade cracking. "Johnny, if you have information—"

"It's not about information," I cut her off, harsher than intended. "It's about feeling. This town, these people... they never forgot Sarah. And now she's back to haunt us."

Liz's lips thin. "We deal in facts, not feelings. The community's reaction is secondary to the evidence."

I stand abruptly, needing space. "Maybe for you, Liz. But I have to live here. Long after you've packed up your fancy forensics kit and gone back to the city."

She doesn't respond, just watches me with those sharp eyes as I walk away. The crowd parts, their whispers falling silent. I feel their silence more than their stares, heavy with questions no one dares to ask.

At the edge of the property, I stop. The old Thompson house looms in the distance, a dark silhouette against the star-studded sky. I close my eyes, and for a moment, I'm twenty-four again—young, eager, still blind to the darkness lurking in small towns.

"I'm sorry, Sarah," I whisper to the night. "I should've done more. Should've seen..."

The guilt rises like bile in my throat. How many nights have I lain awake, replaying every moment of that investigation? How many leads did I miss, clues I overlooked in my inexperience?

A hand touches my shoulder, and I nearly jump.

"Sheriff?" It's Liz, her face uncharacteristically soft in the dim light. "We need you back there."

I nod, swallowing hard. "Yeah, I'm coming."

As we walk back to the grave, I steel myself. The past has come calling, but I'm not that green kid anymore. This time, I'll get it right.

I have to.

The murmur of the crowd washes over me as I approach, a tide of whispers and half-formed theories. Ashley stands at the forefront, her petite frame rigid with determination. She's positioned herself between the onlookers and the excavation site, arms crossed, chin lifted in defiance of her visible nerves.

"Folks, please step back," she calls, her voice wavering slightly. "This is an active crime scene."

I watch as she gently guides old Mrs. Hendricks away from the yellow tape, her hand soft on the elderly woman's arm. "I know you're worried, ma'am, but we need space to work. I promise we'll keep everyone informed."

Pride swells in my chest, tempered by concern. Ashley's eager to prove herself, but this town has teeth. I've seen it chew up tougher souls than hers.

"You're doing fine, Deputy," I murmur as I pass. She beams, freckles stark against her flushed cheeks.

"Thanks, Sheriff. I'm trying to—"

A commotion erupts at the back of the crowd. Frank Thompson, the property owner, pushes forward, his face twisted with anger.

"This is my land!" he bellows. "You can't just dig it up without—"

I quietly intercept him before he breaches the perimeter. "Frank, I know this is tough, but we have a court order. Let us do our job."

He glares at me, eyes bloodshot. I catch a whiff of whiskey on his breath. "You're gonna regret this, Johnny," he hisses. "Some things are better left buried."

My skin prickles. Is it a threat or a warning?

As Frank stumbles away, the whispers intensify. I catch snippets of conversation, each one stoking the unease beneath my skin.

"...always knew there was something off about that family..."

"...wonder if it's connected to those girls who went missing in '85..."

"...bet the Sheriff knows more than he's letting on..."

I clench my jaw, resisting the urge to snap at them. They don't know. They can't know how this cuts deep, how the ghosts of my past failures circle like vultures.

Liz appears at my side, her presence a sharp reminder of the task at hand. "We need to control the narrative," she says, her eyes scanning the crowd. "Before speculation turns to panic."

I nod, knowing she's right. But as I turn to address the townsfolk, it feels like we've cracked Pandora's box wide open—and the darkness spilling out won't be contained. In Stormy Valley, secrets don't just linger. They rot. And they take root.

I meet Liz's eyes, we don't need words. We both know what lies ahead—a journey into the abyss of Stormy Valley's secrets and our own haunted pasts.

"Well, Detective," I drawl, my voice rougher than intended, "looks like we've got one hell of a mess."

Liz's lips twitch, almost a smile. "That's putting it mildly, Sheriff."

We stand side by side, staring at the remains. Lit by floodlights, the grave looks like something from a macabre painting—unreal, grotesque, and far too familiar. I can't help but wonder how many more skeletons we'll unearth before this is over.

"You know," I muse, half to myself, "I always feared this day would come. Hoped it wouldn't, but..."

"The past has a way of clawing to the surface," Liz finishes, her voice soft.

I nod, swallowing hard. "Like a damn zombie in a B-movie."

The joke falls flat, drowned by the gravity of the moment. My badge feels heavy on my chest, a reminder of duty and failures alike. How many times have I looked away, buried my head in the sand?

"Johnny," Liz says, her tone gentle but firm, "whatever this is, I'm in. For now."

I want to believe her. God, I want to. But the phantoms of my past whisper otherwise, their accusing voices a relentless drone in my mind.

"Yeah," I mutter, avoiding her eyes. "Together."

The wind picks up, carrying the scent of decay and long-buried secrets. Stormy Valley seems to hold its breath, waiting for the horrors we'll unleash.

And deep in the darkest corners of my soul, I fear I might be the biggest monster of all.

3
The Outsider Arrives

The floorboards creak under my boots as I step into the sheriff's office, the sound echoing through the stillness. Morning light filters weakly through dusty blinds, casting long shadows across faded photos on the wall. My gaze lingers on faces frozen in time—smiling deputies, solemn judges, grim mugshots. Each one a chapter in Stormy Valley's history. Each one a mirror of my sins.

I run my fingers over the familiar contours of my badge, its weight a constant reminder of duty and redemption. The ghosts of my past whisper accusations, but I silence them with a practiced breath. Not now. There's work to do.

The door swings open, and I turn to see Detective Elizabeth Montgomery stride in. Her eyes, sharp as flint, meet mine in a brief nod. No words needed; we both know why we're here.

"Morning, Detective," I say, my voice rough from disuse. "Coffee's fresh if you want some."

She shakes her head, all business. "Let's get started, Sheriff. Time's wasting."

I admire her focus, even as part of me recoils from her intensity. It's like seeing my younger self—driven, uncompromising, blind to the pitfalls ahead.

"Right," I mutter, moving toward my desk. "The files are—"

Something sharp catches my attention, cutting me off mid-sentence. For a heartbeat, I swear I see a shadowy figure in the corner of my eye, familiar and accusing. But when I turn, there's nothing but empty air and fading memories.

"Sheriff? You alright?" Liz's voice slices through my lapse.

I force a smile, hoping it doesn't look as brittle as it feels. "Fine. Just... remembering."

She doesn't look convinced but lets it drop. As we settle in to work, I can't shake the feeling that we're about to unearth something best left buried. In Stormy Valley, the past never stays silent for long.

I pull open the bottom drawer of my desk, the metal scraping like a rusty scream. The yellowed files within seem to pulse with malevolent energy, each one a chapter in Stormy Valley's dark history. As I lay them on the desk between us, the legacy of each unsolved case settles between us like ash.

Liz leans forward, her eyes narrowing as she pulls the first file toward her. "Tell me, Sheriff," she says, not looking up, "what makes you think these old cases are connected?"

I watch her methodical approach, resisting the urge to blurt out my suspicions. My gut screams there's a pattern, a thread of darkness weaving through our town's past. But I've learned the hard way that instinct isn't enough. Not anymore.

"Just... a feeling," I admit, the words tasting like failure. "Something in the air, maybe. Or in the shadows."

Liz's eyebrow quirks, skepticism etched into her face. "Shadows don't solve cases, Sheriff."

"No," I agree, I glance toward the window, where morning mist clings to the trees. "But sometimes they hide the truth."

As Liz continues her meticulous examination, I'm lost in thought. Old failures whisper from the corners of my mind, reminding me of the cost of rushing to judgment. Yet beneath that caution, a familiar itch grows—to act, to protect, to make things right.

I clear my throat, breaking the silence. "Detective, I know you prefer hard evidence, but—"

"Then give me hard evidence," she interrupts, her tone sharp yet not unkind. "Show me what you see in these files that I'm missing."

For a moment, I'm tempted to lay it all out—the patterns only I see, the connections dancing just beyond proof. It wasn't duty that stopped me. It was the town, pressed into metal, pinned over my heart. We do this by the book, or not at all.

"Take your time," I say, settling back in my chair. "The truth will come out. It always does in Stormy Valley."

As I watch Liz work, I feel it again—that low thrum beneath the surface. The sense that something's coming, and we're already too late. And somewhere in my mind, a voice too much like my own whispers, What if the truth is worse than the lie?

The creak of the door cuts through my dark thoughts. Mike Langley's familiar bulk fills the frame, his mustache twitching with an uneasy smile. "Morning, Johnny," he rumbles.

I nod, noting the slight tremor in his hand as he adjusts his belt. "Mike. Good of you to join us."

Liz's gaze snaps up, sharp as a hound catching a scent. "Mr. Langley," she says, her voice cool and professional. "I was hoping we could discuss your statement from the original investigation."

His smile falters, glancing at me before answering. "Of course."

I watched the exchange unfold, a knot forming in my belly. Liz, relentless as ever, fires questions with surgical precision. Michael responds with his usual straightforward honesty, but something's off in his tone—a hesitation here, a too-quick answer there.

"And you're certain you saw nothing unusual that night?" Liz presses.

I've known him for decades, from a rookie deputy to a pillar of the community. But now, I see him as if for the first time: the sheen of sweat on his brow, the way his fingers twitch toward a pocket where a pack of cigarettes once rested.

What are you hiding, old friend? And why?

The unease in the room is palpable, a living thing writhing between us. I want to trust him, to believe in the man I've worked alongside for so long. But doubt, once planted, grows like a weed.

As Liz presses her interrogation, I'm adrift in a sea of memories and half-formed suspicions. The truth hides in the darker corners of Stormy Valley, but as I watch him squirm under her questioning eyes, I can't help wondering: are we ready for what it might reveal?

I clear my throat, the sound cutting through the tense silence of the office. "Look," my voice rough with unsaid things, "we're missing something. This isn't just about what happened that night. It's about patterns, about undercurrents we've felt but never named."

Liz's eyes narrow, her analytical mind dissecting my words. "What are you getting at, Sheriff?"

I lean forward, the old chair creaking beneath me. "Think about it. The jogger's death, the road rage incidents, even last year's standoff. They're connected, somehow—ripples spreading from a dark center we can't yet see."

Mike shifts uncomfortably while glancing around the office, but I press on. "This town's changing. A darkness is creeping in, seeping into cracks we've tried to ignore."

My words hang in the air, heavy with implication. Liz's face is a mask of concentration, but I see the wheels turning in her eyes. She's starting to glimpse it too—the bigger picture that's haunted me for months.

For a moment, we lock eyes across the cluttered desk. In that silent exchange, something shifts between us—a grudging respect, perhaps, or the recognition of a shared burden. We're different, Liz and I—she with her cold logic, me with gut instincts honed by years on these streets. But in this moment, we're united by a common purpose.

The silence stretches, thick with unspoken understanding. We'll need each other to unravel this mystery, to face the darkness threatening to swallow Stormy Valley whole. And as I look at Liz, I see the same grim determination in her eyes.

God help us if we're right about what's coming.

I stand abruptly, the chair scraping against the worn linoleum. The sound echoes in the small office, breaking the strained quiet.

"We need to go," I say, my voice rough with urgency. "The scene won't wait forever."

I gather the yellowed files, feeling their weight—not just in my hands, but on my conscience. Each page a reminder of lives torn apart, of justice delayed. How many more will suffer before we put this to rest?

"Let's move," I growl, gesturing to Liz and Mike.

They rise, Mike's face etched with worry, Liz's set in stone. We file out of the office, a grim procession of the determined and the damned. Outside, Liz follows me to the cruiser.

The next thing I know, the cruiser's rumbling down Main Street, its familiar vibrations doing little to calm my nerves. Liz sits beside me, her posture rigid, eyes scanning the storefronts as if searching for hidden clues.

"Johnny," she starts, her voice low and measured, "I need to understand your connection to this case. Your... history here."

I grip the steering wheel tighter, my knuckles whitening. The urge to reach for a flask that's no longer there claws at my gut.

"It's not pretty," I warn her, the truth cutting on the way out. "I was a different man back then. Angry. Drunk more often than sober."

"And now?" Liz asks, her gaze sharp enough to slice.

A humorless chuckle escapes me. "Now? I'm just trying to make amends. To the town. To myself."

The silence that follows hangs heavy, thick with unasked questions.

Michael clears his throat from the backseat, his voice carrying forced cheer. "Say Liz, did I ever tell you about old man Wilson's prize-winning pumpkins? Swears the secret's in the soil."

I catch Liz's eye-roll in the rearview mirror, but I'm grateful for his inter-jection. His rambling about local gossip fills the car, a temporary reprieve from the unease clinging to every turn in the road.

As we near the outskirts of town, his stories shift to a somber tone. "This area's changed since the incident," he muses. "Folks avoid it now. Too many bad memories, I reckon."

I nod, my throat tightening. The road ahead blurs, and for a moment, I see it as it was years ago—stained with blood and regret.

"We're here to change that," I force out, more to convince myself than anyone else. "To lay those ghosts to rest."

But as we near our destination, a creeping dread warns that some ghosts aren't ready to be silenced.

The cruiser's tires crunch on gravel as we pull up to the scene. I kill the engine, and an eerie silence settles. The air feels thick, oppressive, as if it's trying to smother us.

"Christ," Liz mutters, her eyes scanning the overgrown lot. "It's like time froze here."

I step out, my boots sinking slightly into the damp earth. The scent hits me immediately—decay and something darker, something that makes my skin crawl.

"Watch your step," I warn, more from habit than necessity. "The ground's uneven."

Michael lumbers out behind us, his face pale. "Johnny, you sure about this? This place gives me the creeps."

I don't answer. Can't. My eyes are fixed on the dilapidated structure before us, its weathered boards a patchwork of shadows and secrets.

Liz doesn't move, her eyes locked on the field where she was found last night, a shiver visibly running down her spine. Wordlessly, we exchange a knowing glance before deciding to enter the house for potential clues. Memories of that fateful night surge back—the urgent phone call echoing in my ears, mingling with the metallic tang of blood and dread still lingering in the air. The image of her pleading eyes from the missing poster haunts me, an unspoken cry for justice.

I shake my head, trying to focus. "Let's do this," I growl, more to myself than the others.

But as I reach for the door, my hand trembling slightly, I can't shake the feeling that we're not alone. That something is watching, waiting.

And maybe, just maybe, it's been waiting for me all along.

I pause, my hand hovering over the rusted doorknob. The air feels thicker here—charged, expectant, like the house remembers.

"Johnny?" Liz's voice cuts through my thoughts. "You okay?"

I turn to her, forcing a grim smile. "Never better."

As we step inside, the floorboards creak beneath our feet, a mournful sound echoing through the empty rooms. Dust motes dance in the thin shafts of light piercing the boarded-up windows.

"Jesus," Michael whispers, his eyes wide. "It's like a tomb in here."

"What do you see?" Liz asks, her voice hushed.

I close my eyes, letting the scene play out in my mind. "Pain," I murmur. "Fear. And... something else. Something darker."

When I open my eyes, I catch a flicker of movement in the cracked mirror. For a split second, I see her face—pale, accusing. But when I blink, it's gone.

My heart races. Am I losing it? Or is this place playing tricks?

"We need to be thorough," I say, trying to steady my voice. "Leave no stone unturned."

As we push deeper into the house, the air thickens, the walls groaning as if we've stirred something best left buried. Every creak underfoot sounds like a warning. This place isn't just hiding secrets—it's waiting for us to unearth them.

God help us if we're not ready for what we find.

4

Whispers of the Past

The diner's neon sign casts an eerie glow across the rain-slicked parking lot. Detective Montgomery's lithe figure emerges from her car, her steps purposeful as she approaches the entrance. My gut tightens. Something about her determined gait sets my teeth on edge.

I mutter under my breath, "Easy, Johnny. She's just doing her job." But the words ring hollow even to me.

Liz pauses at the threshold, her sharp eyes scanning the interior. I can almost see the gears turning in her analytical mind. She's hunting, searching for familiar faces, for anything out of place.

My fingers drum an anxious rhythm on the steering wheel as Liz disappears inside. The urge to follow, to keep watch, gnaws at me. But I resist. This is her show now.

Through the fogged window, I catch glimpses of the detective's progress. She weaves between worn booths and chipped Formica tables, her gaze locking on a solitary figure in the far corner.

Emma Martinez. Her very presence sends a chill down my spine, stirring memories best left buried.

I lean forward, straining to hear their exchange over the diner's ambient noise. Liz's voice carries just enough for me to catch fragments:

"Ms. Martinez, thank you for meeting me."

"Detective Montgomery. I... I wasn't sure I should come."

"I understand your hesitation. But your insight could be invaluable."

Emma's response is lost to me, her soft voice drowned by the clatter of dishes and murmurs of other patrons. But I see her hunched shoulders, her fingers worrying at the frayed edge of a paper napkin.

Unspoken truths hang heavy between them. Even from here, I feel it pressing on my chest, threatening to suffocate me with guilt and regret.

As Liz slides into the booth across from Emma, I whisper a silent prayer. For what, I'm not sure. Justice? Absolution? Or maybe just the strength to face whatever ugly truths this investigation might unearth.

One thing's certain: the ghosts of Stormy Valley won't rest easy tonight.

I watch as Liz leans in, her voice calm and practiced—like she's mimicking me. "Emma, I need you to think back to that night. Every detail, no matter how small, could be vital."

Emma's eyes flutter closed, her brow furrowing. When she speaks, her voice trembles, weighed down by things she's never said aloud. "It was... raining. I remember the sound on the roof, like whispers in the dark."

My gut twists. I know that sound all too well—the patter of raindrops that sometimes turns into accusatory murmurs in the dead of night.

"Go on," Liz urges gently.

"There was a scream. Or... maybe it was just the wind." Emma's voice wavers. "Everything after that is... fragments. Flashes of red. The smell of copper."

I turn away from the window, leaning against the diner's cold metal exterior, dread coiling tight in my gut. The coppery scent of blood fills my nostrils, a phantom memory that never fades.

I look at my cruiser, parked across the street. For a moment, I'm tempted to climb in, to drive away from this town and its secrets. But I can't. I'm bound to Stormy Valley, for better or worse.

A gust of wind rustles through the pines, carrying a whisper that sounds eerily like my name. I shudder, forcing myself to look back through the diner's window.

Liz is still questioning Emma, her pen scratching across her notepad. But it's Emma who holds my attention now. There's something in her eyes—a flicker of recognition? Fear?

For a heartbeat, I swear she's looking right at me. And in that moment, I feel exposed, as if all my sins are laid bare for her to see.

I stumble back, my heart pounding. What does she know? What does she remember?

The wind whispers again, and this time I'm certain it's not my imagination. It carries a warning, a promise of a reckoning long overdue.

God help us all when the truth comes to light.

Emma's lips move, forming a name that chills my bones: Michael Langley. I can't hear her words, but I see Liz's reaction. Her posture stiffens; her pen pauses mid-stroke. She leans in, her eyes narrowing with renewed intensity.

I press closer to the glass, straining to catch a fragment of their conversation. But the diner's bustling ambiance drowns their words, leaving me with only my tumultuous thoughts.

Michael Langley. My friend. My confidant. The man who stood by me through the darkest chapters of my life. Could he be...? No. I can't let myself consider it.

The diner's bell chimes, startling me. Liz emerges, her face a mask of professional detachment. But I know her too well. I see the subtle tightening around her eyes, the faint furrow of her brow.

"Johnny," she says, her voice low and controlled. "We need to talk to Michael."

I nod, unable to trust my voice. As we walk toward Michael's house, each step feels like sinking deeper into quicksand. The silence grows thick between us, swelling with every word we're not saying.

"What did Emma say?" I manage to ask, my voice rougher than intended.

Liz's eyes flick toward me, then away. "Enough to raise questions. Questions we need answered."

I swallow hard, tasting bitter regret. "And you think Michael...?"

She doesn't respond immediately. Her words, when they come, are carefully measured. "I think we need to keep an open mind. No matter where it leads."

No matter where it leads. The phrase echoes in my mind, a grim promise of truths I'm not sure I'm ready to face. As we near Michael's house, my steps grow heavier, my thoughts darker.

What if the killer has been right under our noses all along? What if, in my desperation to protect this town, I've been blind to the very evil I swore to fight?

The wind's whisper returns, louder now. It sounds like laughter—cold, mocking, and terribly familiar.

Michael's modest home looms before us, a weathered sentinel against the encroaching twilight. The porch light flickers to life as we approach, casting warped silhouettes over the grass—familiar, but wrong in a way I couldn't name. My throat tightens, memories of shared beers and easy laughter on that porch flooding my mind.

I rap my knuckles against the peeling paint of the door, each knock a thunderclap in the deepening darkness. The door creaks open, and there's Michael, his bushy mustache twitching as he forces a smile that doesn't reach his eyes.

"Johnny," he says, his voice warm but strained. "What brings you by so late?"

I clear my throat, gesturing to Liz. "Michael, this is Detective Montgomery. We'd like to ask you a few questions, if you don't mind."

Something flickers in Michael's eyes—fear? Resignation?—before he nods, ushering us inside. The living room is a cluttered shrine to small-town life, family photos and dusty knickknacks crowding every surface. We settle onto a worn couch, its springs groaning in protest.

Liz leans forward, her posture deceptively relaxed. "Mr. Langley, can you tell me where you were on the night of April 15th, twenty-five years ago?"

Michael's brow furrows. "That's... a long time ago, Detective. I'm not sure I can—"

"The night Sarah Lawson was murdered," Liz interjects softly.

The color drains from Michael's face. I watch him closely, searching for the friend I thought I knew. But in this moment, he's a stranger.

"I... I was home," Michael stammers. "Watching the game, I think. Yeah, must've been."

Liz's pen scratches across her notepad. "Can anyone confirm that?"

Michael's eyes dart to mine, pleading. I look away, shame burning like acid. How many times have I vouched for him without question? How many loose threads have I refused to pull, fearing what might unravel?

"No," Michael admits, his voice fraying at the edges.

The silence that follows is deafening. In it, I hear echoes of every lie I've told myself about this town, about justice, about the man I thought I was.

Liz's voice cuts through the quiet, sharp as a blade. "Mr. Langley, I need you to walk me through that night. Every detail you can recall."

As Michael speaks, his words halting and uncertain, I feel the foundations of my world crumbling. The wind's whisper grows louder, a chorus of accusation. I've spent so long protecting this town, but what if I've been protecting the wrong people all along?

I shift in my seat, the leather creaking like a dying animal. Michael's voice drones on, a litany of half-truths and maybes. Each word drives another nail into the coffin of our friendship, of my faith in this town.

"I might've stepped out for a smoke," Michael says, his fingers drumming an anxious rhythm on his knee. "Can't rightly recall."

Liz's eyes narrow. "At what time, approximately?"

Beads of sweat glisten on Michael's brow, each one a quiet admission he's too scared to say out loud. My stomach churns, bile rising in my throat. How many times have we shared a drink on this porch, laughing about nothing and everything? Now, those memories feel tainted, poisoned by doubt.

"Around nine, maybe?" Michael's voice cracks. "Or was it ten?"

Liz's pen pauses, hovering over her notepad like an executioner's axe. "That's quite a discrepancy, Mr. Langley."

I close my eyes, willing myself to disappear. The room feels smaller, the walls closing in. The whispers in my head grow louder, a cacophony of accusation: You knew. You've always known.

"Johnny," Michael's plea cuts through my torment. "You remember, don't you? We talked that night."

I open my eyes, meeting his desperate gaze. For a moment, I'm tempted to lie, to protect him one last time. But duty wins—stone-faced and silent. Like the badge I don't remember losing.

"I'm sorry, Michael," I say, each word tasting like ash. "I don't recall any conversation that night."

The look of betrayal in his eyes will haunt me till my dying day.

Liz rises, her voice cutting through the thick silence. "Thank you for your time, Mr. Langley. We'll be in touch if we need anything further."

Michael nods, relief washing over his face like a curtain falling. "Of course, Detective. Anything to help." His eyes dart to mine, reflecting something unreadable—fear? Gratitude?—before he looks away.

We step into the crisp autumn air, leaves crunching beneath our feet. The wind whispers through the pines, carrying secrets I'm not sure I want to hear. Liz walks beside me, her presence a grounding reminder of the chasm between duty and loyalty.

The silence stretches, taut as a wire. I feel the words gathering against my chest, a dam about to burst. Finally, I can't hold back.

"Liz, I—" My voice cracks. I clear my throat and try again. "I've known Michael for damn near thirty years. We've been through hell together. The thought of him being involved..."

She doesn't look at me, still staring toward the horizon. "And if he is?"

The question hits like a gut punch. I think of the bodies we've found over the years, the broken families left behind. The badge suddenly feels twice as heavy — not with duty, but with brotherhood. With history.

"Then I'll do what needs to be done," It doesn't feel right, even as I say it. "But God help me, I hope we're wrong."

Liz nods, her expression unreadable. As we walk, I can't shake the feeling that each step buries a piece of myself alongside the truth in this quiet, haunted town.

Liz's eyes meet mine, their usual sharpness softening for a moment. "Johnny, I understand this isn't easy. But we're not here to judge. We're here to uncover the truth."

I nod, swallowing hard. The truth. A simple word for a complex, terrifying thing.

"And if that truth destroys everything?" I ask, the words escaping before I can stop them.

She pauses, considering. "Then it was built on lies to begin with."

We reach the crossroads where our paths diverge. The wind picks up, carrying the scent of pine and something darker, something unnameable. Liz turns to me, her face etched with determination and, perhaps, empathy.

"We'll find answers, Johnny. No matter how deep we have to dig."

As she walks away, her words echo in my mind. I stand there, watching her fade into the gathering dusk. I turn toward home, each step heavier than the last. Whatever resolve I had left sinks with them, buried beneath everything I still haven't said. In the distance, a lone crow calls, its cry a mournful reminder of the secrets buried in this town—and in my heart.

5
Silent Witness

The crunch of gravel under our feet echoes like a funeral march as Liz and I step out of my cruiser and approach Michael's weathered front door. Each step feels heavier than the last, weighed down by new suspicions and the bitter taste of betrayal coating my tongue.

Liz's voice cut through my brooding. "You ready for this, Johnny?"

I nod, not trusting my voice. How could I have been so blind? Michael, my friend, my deputy... a liar? The thought makes me sick, not just at him—but at myself, for not seeing it sooner.

My knuckles rap against the peeling paint, the sound hollow and ominous. As we wait, my mind races. What else have I missed? What other secrets lurk beneath the surface of this quiet town I've sworn to protect?

The door creaks open, and we step into Michael's living room. The space closes in, suffocating with its claustrophobic clutter. Stacks of newspapers teeter precariously, old coffee mugs leave rings on every surface, and the air hangs thick with the musty scent of long-kept secrets.

My eyes dart from corner to corner, unable to settle. Each pile of junk mocks me, a physical manifestation of the chaos swirling in my head. How many clues have I overlooked? How many lies have I swallowed whole?

"Quite a collection you've got here, Michael," I manage, my voice strained even to me.

Michael shuffles nervously, his gaze flitting between Liz and me. "Yeah, been meaning to clean up. Just haven't found the time, you know?"

I do know. Time has a way of slipping away, burying truths beneath layers of dust and neglect. But now, standing in this cramped room a pall of suspicion settles over us, I realize time has run out for us all.

Liz's sharp eyes scan the room, her analytical mind cataloging every detail. I can almost hear the gears turning, piecing together the puzzle we've stumbled into.

As Michael fumbles with his hearing aids, my body stiffens. How much did he truly hear that night? And more importantly, what did he choose not to hear?

The walls press closer, the clutter morphing into accusing fingers pointing at our collective guilt. In that moment, surrounded by the debris of a life half-lived, every secret, every lie, every unspoken truth seems to hang in the air—thick, suffocating, impossible to ignore.

Michael greets us, lips twitching into something that might've been a smile on a better day. "Johnny, Detective Montgomery," he says, his voice quavering like a leaf in autumn. "What brings you by?"

My jaw clenches, anger simmering beneath the surface. I force out a terse, "Evening, Michael."

Liz didn't flinch. She stepped forward, calm and clinical, as if the tension between him and me didn't faze her. "Deputy Langley," she begins, her tone measured yet probing, "we need to discuss the night of Sarah Lawson's murder."

I watch his face, searching for a flicker of guilt, a telltale twitch. But all I see is mounting anxiety, his eyes darting between us like a cornered animal.

Liz continues, her words precise as a scalpel. "Your previous statement mentioned hearing nothing unusual that night. However, we've uncovered some... inconsistencies."

The room shrinks, the walls closing in as Liz methodically lays out the discrepancies. Each point hits like a hammer blow, chipping away at the trust I've built with him over the years.

I'm adrift in a sea of doubt. How well do I really know this man? The thought gnaws at me, a relentless whisper in the back of my mind. As Liz's questioning persists, I feel it—that lurching sense of vertigo, like we're tee-tering on the edge of a precipice, about to plunge into depths from which we might never resurface.

Michael's facade crumbles before my eyes, his hands trembling as they reach for his hearing aids. The slight tremor in his fingers betrays his inner turmoil. I watch, a maelstrom of frustration and empathy churning, pulling me apart from the inside, as my old friend struggles to maintain his com-posure.

Michael's shoulders slump as he grips the table's edge. "I... I took out my hearing aids that night."

Liz leans forward, her voice sharp. "You did what?"

"Jess was colicky. Wouldn't stop crying. I was exhausted, frustrated." Michael's words tumble out. "I just wanted some peace."

A silence fills the room. Liz's jaw clenches, her fingers tapping rhythmi-cally on her notepad.

"So you heard nothing?" she presses.

Michael shakes his head, shame etched across his face. "Not a sound."

Liz's pen scratches furiously across the page. "And Rebecca?"

"Sound sleeper. Always was." Michael's voice cracks. "She never knew I did it."

"Christ, Langley," Liz mutters. "You realize what this means?"

Michael nods, his face ashen. "I might've heard something. Could've... could've helped Sarah."

Liz exhales slowly, watching Michael. "You understand I'll need to verify this?"

"Of course," he whispers. "I'll cooperate fully."

"Why?" I ask, my voice rough with emotion. "Why didn't you tell me?"

Michael's hands trembled. "Guilt. Fear. I convinced myself it wouldn't have mattered."

He looked up, his eyes pleading. "I was ashamed, Johnny. I didn't want to listen to Jess crying, and I thought... if I'd let them in, maybe I could've heard something, done something..."

"You might have," Liz said sharply.

"I know that now," Michael admitted, his voice breaking. "God, I know."

Liz stood, pacing the room's length. "We'll need to reexamine the timeline and check for disturbances that night."

Michael nodded numbly. "Whatever you need."

"This changes things, Langley," Liz said, her voice voice measured, edged with caution. "You understand that, right?"

Michael met her gaze, his expression haunted. "It's been eating away at me for years."

Liz paused, choosing her next words carefully. "There could be consequences."

"I know," Michael whispered. "I'm ready for that."

Liz's pen hovered over her notepad. "Is there anything else you're holding back? Anything at all?"

Michael hesitated, his brow furrowed. "I... I'm not sure. It's all a blur now."

"Take your time," Liz urged gently. "Even the smallest detail could be crucial."

Michael closed his eyes, focusing. "I remember... a car. Late that night. Unusual for our street."

Liz's pen raced across the page. "What kind of car?"

"Old. Ran rough." Michael's voice grew distant. "It struck me as odd, but..."

"But you couldn't hear it," Liz said, her voice firm.

Michael nodded, his expression pained. "Rebecca mentioned it the next morning. I played along, as if I'd heard it too."

Liz's tone grew sharper. "And you never thought to mention this before?"

"I didn't think it mattered," he replied, his voice faltering. "It was just a car."

The admission struck me like a physical blow. Anger flared, white-hot and searing, at his deception. How could he? After everything we'd been through?

But as quickly as it came, the rage faded, leaving a hollow ache in its wake. I saw not just my deputy but a man I'd known for decades—a man who'd stood by me through my battles with the bottle, who'd seen me at my lowest and never judged.

"In a case like this, everything matters," Liz said firmly. "You know that, Deputy."

Michael flinched at the title. "I do. I should've known better."

Liz's pen stilled. "We'll need to track down that vehicle. Any other memories surfacing?"

Michael shook his head. "Nothing concrete. Just... a sense of unease."

"Unease about what?" Liz pressed.

"The whole night," Michael admitted, his voice low. "Like something was off, but I couldn't pin it down."

Liz nodded, her expression unreadable. "We'll dig deeper into this. You understand you'll need to make an official statement, right?"

"Yes," Michael whispered. "I'm ready."

Liz gathered her notes. "This conversation isn't over, Langley. Not by a long shot."

He nodded, his shoulders slumped. "I know. And Liz? I'm sorry. For everything."

Liz paused at the door, her voice low. "Save it for Sarah's family. They deserve the apology."

I closed my eyes. In Michael slumped frame, I saw a reflection of myself—fractured by shame and secrets, cracked by years of carrying things we never said aloud. Were we not both haunted men, chasing redemption for sins we could never fully absolve?

The case twisted in my mind like a labyrinth. How much had we missed? What else lay buried in the silence of that night?

A sharp pang gripped my chest, a blend of betrayal and self-recrimination. How had I not noticed? I'd known him for years, trusted him with my life. Yet here we were, strangers in familiar skin.

"Johnny?" Liz's voice cut through my spiraling thoughts. "You coming?"

I nodded, my voice untrustworthy. The room felt smaller, its walls closing in. I wanted to reach out, to offer some word of comfort or understanding, but the badge on my chest felt heavy, a reminder of the professional distance I had to maintain.

"We'll need a full statement," I managed, my words sounding hollow even to myself.

He looked up, his eyes searching mine. I saw fear there, a plea for forgiveness—but beneath it, something else. A reflection of my own haunted eyes staring back.

I rose from my seat, the old floorboards creaking beneath me. The sound reverberated in the cramped living room, a jarring note in the stifling quiet.

"We'll be in touch, Michael," I said, my voice rougher than intended. "Don't leave town."

I watched him as we prepared to leave. His shoulders slumped, defeat etched into every line of his face. I felt a pang of something—pity, perhaps, or a twisted sense of kinship. Were we not both men burdened by our secrets?

"Johnny," he called as we reached the door. I turned, meeting his eyes. "I'm sorry. For everything."

I nodded, words failing me. In that moment, I made a silent vow: to seek justice, no matter the cost to myself or those I once called friends.

The door creaked open, and we stepped into the fading evening light. The air felt thick and oppressive, mirroring the unresolved tension that clung to us like a spider's web.

"What now?" Liz asked, eerily calm for the situation.

I opened my mouth to respond, but the words died before they lived. A shadow slipped through my periphery, pulling my attention from Liz and our next steps. My hand instinctively moved to my holster as twilight engulfed the area.

"Did you see that?" I murmured, eyes narrowing.

A figure emerged from the gloom, tall and lanky, with a disheveled mane of blond hair. Samuel Thompson. My gut clenched, instincts screaming danger as I studied his inscrutable expression. Sam's presence here, now, felt like a dark omen.

"Well, well," Sam drawled, his voice grating. "If it isn't our illustrious sheriff and his new pet detective. Awfully late for a social call, isn't it?"

I felt Liz tense beside me. "Just following leads, Sam," I replied, keeping my tone even. "Nothing for you to worry about."

Sam's lips curled into a sneer. "Oh, I think there's plenty to worry about in this town, Sheriff. Plenty of secrets just waiting to be dragged into the light."

My instincts kicked in, reading every twitch of his face. Was this just his usual antagonism or something more sinister? No... this wasn't just Sam being Sam. He was here for a reason, and it wasn't good.

"Is there something we can help you with, Mr. Thompson?" Liz's cool voice sliced through the tension.

I glanced at her, catching the sharp glint in her eyes. Without a word, we exchanged a silent understanding. She'd sensed it too—the wrongness of this encounter, the potential for trouble coiled tightly in Sam's lean frame.

"Help me?" Sam barked out a harsh laugh. "Nah, I don't need anything from the likes of you. Just keeping an eye on things, you might say. Someone's got to watch the watchmen, right?"

The hairs on the back of my neck prickled. "We're done here," I said firmly, placing a hand on Liz's elbow to guide her toward the cruiser. "Have a good night, Sam."

As we walked away, I felt Sam's gaze boring into my back. Something clung to me as we walked—like eyes I couldn't shake, or danger just out of frame, leaving me to wonder: how many more shadows lurked in Stormy Valley, waiting to engulf us all?

The crunch of gravel under our boots sounded unnaturally loud as we reached the cruiser. My mind churned, a maelstrom of half-formed theories and nagging doubts.

"Johnny," Liz said, her voice low and urgent. "What do you make of this?"

I ran a hand through my hair, "I don't know, Liz. But I'll be damned if I let this town down again."

A phantom accusation echoed in my mind, a spectral whisper that sent chills down my spine: You failed us once, Johnny. Can you protect them now?

I shook my head, trying to banish the voice. "We need to dig deeper. Michael's confession, Sam's presence... it's all connected somehow."

Liz nodded, her eyes scanning the darkening street. "And the hearing aid? That changes everything."

"Yeah," I muttered, the betrayal souring everything. "How did I not notice? Some friend I've been."

We reached the cruiser, its worn frame a familiar comfort in the gathering gloom. As I opened the door, movement caught my eye—a figure darting between houses, gone in an instant.

"Did you see that?" I asked, my hand instinctively reaching for my holster.

Liz shook her head, her brow furrowed. "No, what was it?"

I hesitated, doubt gnawing at me. "Nothing. Probably just my imagination."

As we climbed into the cruiser, the silence between us was suffocating with unspoken fears and half-formed plans. The engine roared to life, its determined growl echoing my own resolve.

"We'll get to the bottom of this, Johnny," Liz said, her voice firm. "Whatever it takes."

I nodded, her face half-shrouded in shadow. "I know we will, Liz. But at what cost?" My knuckles whitened on the steering wheel.

As we pulled away, the streetlights flickered to life, bending the road into strips of light and dark. The town pulsed with secrets, its silence loaded, its darkness hungry.

6

Shadows of Suspicion

Gravel crunched under our boots, each step a whisper of accusation. Liz and I approached Sam Thompson's trailer, a rusted tin can nestled among Stormy Valley's shadowed pines. The pressure of the case bore down on me, heavier than the gun at my hip.

My mind raced. Would this moment crack the case open? Or was I leading us into the maw of danger?

I raised my fist to knock, hesitating. "Liz, stay sharp. Something's off."

She nodded, scanning the surroundings like a searchlight. "I've got your back, Johnny."

My knuckles rapped on metal, the sound echoing in the unnatural stillness. No birds sang. No wind stirred the trees. Only my heart thudded, a countdown to confrontation.

Memories flashed—Sarah Lawson's broken body, a grieving family, years of dead ends. Now, a lead, at last. But at what cost?

"You sure about this?" Liz's voice was low, taut.

I didn't answer. Couldn't. Regrets crowded close, whispering doubts. What if I was wrong? What if this was another dead end, another disappointment to heap on the pile?

No. I couldn't think like that. Not now. Not when we were this close.

The silence stretched, suffocating. I knocked again, harder. The hollow sound mocked me, a taunt from the past.

"Come on, Sam," I muttered. "Face the music."

My fingers twitched, itching for my gun. But that path led to madness. We had to do this right. By the book. No matter how much the darkness within me craved another kind of justice.

I closed my eyes, drawing a steadying breath. When I opened them, the world sharpened—the rusted trailer, the overgrown yard, the shadows writhing at the edges of my vision.

"Johnny," Liz said, her voice urgent. "Movement inside."

My body tensed, coiled, ready. This was it. The moment of truth. Whatever lay behind that door, one thing was certain—nothing would be the same.

The door creaked open, revealing Sam Thompson's gaunt face. His bloodshot eyes met mine, a flicker of recognition masked by disdain.

"Well, if it ain't the town's finest," Sam drawled, his words dripping sarcasm. "Come to harass me again, Sheriff?"

I held his gaze, unflinching. The stench of stale beer and unwashed clothes wafted from the trailer, churning my stomach. But it wasn't just the smell that set me on edge. A feral glint in Sam's eyes spoke of desperation and barely contained violence.

"Evening, Sam," I said, keeping my voice even. "Mind if we come in?"

He sneered but stepped back, granting us entry. As Liz and I crossed the threshold, the trailer's oppressive atmosphere hit like a physical force. Dust hung in the air, catching in the dim light that revealed a battlefield of empty bottles, grease-stained takeout boxes, and the quiet decay of loneliness.

My senses sharpened, cataloging every detail. A faded photo on a shelf caught my eye—I'd need to inspect it later. The air felt thick, loaded with secrets and unspoken threats.

"Make yourself at home," Sam muttered, slumping into a worn armchair. "Not much hospitality to go around."

I stayed standing, keenly aware of Liz's presence at my back. The walls seemed to close in, shadows deepening with each passing moment. Every instinct screamed danger, but I suppressed it. We had a job to do.

"You know why we're here, Sam," I said, my voice sounding distant to my own ears. The ghosts of the past whispered again, a cacophony of accusation and regret. I pushed them aside, focusing on the man before me—the key to unraveling this twisted mess.

Sam's lip curled. "Do I? Enlighten me, Sheriff. What new crimes are you pinning on me today?"

I steadied myself, the floorboards creaking beneath my boots. "Let's talk about the night Sarah Lawson disappeared. Where were you?"

Sam's eyes darted aside. For a second, he looked cornered—fear in his eyes, or maybe just the shame I needed to believe in. "Christ, that again? It was years ago. I told you everything back then."

"Humor me," I pressed, my voice calm despite the storm brewing within. "Walk me through it again."

He leaned back, arms crossed defensively. "I was at Rosie's," he snapped. "You know that. I—" He faltered, eyes darting to the wall. "I was waitin'... didn't matter. Never showed."

His words rang hollow, warped by years of pain. "All night?" I prodded.

"What're you getting at? You think I had something to do with *Sarah*?" Sam spat, his voice cracking halfway through. "Jesus, she was—" He bit the rest back, jaw clenched tight.

From the corner of my eye, I caught Liz's subtle shift. She zeroed in on Sam, dissecting every twitch, every inflection. We'd worked together long enough that I could read her silent cues. Something in Sam's story wasn't adding up.

"Just trying to get the facts straight," I said, striving to keep my voice neutral. The shadows in the room deepened, pressing in from all sides. "Anyone who can corroborate your story?"

Sam's laugh grated, harsh and jagged. "After all this time? Hell, half the regulars from back then are dead or gone."

I felt Liz tense behind me, her presence a silent anchor in the suffocating atmosphere. Sam's story unraveled, thread by thread. But how far could we push before he snapped?

The ghosts whispered again, a chorus of accusation. You're just like him, they hissed. A liar. A killer.

I clenched my fist, nails biting into my palm. Not now. I couldn't lose focus, not when we were this close to the truth.

"Sam," I said, leaning in, "it's time you told us what really happened that night."

Sam's face contorted, rage flashing in his eyes like lightning in a storm. "You're harassing me!" he bellowed, slamming his fist on the rickety table. The sound reverberated through the cramped trailer, making my skin crawl.

I held my ground, though my heart raced. "Calm down, Sam. We're just asking questions."

"Questions? This is a goddamn witch hunt!" His voice hit a fever pitch, spittle flying.

I felt the old urge to reach for the bottle, to drown the chaos. But I suppressed it, steeling myself. "I'm not here to persecute you, Sam. I'm here for the truth."

His eyes darted wildly, a cornered animal seeking escape. Violence crackled in the air like static electricity.

"Take it easy," I said, my voice low and even. "Let's all take a breath."

As Sam's chest heaved, his gaze locked on something behind me. I turned, following his line of sight to a cluttered shelf. Amid the dust and debris, a glint of silver caught my eye.

My blood ran cold as I focused on the photograph: a younger Sam, grinning broadly, his arm around a woman I knew all too well—Sarah Lawson.

The pieces fell into place with sickening clarity. The suspect description from all those years ago... it was Sam. It had always been Sam.

I turned to face him, my mind reeling. The trailer's walls seemed to close in, the air thick with unspoken accusations and long-buried secrets.

"Sam," I said, the threat buried just beneath the calm. "You need to explain this photo."

I caught Liz's eye, giving her a subtle nod. To anyone else, it would've been imperceptible, but Liz and I had been in enough tight spots together; she knew exactly what it meant. Her stance shifted slightly, poised to act at a moment's notice.

My heart pounded as I faced Sam again, the photograph clutched in my hand. "Care to explain this, Sam?" I asked, my voice rising but taut as a wire.

Sam's eyes darted from me to the photo and back again. His face contorted into a mask of rage and fear. "Where the hell did you get that?" he snarled, lunging forward.

I held my ground, though my instincts urged me to step back. "It doesn't matter where I got it. What matters is you're in it, with Sarah—the woman you claimed not to know."

"You don't know anything!" Sam roared, his fists clenching and unclenching at his sides. "You're twisting everything, trying to pin this on me!"

The room seemed to shrink, its walls closing in. I could smell Sam's fear-sweat, hear Liz's rapid, shallow breaths behind me. My pulse thundered in my ears.

"I'm not trying to pin anything on you, Sam," I said, struggling to keep my voice calm. "I just want the truth. Where were you the night Sarah disappeared?"

Sam's face twisted into a rictus of pain and fury. "I don't have to tell you anything! Get out! Get the hell out of my house!"

As he advanced, spittle flying from his lips, I felt the old, familiar itch—the urge to reach for my gun, to end this confrontation before it spiraled out of control. But I held back, knowing one wrong move could unravel everything.

The air crackled, charged and choking, like static in a thunderstorm. Sam's eyes darted wildly, like those of a cornered animal. I shifted my weight, braced for action if he lunged. My mind raced, assessing angles and potential weapons within reach. The old instincts, honed by years on the job, never truly faded.

"Sam," I began, "we don't want this to—"

But before I could finish, Liz stepped forward, her presence a sudden balm in the charged atmosphere.

Liz didn't speak, but I could almost hear her voice in my head—measured, grounding. *We understand this is difficult... but the photo raises questions we can't ignore.*

I watched Sam's face, catching a flicker of uncertainty passing over it. Liz spoke, reiterating our goal.

"Mr. Thompson," she said, her tone firm yet calming, "we understand this is difficult. But the photo raises questions we can't ignore."

As she spoke, I felt a pang of admiration. Liz had a knack for cutting through tension, reaching people at their most volatile. It was a skill I'd never quite mastered.

Sam's shoulders sagged slightly, some of the fight draining from him. But I stayed on edge. In my experience, this moment—when a suspect teetered between rage and resignation—was often the most volatile.

"You don't understand," Sam muttered, his voice cracking. "You can't possibly..."

I held my breath, waiting to see which way he'd tip.

Sam's eyes darted around the room, wild and desperate. For a heartbeat, I glimpsed something else—a flicker of doubt, a crack in his defiant facade. My pulse quickened. This was it.

"Sam Thompson," I said, my voice slicing through the thick silence, "you're under arrest for the murder of Sarah Lawson."

The words hung in the air, sharp and final. Sam's face crumpled, fear and resignation washing over him. Still, I couldn't lower my guard. Not yet.

"You have the right to remain silent," I continued, stepping forward. "Anything you say can and will be used against you in a court of law."

As I recited the familiar words, my mind raced. How many times had I done this? How many men and women had I watched crumble, dragged down by ghosts they tried to outrun? Yet each time felt like the first—raw, unpredictable, and dangerous.

Sam's hands trembled at his sides. I tensed, braced for him to lash out, to make a desperate grab for something—anything—to use as a weapon. But he stood frozen, eyes glassy, as if staring beyond the cramped confines of his trailer.

Out of the corner of my eye I saw Liz positioning herself near the door. Always one step ahead. I felt a surge of gratitude for her presence, even as I kept my focus on Sam.

"Do you understand these rights as I've explained them?" I asked, my voice sounding distant even to myself.

Sam's gaze snapped back to me, something unreadable flickering in its depths. My throat tightened. In that moment, I realized the true horror lay not in the act of arrest but in the uncertainty of what followed—a knife's edge where one misstep could send everything spiraling into chaos.

"I..." Sam began, his voice barely a whisper. "I didn't..."

7

Standoff at Sunset

The stench of stale beer and desperation clung to Sam as we led him from the trailer. His eyes darted wildly, searching for a way out.

"You don't understand," Sam muttered, his voice cracking. "I loved her. Sarah was everything."

I tightened my grip on his arm. "We know, Sam. Come with us now."

But his ramblings grew frantic. "No, no, you don't get it. It wasn't supposed to end like this!"

In a burst of manic energy, Sam wrenched free from my grasp and bolted toward a rickety shed. My heart pounded as he vanished inside.

"Liz, get in the cruiser!" I shouted, yanking open the door.

We scrambled inside, slamming the doors shut. My hands gripped the steering wheel, knuckles whitening with tension. Where was Sam? What was he planning?

Then I saw him, standing in the middle of the drive, a shotgun clutched in trembling hands. His wild gaze locked with mine through the windshield.

My throat went dry. This was it, the moment I'd dreaded since taking this job: an unhinged suspect, armed and dangerous. Not fear. Not duty. Just that terrible silence between what I should do—and what I never could.

I had to protect this town. These people trusted me to keep them safe. But as I stared down the barrel of that gun, doubt crept in. Was I truly the right man for this? My demons whispered I'd fail, just as I had before.

No. I couldn't let the past paralyze me. Not now, with so much at stake.

I took a deep breath, steeling myself. "Liz, call for backup," I said, my voice steadier than I felt. "I'm going to try to talk him down."

As I reached for the door handle, Sarah's accusing eyes flashed in my mind. But I pushed the vision away. I had a job to do, come hell or high water. And may God have mercy on us all.

The air erupted with the deafening crack of gunfire. Glass shattered, raining razor-sharp shards as the windshield disintegrated. My body reacted before my mind could process—ducking low, heart hammering against my ribs.

"Damn it!" I hissed, adrenaline surging through my veins. The acrid smell of gunpowder stung my nostrils. Another shot rang out, pinging off the hood.

I risked a glance. Sam pumped the shotgun with a snap of metal on metal, his face twisted with rage—or was it fear? The line between the two blurred, memories of my own desperation rising unbidden.

Slicing through the chaos, Liz shouted "Johnny! He's aiming for the gas tank!"

I twisted to see her, crouched in the back seat. Her eyes were wide, but her voice remained steady—always the analyst, even now.

"How many shots has he fired?" I asked, my mind racing through options.

"Three," she replied without hesitation. "His hands are shaking. He's scared, Johnny. Look at his eyes."

I peered through the spiderweb of cracks in what remained of the windshield. Sam's eyes twitched side to side, like he was searching for something. Was he seeing us or his own ghosts?

"Sam!" I shouted, my voice hoarse. "It doesn't have to end like this!"

Another shot rang out. The cruiser rocked with the impact. Grabbing the radio, I called for backup: "Code 8, Thompson Trailer!"

"Damn it," I muttered. How had it come to this? A simple arrest spiraling into a firefight. Just like that night years ago—one breath too slow, one decision not to draw, and everything went to hell.

No. Focus. I couldn't let the past cloud my judgment. Not now.

"What's your play, Sheriff?" Liz asked, her tone clipped yet concerned.

I met her gaze in the rearview mirror. "We wait him out. He's got to run out of shells eventually."

But as another shot rang out, doubt gnawed at me. Would we survive long enough to find out?

The acrid stench of gunpowder mingled with my own fear-sweat as I gripped the steering wheel. My knuckles blanched. Blood flecked my sleeve—bright, unreal—like it belonged to someone else. The pain in my arm dulled to a throb, overshadowed by the adrenaline surging through my veins.

"To hell with waiting," I growled, my resolve hardening like steel.

Without warning, I slammed my foot on the accelerator. The cruiser lurched forward with a roar, tires spitting gravel from the drive. Sam's eyes widened in shock, his shotgun wavering.

"Johnny, what are you—" Liz's words cut off as we hurtled toward Sam.

Time seemed to slow. I saw every detail of Sam's face—the stubble on his chin, the wild desperation in his eyes. For a moment, I glimpsed myself reflected there, a man pushed to the edge.

The impact came with a sickening crunch. Metal shrieked as the cruiser's front end crumpled. The air thickened with the acrid scent of burnt rubber and the metallic tang of blood. Sam's scream pierced the air, a sound destined to haunt my dreams for years to come.

As we skidded to a halt, my heart pounded in my ears. "Damn it," I whispered. "What have I done?" Even I barely heard it over the hissing engine.

The question hung unanswered in the air. I knew this moment would linger, another scar layered onto a burden I'd long stopped counting. Yet in that instant, as the dust settled around us, I couldn't shake the sense that this was only the start of a darker journey.

The world spun, a kaleidoscope of pain and fading light. I slumped back, my head thudding against the seat. Warm blood seeped through my shirt, a crimson bloom spreading across my chest.

"Johnny! Oh God, Johnny!" Liz's voice sliced through the haze, sharp with panic. Her hands, trembling yet determined, probed my wounds. "Stay with me, you stubborn bastard."

I tried to laugh, but it came out as a wet, ragged cough. "Not... going anywhere, Liz. Too much... paperwork if I clock out now."

Her gaze locked with mine, a storm of worry and exasperation. "This isn't funny, McCallister. We need backup." She fumbled for the radio, her words clipped and professional despite the tremor in her voice. "Officer down, suspect neutralized. We need immediate medical assistance..."

As Liz's voice faded into the background, I stared through the shattered windshield. Through the spiderweb of cracks, I saw Sam's crumpled form on the road. Was he dead? The thought should have troubled me more than it did.

In the distance, a siren's wail rose, a mournful cry echoing through the valley. It recalled Emma's scream the night she died, a sound that had haunted me. Now it mingled with Sam's final cry, a cacophony of guilt and regret.

My vision blurred, the edges of the world softening into darkness. The pain receded, replaced by a numbing cold creeping through my limbs. It was almost peaceful, in a way.

"Don't you dare, Johnny," Liz's voice sliced through the din. "Stay awake. That's an order."

I blinked, forcing my gaze to focus on her face. "Since when... do you give me orders, Detective?"

She managed a tight smile. "Since you decided to play demolition derby with our only suspect."

The sirens grew louder, their urgent wail a counterpoint to my heart's thudding. As my consciousness wavered, one thought crystallized with chilling clarity: the immediate threat might be over, but our troubles were only beginning.

I felt Liz's hands pressing against my chest, her fingers slick with my blood. Pain flared, hot and sharp, pulling me back from the brink of oblivion.

"Talk to me, Johnny," she commanded, her voice steady despite the tremor in her hands. "Why this town Johnny, why'd you become sheriff here?"

I coughed, tasting copper. "Thought I could... make a difference. Protect people."

Liz's dark eyes locked with mine, a storm of concern and—disappointment? "And have you? Protected them?"

Her question struck harder than Sam's bullets. Images flashed through my mind: Sarah's lifeless body, the jogger's mangled corpse, Sam's desperate face moments before impact. Each failure, each life I couldn't save, weighed on me like stones.

"I've tried," I whispered, more to myself than to Liz. "God knows I've tried."

Even as I spoke, doubt crept in. Had I truly done all I could? Or had I been fleeing my own demons, hiding in this quiet town, pretending to be a hero?

The world began to fade again, and with it came a familiar presence. "You can't hide forever, Johnny," she whispered, her voice a mix of accusation and pity. "The truth always surfaces in the end."

I tried to respond, to deny her words, but my mouth wouldn't cooperate. The last thing I heard before oblivion claimed me was Liz's frantic voice calling my name.

The wail of sirens pierced through the disorientation, pulling me back to consciousness. Red and blue lights sliced through the shattered windshield, casting eerie shadows across the wreckage. I blinked, struggling to focus as uniformed figures swarmed around us, their movements urgent yet purposeful.

"Johnny? Can you hear me?" Liz's voice was tight with worry. I grunted, tasting blood. "Yeah. I'm here."

Officer Miller's face appeared at my window, eyes wide. "Damn it, Sheriff. What happened?"

"Sam Thompson," I managed, my words clipped. Every breath was agony. "Cold-case suspect. Armed. Dangerous."

Miller nodded, barking orders to secure the perimeter. I fought the pain, forcing myself to stay alert. Too much was at stake to slip away now.

"The shotgun," I rasped. "By the shed. Evidence."

Liz's hand squeezed my shoulder. "Johnny, you need to rest. Let them handle it—"

"No," I cut her off, harsher than intended. "Need to make sure... it's done right."

As paramedics swarmed the cruiser, I glimpsed Sam's crumpled form on the asphalt. Nausea surged—sharp, fast, unstoppable. Not from pain. From the awful truth clawing at my chest: I hadn't talked him down. I hadn't tried hard enough. Because maybe, deep down, I'd already decided he was guilty.

Voices swirled around me—urgent, official. Someone mentioned the trailer. Something about evidence. I struggled to focus on the words, my mind drifting to Sarah's case, the jogger, and all the loose threads I'd failed to tie up. Beneath it all, a gnawing fear lingered: this was only the start. The real reckoning was yet to come.

"Stay with us, Johnny," Liz pleaded, her voice fading as the world dimmed again.

I wanted to reassure her, to say everything would be alright. But the lies caught in my throat, strangling me with all I hadn't said.

The sun sank lower, painting the sky in crimson hues that echoed spilled blood. Through the shattered windshield, I watched it descend, each shard catching the dying light like a kaleidoscope of accusation.

"Johnny," Liz's voice pierced the haze. "They're ready to move you. Can you hear me?"

I grunted, unwilling to tear my gaze from the horizon. "Yeah. I hear you."

But louder still was the whisper of doubt, slithering through my mind like smoke. Had I done enough? Or had I merely delayed the inevitable?

As they loaded me onto the stretcher, I glimpsed the scene—flashing lights, bustling officers, the dark stain where Sam had fallen. It felt distant, unreal, like a nightmare I couldn't fully escape.

"Sheriff," Brooks jogged to my side, out of breath, his face pale beneath the brim of his hat. "We found something inside—back room of the trailer. Could be big."

I turned my head slightly, the motion costing more than it should. "Not now," I rasped, each word dragging pain in its wake. "Secure it. All of it. Chain of custody, full log."

Brooks nodded, but his eyes lingered—uncertain, too green to hide it.

You're not ready for what comes next, I thought, but said nothing.

As they lifted me into the ambulance, I caught one last glimpse of the blood-red sun. It hung there, mocking me with its finality. Tomorrow would come, sure as death. But what terrors would it bring?

The doors slammed shut, and the void swallowed me whole. In that moment, I couldn't tell if it was the ambulance or my own damned soul.

8

Healing and Connection

The crunch of gravel beneath our wheels shatters the eerie silence of Stormy Valley's winding roads. Liz and I pedal our bicycles in sync, our movements a tentative dance of trust. I steal glances at her, noting the sharp focus in her eyes as she navigates the path ahead. Her long, dark ponytail sways with each push of the pedals, a pendulum marking the passage of time in this fleeting moment of peace.

"Nice to get away from it all, isn't it?" I say, my voice slicing through the still air. "Almost makes you forget the chaos back in town."

Liz's lips curl into a wry smile, a fleeting warmth in her otherwise guarded demeanor. "Almost," she replies, her tone laced with caution. "But the silence out here... it's deafening. Makes me wonder what secrets these hills hold."

Her words sink in, cold and unwelcome, mirroring the unease gnawing at me since the standoff. I force a chuckle, trying to dispel the creeping dread. "Come on, Liz. Can't we just enjoy the ride?"

But even as I speak, I know she's right. The countryside's tranquility is a fragile veil, barely concealing the decay beneath. I feel it in the air, taste it on my tongue—the bitter tang of unspoken truths and buried sins.

We pedal on, the rhythm of our movements at odds with the turmoil in my mind. My badge presses harder against my chest with each mile, a constant reminder of everything I still carry. Yet as I watch Liz's determined profile, something loosens in my chest—barely there, almost absurd. Maybe it's hope. Can we possibly unravel the web of secrets threatening to choke our little town?

But for now, we ride. The road stretches before us, a ribbon of uncertainty winding deeper into the heart of Stormy Valley's mysteries. With each turn of the wheels, I can't shake the sense that we're pedaling toward a reckoning long overdue.

I clear my throat, pushing back the encroaching gloom. "Hey, Liz," I call, my voice laced with forced casualness. "Ever been down Hillcrest Road?"

She glances over, her gaze sharp and inquisitive. "Can't say I have. Why?"

"There's this hill…" I trail off, memories of simpler times flickering through my mind. "It's got a kick to it. Used to ride it when I needed to clear my head."

Liz's eyebrow arches, a hint of intrigue piercing her guarded facade. "That so? Sounds like you could use a clear head right now, Johnny."

I bark out a laugh, hollow and brittle. "You've got no idea." I pause, weighing my words carefully. "Want to give it a go?"

She hesitates, her analytical mind visibly turning. Then, to my surprise, she nods. "Lead the way, Sheriff."

We veer off the main road, gravel crunching beneath our wheels. As we approach the hill, a familiar thrill buzzes against my sternum, a stark contrast to the weight crushing me for days.

"Here we go," I mutter, more to myself than to Liz.

The descent starts slowly, then surges with momentum. The wind whips past, carrying away the stench of fear and consequence—if only for a moment. I hear Liz's sharp intake of breath, see her white-knuckled grip on the handlebars.

For a fleeting instant, hurtling down the hill, I feel… free. The burden of my past, the looming threats, the whispers of accusation haunting my dreams—all fall away, lost in the rush of adrenaline and the roar of the wind.

We hit the bottom with a jolt, our bikes bouncing and swerving on the uneven road. I let out a whoop of exhilaration. "Damn, Liz, that never gets old!"

But even as I revel in this brief respite, I know it can't last. Reality rushes up to meet us, as swift as our descent. A chill, unrelated to the wind, grips me as I wonder what darkness awaits when our wheels touch level ground.

As we rejoin the main road, the exhilaration fades like mist in the morning sun. A menacing growl shatters the quiet country air, growing louder with each second. I glance over my shoulder, my heart sinking as I spot the pickup truck, its engine snarling like a beast on the hunt.

"Liz," I call, my voice taut. "We've got company."

She doesn't respond, but her shoulders tense, her posture shifting subtly. The truck looms closer, its presence an unwelcome intrusion into our fleeting moment of peace.

As the truck pulls alongside us, I glimpse the driver's face, twisted with rage. His bloodshot, wild eyes lock with mine. For a moment, I'm thrown back to that night, staring down a gun's barrel, the consequences of my inaction crushing me.

"Get off the damn road!" the man bellows, his words slicing through the air like shrapnel. "You cyclists think you own the place!"

I raise a hand, signaling Liz to slow. She complies, her eyes flicking between me and the agitated driver. Her analytical mind churns, assessing the threat, formulating a strategy.

"Easy now," I say, my voice even despite my hammering heart. "We're just out for a ride. No need for—"

"No need?" The man's face flushes a deep crimson as he cuts me off. His arms flail as he steps from the cab, slamming the door behind him. "You're blocking traffic, endangering lives!"

As I prepare to respond, a chill grips my spine. The man's face blurs, morphing into another—one that's haunted me for years. I blink hard, forcing the vision away. Now's not the time for ghosts, I tell myself. Yet a part of me wonders if there'll ever be a time they don't lurk at the edge of my vision, waiting to drag me into the abyss. I swallow hard, shoving the specter aside.

My palms sweat as I grip the handlebars tighter. This guy's clearly unstable, and I don't want to provoke him further. "Sir," I begin, keeping my bicycle ready, my voice carrying the authority I've honed for years, "I'm Sheriff Jonathan McCallister. I understand your frustration, but we're not here to cause trouble."

"You cyclists, always hogging the road like you own it," the man spits, his voice laced with frustration as he kicks the gravel.

His eyes widen as he stares at me, his balled fists loosening slightly. I see his mind churn, reassessing the situation. Liz watches intently, her gaze narrowed, cataloging every detail.

"Sheriff?" the driver stammers, his anger deflating like a punctured tire. "I... I didn't realize..."

"It's alright," I say, offering a smile that doesn't reach my eyes. Ghosts of past confrontations flicker at the edges of my vision, but I shove them back. "Look, if you've got concerns about cyclists, I'd be happy to discuss them. Why not follow us to the station? We can file a formal complaint, talk it through properly."

The man hesitates, conflict etched across his face. I hold my breath, keenly aware of how quickly situations like this can spiral. Responsibility clings to me like a second skin — tight, hot, impossible to shed. I'm just one wrong word from this turning into something else entirely.

"I... yeah, okay," the driver concedes, his shoulders sagging as he retreats to the truck's cab. "I'll follow you."

I exhale slowly, tension draining from my body. Yet even as relief washes over me, a nagging voice whispers that this is only the start. In Stormy Valley, peace is a fragile veil, ready to shatter at the slightest touch.

The truck's engine rumbles as it falls back, a growling beast momentarily tamed. Liz and I resume our ride, gravel crunching beneath our tires—a sound too ordinary for the tension still lingering in the air. I feel her gaze on me, analyzing, dissecting.

"That was... impressive," Liz says, her voice laced with admiration and something else—curiosity, perhaps, or suspicion. "What was he complaining about, blocking traffic? No one's on the road but us."

I let out a dry chuckle, hollow in my ears. "That's just the surface," I say, my grip tightening on the handlebars as we navigate a sharp bend. "Folks around here harbor contentious feelings toward cyclists. They see us as a nuisance, slowing traffic, taking up space. Some even think we're deliberately making their lives harder."

Liz nods, something shifting in her expression. "And they take that frustration out on you."

"Sometimes," I admit, my tone grim. "Mostly it's just words. But sometimes, things escalate into physical confrontations, like what nearly happened back there."

"You've got a knack for defusing volatile situations, Sheriff."

"Knack? More like a curse. It's a daily tightrope walk in this town, Liz. One wrong step and..."

My words trail off as memories of past missteps flicker through my mind like a grim slideshow. I shake them away, focusing on the road ahead.

"Sounds like more simmers beneath Stormy Valley's quaint surface than meets the eye," Liz probes, her tone casual but her intent razor-sharp.

"You have no idea," I quietly admit. "This place... it's a powder keg. Everyone harbors secrets, grudges. One spark, and the whole damn town could ignite."

As we pedal on, the countryside's tranquility masks the deterioration lurking beneath. I wonder, not for the first time, how long I can hold the peace before it all crashes down around me.

The police station looms ahead, a weathered sentinel of law and order. My thoughts drift to the standoff with Sam, the echo of gunfire still ringing in my ears. Memories of that day settles on my shoulders like a leaden blanket.

"Johnny?" Liz's voice nudged me from my daze. "You went somewhere else for a moment."

I blink, forcing a wan smile. "Just... remembering. That standoff changed things. People look at me differently now, like I'm some kind of hero."

"Aren't you?" Liz asks, her gaze searching mine.

I laugh, a hollow sound devoid of humor. "Heroes don't wake up in cold sweats, haunted by ghosts of the past." The words slip out before I can stop them.

Liz's hand brushes my arm, a fleeting touch that speaks volumes. "We all have demons, Johnny. It's how we face them that matters."

Her words strike deep, stirring something in my chest. As we pull into the station's lot, I glimpse the pickup in my peripheral vision, a looming reminder of unfinished business.

"Looks like our friend took you up on that complaint," Liz observes.

I nod, steeling myself. "Time to play peacekeeper again. Some days, I feel more like a damn shrink than a sheriff."

Liz's lips quirk in a half-smile. "Maybe that's exactly what this town needs."

As I dismount my bike, the road feels alien beneath my boots—like I'm balancing on a knife's edge. One wrong move, and I'll cut myself open, spilling my secrets for the world to see. But for now, I have a job to do. Time to don the mask of Sheriff Johnathan McCallister and face whatever demons come knocking.

9

Jogging into Darkness

The rhythmic crunch of gravel beneath our feet echoed through the misty air as Liz and I jogged side by side along the Stormy Valley trail. Our breath billowed in frosty plumes, dissolving into the pale morning light. The recent closure of the cold case that had haunted me for years should have brought relief. Instead, an uneasy hollowness lingered.

"Beautiful morning," Liz remarked, her ponytail swaying with each stride.

I grunted, my mind drifting to darker places. Had we truly solved the mystery, or merely scratched the surface of something far more sinister? The forests looming on either side of the path watched us with ancient, knowing gazes.

Up ahead, a cluster of joggers in eye-searing neon gear rounded a bend. Their synchronized footfalls wove a hypnotic rhythm—thud, thud, thud. One man stood out—his eyes wild, movements erratic. A chill gripped my spine, unrelated to the crisp air.

"Quite the turnout today," I observed, trying to dispel my growing sense of foreboding.

Liz nodded. "Safety in numbers."

If only she knew how false that sentiment was. In Stormy Valley, darkness crept in, no matter how brightly we shone our lights against it. As we fell in step with the group, I couldn't shake the sense that we were moths drawn to an invisible flame, unaware of the inferno awaiting us.

"We make quite the team, don't we?" Liz said, her breath forming small clouds in the crisp air. "Cracking that cold-case... I never thought we'd see it solved."

I forced a smile, scanning the path ahead. "Yeah, we did good work." The words rang hollow, as if I were convincing myself more than her.

Liz glanced at me, eyes sharp and unreadable. "But...? I sense there's more on your mind, Sheriff."

I hesitated, weighing how much to reveal. "It's just... cases like that leave scars. Even when they're closed."

She nodded, her expression softening slightly. "I get it. The burden doesn't vanish overnight."

We ran in silence for a moment, gravel crunching beneath our feet, filling the air. I was about to respond when a blur of movement caught my eye.

The man I'd noticed earlier—the one with manic energy—sprinted past us. His eyes were wide, unfocused, a primal glint flickering in it as he flew by.

My muscles tensed, a lifetime in law enforcement urging caution. "Did you catch that?" I whispered to Liz, tracking the man as he hurried away. "That runner... doesn't he remind you of someone?"

Liz followed him with narrowed eyes, already putting the pieces together. "You mean the road rage guy from before?" Her voice held a hint of concern, mirroring my unease.

I nodded tersely, struggling to convey the unease coiling in my stomach. "Exactly. There's something off about him. He looks... like he's on edge."

As we watched, the man disappeared around a bend in the trail, leaving behind only the echo of his frenzied footsteps and a growing sense of unease.

The road rage man barreled past the last woman in our group, his ragged breathing echoing in the crisp morning air. I couldn't shake the sense that something was terribly wrong. My eyes darted to the ground, where neon running markers jutted from the dirt like strange, fluorescent blooms.

"What the hell?" I muttered, my brow furrowing.

Liz edged closer. "Johnny? What's going on?"

I opened my mouth to respond, but nothing came out. A chill gripped my spine, instincts screaming danger. Before I could react, a weight slammed into my back, throwing me off balance.

"Shit!" I grunted, stumbling forward. The road-rage man had circled back, attacking from behind. My mind raced, years of training kicking in as I fought to regain balance.

"Johnny!" Liz's voice rang distant, muffled by the rush of blood in my ears.

I spun, hands raised defensively. The man's gaze was wild, unfocused. In that moment, I wasn't just fighting an attacker—I was battling ghosts, every failure I thought I'd buried rising with a voice of its own. The whispers were louder now, impossible to ignore.

"Stand down!" I barked, voice rough with exertion. But there was no reasoning with him. He lunged again, and I braced myself, determined to shield the others.

As we grappled, a voice in my head whispered, "You can't outrun your demons, Johnny. They always catch up." I shoved the thought aside, focusing on the immediate threat. Yet deep down, I knew it spoke truth. Some battles never end.

The man's fist slammed into my jaw, pain bursting through my skull. I tasted blood, coppery and bitter. My vision blurred, but instinct took over. I drove my knee into his gut, hearing the air rush from his lungs.

"Why are you doing this?" I growled, grappling for control.

He snarled, a feral sound that chilled me to the bone. We stumbled, a tangle of limbs and desperation, gravel biting into my skin as we fell.

My fingers caught his shirt, and I rolled, pinning him beneath me. "Stop!" I commanded, but the madness in his eyes told me he was beyond reason.

He thrashed, his elbow slamming into my ribs. Pain erupted in my side, and for a moment, stars danced before my eyes. In that split-second distraction, he surged upward, hands wrapping around my throat.

Panic clawed at me as I fought to breathe. The world narrowed to a pinpoint, and in that instant, I saw not just this man, but every mistake I'd made, every demon I'd tried to outrun.

"No," I choked out, more to myself than him. "Not like this."

With a surge of desperate strength, I broke his grip and shoved him back. A sickening crack echoed as his head struck a rock, and he went limp.

The silence that followed was deafening.

"Oh God," I whispered, hands trembling as I checked for a pulse. Nothing. "No, no, no."

The horror of what I'd done crashed over me like a tidal wave. I'd taken a life. Again. Not in defense. Not with honor. Just a blur of rage. The very thing I'd sworn to protect.

"Johnny?" Liz's voice trembled. "Is he...?"

I couldn't meet her gaze, dreading the horror in her eyes. "I didn't mean to," I murmured, voice barely audible. "I was just trying to stop him."

But intentions meant nothing against the cold, hard reality. As I knelt, the early morning mist swirling around us, I felt the fragile peace I'd built in Stormy Valley crumble away.

What have I done?

The mist clung to my skin like a cold, damp shroud as I stood over the lifeless body. My breath came in ragged gasps, each a stark reminder of the struggle that ended moments ago. The trail, once a sanctuary of morning solitude, now loomed alien and hostile.

"We need to call this in," Liz said, her voice cutting through the blur of panic and guilt clouding my thoughts.

I nodded, unable to form words. I swept the scene, desperately seeking something—anything—to make sense of what had happened. That's when I saw it: a glint of metal peeking from beneath the attacker's jacket.

"Wait," I muttered, kneeling beside the body. With trembling hands, I reached for the object.

"Johnny, don't—" Liz began, but her words faltered as I drew a rusted hunting knife.

"He was armed," I said, voice hollow. "He would've..."

My words trailed off as my gaze drifted past the body. There, half-hidden in the undergrowth, a pale, lifeless hand protruded.

"Oh, Christ," I whispered, stumbling to my feet. "Liz, there's—"

"I see it," she said, her face ashen. "Over here, too."

As if in a trance, we moved deeper into the woods. With each step, the horror grew. Desiccated limbs jutted from the earth like grotesque saplings. The stench of decay, masked by the crisp morning air, now struck in nauseating waves.

"This can't be real," I muttered, bile rising in my throat. "This isn't possible."

The evidence was undeniable. Our quiet jogging trail had turned into a graveyard, each step unveiling fresh horrors. I'd seen death before—hell, I'd caused it—but this... this was something else entirely.

"How long has this been here?" Liz asked, her analytical mind already churning. "How did we never notice?"

I shook my head, unable to process it. "I don't know. But whoever that man was"—I gestured toward the body on the trail—"he knew. He was trying to keep us away."

The realization struck like a punch to the gut. In my desperation to survive, I'd killed the one person who might've held answers.

"What have we stumbled into, Liz?" I asked my voice frayed with disbelief.

She met my eyes, reflecting my dread. "I don't know, Johnny. But I fear this is only the beginning."

Surrounded by death and decay, I couldn't shake the sense that Stormy Valley's quiet facade had cracked, exposing the rot beneath. And I, the town's protector, had just opened Pandora's box.

The world seemed to warp and twist, reality bending like a funhouse mirror. I blinked hard, desperate to clear my vision, but the grotesque scene remained. My mind reeled, clawing for any explanation to make sense of this nightmare.

"Johnny? We need to call this in." Liz shouted, snapping me out of a daze.

I nodded mechanically, my hand trembling as I reached for my radio. Was I losing my grip? After years of sobriety, had I snapped?

"This is Sheriff Johnathan McCallister," I managed, voice rough. "We've got multiple bodies on the Stormy Valley trail. Send everyone."

As I lowered the radio, a chill gripped my spine. The trees loomed closer, their gnarled branches reaching like skeletal fingers. I'd walked this trail countless times, but now it felt alien, hostile.

"You okay?" Liz asked, her brow furrowed with concern.

I forced a weak smile. "Peachy. Nothing like stumbling onto a mass grave to start your day."

She didn't laugh. Smart woman.

"Johnny, about what happened with that man—"

"Not now," I snapped, harsher than intended. I couldn't face it. Not yet. "We need to secure the scene."

As we moved to cordon off the area, my mind raced. How long had this been here? How many had jogged past, oblivious to the horror beneath their feet? And most crucially, who was responsible?

The questions piled up, each more unsettling than the last. Beneath it all, a darker thought whispered: What if I was involved? What if, in my addiction-fueled blackouts, I'd done something unforgivable?

I shook my head, trying to silence the treacherous voice. "Focus, McCallister," I muttered. "One step at a time."

As sirens wailed in the distance, I steeled myself. Whatever was happening here, I'd uncover the truth. I had to—for the victims, the town, and my own sanity.

Yet as I surveyed the grim scene one last time, I couldn't shake the sense that Stormy Valley's secrets ran deeper than we could fathom. Uncovering the truth might destroy us all.

I turned to Liz, my gaze meeting hers. In that fleeting, tense glance, I saw my dread mirrored. The enormity of what lay before us pressed down like the low-hanging clouds before a thunderstorm—charged, oppressive, waiting to rupture.

"We're in for one hell of a ride, aren't we?" I said, voice low and gravelly.

Liz nodded, her lips pressed into a thin line. "This goes beyond anything we've faced, Johnny. We'll need to watch each other's backs."

I laughed, a hollow sound echoing in the stillness. "Careful, Detective. That almost sounds like trust."

"Don't get ahead of yourself, Sheriff," she shot back, but her words carried no real bite.

As we stood there, the wind picked up, rustling through the trees. It carried the stench of decay, a grim reminder of what lay beneath our feet. I suppressed a shudder, my mind drifting to dark places.

How many more secrets did Stormy Valley hold? And how many were mine?

"We should start interviewing the other joggers," Liz said, slicing through my thoughts. "Someone must've seen something."

I nodded, grateful for the distraction. "Right. You take the women, I'll handle the men. And Liz?" I paused, meeting her eyes. "Whatever we find, whatever comes next... we're in this together."

She gave a curt nod and turned away. I couldn't shake the sense we stood on the brink of something vast and hungry—and I had the sinking feeling it had already slipped through the cracks.

Welcome to Stormy Valley, where every shadow hides a secret, and every secret bites.

10

Descent into Doubt

The amber liquid swirls in my glass, mirroring the churning thoughts in my mind. The kitchen's overhead light hums faintly, casting warped shadows across the counter. I take another sip, savoring the burn as it slides down my throat. It does little to dull the sharp edges of memories slicing through my consciousness.

The jogging trail. The scream. The sickening thud. The desiccated limbs.

I squeeze my eyes shut. No use. The images flare brighter behind my lids. I slam the glass onto the counter, harder than intended. Whiskey sloshes over the sides, onto my hand.

"Christ," I mutter, wiping it on my shirt. The house groans around me, its bones settling in the cold.

I need to get it out. Write it down—force it from my head onto the page. That used to help.

I leave the glass and step into the darkened hallway. No need for lights. The desk lamp's amber glow spills from the office, pooling in the corridor like memory.

The carpet crunches faintly underfoot where something spilled—coffee, maybe. It's hard to recall. Case files spill across the floor as I pass the living room, where the TV hums a blue glow to no one.

I tell myself I'll clean it up once this case settles. Once my head does.

The journal waits in its usual spot: beside the unused coaster, beneath a coffee mug ringed with dried sludge from the last time I opened it. Leather-bound, worn at the corners, its pages swollen with ink and memory.

I sit and open it to a blank page.

Liz said the necklace matters. She saw the scratches—same as me. Said it wasn't Sarah's originally. So who wore it first?

I flip forward. More notes. My handwriting twists into frantic, cramped loops.

Emma's story shifted again. Can't tell if she's lying or if it's her meds. Liz thinks the brother knew. Find Frank Thompson.

Farther down, a line stands apart:

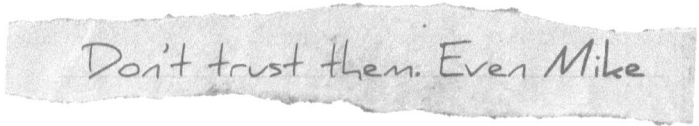

I blink. My finger hovers beneath the words, half-expecting the ink to smear. It's dry. Old. Mine.

"No," I whisper. "I didn't write that. I wouldn't—"

I flip back; diagrams of the Thompson property, a to-do list with "Find locket" circled three times, then scratched out. A page filled with *LIZ MONT-GOMERY* repeated down the margin, beside a sketch of her eyes—sharp, watchful.

The lines blur. I blink once, then again.

She's there

In the doorway, half-shadowed, watching. Liz Montgomery. Same dark coat, arms crossed. Her expression unreadable, but her gaze holds something—judgment or worry?

"You're not listening," she says, voice steady, almost patient.

I freeze. My breath catches.

Did she follow me home?

Had she been with me all along?

"You've seen it. You just keep looking away."

Her words strike like a slap. I open my mouth to respond, to ask what she means—but the lamp flickers.

She's gone.

Only dust motes drift in the lamplight, casting soft shadows that don't belong.

I turn the page.

Blank.

And then—bottom right corner—faint as a shadow:

She was never real.

My heart stutters. I blink again.

Gone.

A wave of cold sweeps over me, sharp and absolute. My skin prickles. The room tilts, as if the floor dropped an inch beneath my feet.

I grip the chair's arms to compose myself, but it's no use. My heart pounds, too loud, too fast. The air thickens, like breathing through wool.

Was she here?

Was she ever here?

I stare into the empty doorway.

The house's quiet hum swells in my ears—pipes ticking, refrigerator cycling, wind pressing the siding like fingers tapping to get in.

I look at the page, but the words have vanished. Blank again. Except where my trembling hand has left faint smudges.

No. No, no. I flip forward, then back, faster, hands shaking. Just paper. Just empty margins. Just static from the living room and the faint tap of heat pipes, pulsing in time with my heart.

I need to do something. Anything.

I reach for the pen.

At the bottom of a fresh page, I write:

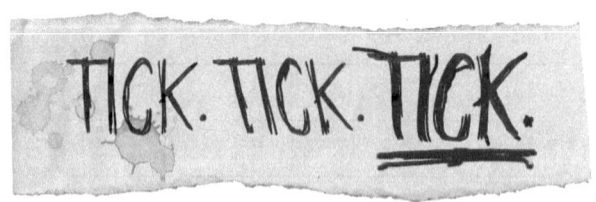

I underline the last line. Again. And again. Until the pen tears into the paper.

I stare at the ink, the frayed fibers beneath. My breath comes in shallow bursts. The house's silence presses in—too quiet, like something holding its breath.

"She wasn't here," I say aloud, needing to hear it, to anchor the thought.

It's not that bad. I've seen worse. Lived worse.

Just a blip. Sleeplessness. Stress. Whiskey.

I press my palm flat on the desk, grounding myself—as if normal people do that. As if stable people do.

It's fine.

Everything's fine.

It's temporary. All of it.

The phone's shrill ring shatters the oppressive silence.

I jerk, the pen goes flying from my hand, clattering to the floor. My chair scrapes violently against the hardwood as I half-stand, heart slamming against my ribs, desperate to break free.

I stare at the phone. Its piercing cry slices through the silence—sharp, alien, wrong.

I swallow hard, reaching for the receiver with fingers that don't feel like mine.

"Sheriff Johnathan McCallister."

"Johnny, it's Deputy Larson. We've got a situation at Stormy Valley Farm. A death."

My stomach lurches, whiskey or news—I can't tell. "Details, Larson. Give me details."

"Farmhand found at the base of the hayloft. It's grim, sir."

I squeeze my eyes shut, willing the room to halt its sluggish spin. "I'll be there in ten."

The receiver clatters into its cradle, the sound echoing in the empty office. I heave myself up, gripping the desk's edge as the floor tilts beneath me.

"Pull yourself together," I mutter, fumbling for my coat. Its familiar weight settles on my shoulders, a frail shield against the chill seeping into my bones.

My fingers brush the cool metal of my badge. I pause, staring at the tarnished star. How many times have I pinned it on, vowing to be better, to do better? How many times have I failed?

"Not this time," I growl, pinning the badge to my coat with trembling hands. "This time, I'll get it right."

I stumble toward the door, each step a fight against the whiskey coursing through my veins. The gray afternoon light, filtering through the blinds, accuses me, exposing every stumble, every weakness.

As I wrench open the door, cold air slaps my face, a stark reminder of the reality beyond these walls. I squint into the overcast sky, my thoughts racing to the scene awaiting me.

What fresh horrors will Stormy Valley unveil today? And am I strong enough to face them?

11

Blurred Lines

The road winds too swiftly beneath my tires, trees blurring at the edges of my vision. I crack the window, hoping the cold air will sober me. Deep breaths. I count them—one, two, three—but they come shallow and hot, offering no anchor. I fumble with the radio, but the static grates worse than the silence. By the time the barn crests the hill, the only thing I've calmed is the lie I keep telling myself: I'm fine.

The hayloft looms as I pull up to Stormy Valley Farm, its dark frame stretching across the ground like skeletal fingers of an ancient, grasping hand. I kill the engine, the sudden silence amplifying the pounding in my skull.

"Christ," I mutter, squinting at the scene before me. Hay litters the ground, golden strands catching the weak afternoon light. There, at the base of the loft, a crumpled form lies motionless.

I force myself out of the cruiser, each step like wading through molasses. The scent of fresh-cut grass mingles with something darker—copper, iron—filling my nostrils.

"Sheriff McCallister," a voice calls. A farmhand, his face a mask of shock. "We... we found him like this. Must've fallen."

I nod, not trusting my voice yet. My eyes scan the scene, taking in details my alcohol-addled brain struggles to process: the angles, the stains, the hay—nothing sits right.

Something feels off. A nagging feeling claws at the back of my mind, cutting through the whiskey's haze.

"Has anyone moved him?" I ask, my voice rough as gravel.

The farmhand shakes his head. "No, sir. We called you straight away."

I crouch, ignoring the creak of my knees. Up close, the wrongness hits me like a freight train: the body's unnatural position, the unscuffed boots, the hay scattered too neatly, too deliberately.

"This wasn't an accident," I mutter, more to myself than anyone else.

"What was that, Sheriff?" the farmhand asks, leaning closer.

I stand, swaying slightly. "Nothing," I lie, the words sliding out like someone else said them. "Just thinking aloud."

But as I survey the scene again, certainty settles in my gut like a lead weight. This poor bastard didn't fall. He was pushed. Or worse.

And now, God help me, I've got to figure out why.

A movement catches my eye, and I turn to see a figure at the edge of the farmyard. Pete Collins. The boy's always been quiet, but today, something's different. His eyes, usually blank, now hold a depth I can't fathom.

Our gazes lock, and a shiver runs down my spine. Recognition flares, followed swiftly by suspicion that burns through the whiskey's haze clouding my mind.

I take a deep breath, steeling myself. "Pete," I call, my voice carrying across the yard. "I need a word with you."

My feet feel like lead as I trudge toward him. The ground seems to sway beneath me, a reminder of the whiskey still coursing through my veins.

"Evening, Sheriff," Pete says softly as I approach. His voice is consistent, betraying nothing.

I study his face, searching for any hint of deceit. "Tell me what happened, Pete. From the start."

Pete's eyes flicker briefly to the crumpled body behind me before returning to mine. "I was in the barn," he begins, his words measured. "Heard a commotion in the loft. By the time I got out here..."

"Did you see anyone else around?" I press, fighting to keep my voice steady. "Anything unusual?"

Pete shakes his head slowly. "No, sir. It was just... quiet. Too quiet, you know?"

I do know. The eerie stillness that follows violence, like the world's holding its breath. But something in Pete's demeanor sets my nerves on edge. Is it guilt lurking behind those inscrutable eyes? Or just the shadow of my own paranoia?

"And you didn't hear anything before the commotion?" I ask, my tone sharpening. "No argument? No struggle?"

Pete's gaze holds firm, but I catch a subtle shift in his posture. "No, Sheriff. Like I said, it was quiet."

I step closer, crowding Pete's space. "You sure about that, Pete? Because something doesn't add up."

His eyes narrow slightly. "What're you implying, Sheriff?"

I growl, my patience fraying. "I'm asking for the truth. What're you holding back?"

Pete's jaw tightens, a flicker of something—fear? defiance?—crossing his face. "I've told you all I know," he says, his soft voice carrying an edge now.

I lean in, too close. The whiskey hums in my blood, blurring the hard lines of his face until he swims like smoke. My vision snaps in and out of focus, and with each blink, he looks less like a man and more like a shadow I almost recognize.

"You're drunk, Sheriff. This isn't the time."

The words spark something raw. Who the hell is he to dismiss me? A farmhand. A nobody. Talking down to the sheriff?

"Don't tell me what to do." My hand fists his collar before I know it. The room lurches. My balance falters. I let go—but I can't let go of that *look*.

"In your eyes..." My voice drops to a whisper, trembling somewhere between fury and dread. "I've seen it before. At the fair... by the ferris wheel. Watching Sarah."

Pete backs off fast, eyes wide. "Sheriff—please. You're not yourself."

Am I not? The thought cuts through the fog. What am I doing? But the doubt slips away, drowned in the rising tide of suspicion.

"I know you're hiding something," I rasp. "And I'll find out what."

But the moment hangs too long. My grip on reality slips. What's real? What's imagined? I'm lost in the mirror maze of my mind.

"I've told you everything, Sheriff," he says softly. "I found him like that when I came to start the morning chores."

But a tremor in his hand, so slight I nearly miss it, betrays him. My instincts scream to push harder, to tear down his composed facade.

"You expect me to believe that?" I snap, struggling to keep my balance. The whiskey churns in my gut, stoking my anger. "A man doesn't just fall from a hayloft, Pete. Not like this."

Pete glances at the crumpled body, then back to me—too quick to be casual. "Accidents happen, Sheriff. You know that better than most."

His words hit like a physical blow. Does he know? About the jogger, about my sins? The world spins, and I fight to focus on Pete's face. Pete tilts his head, a ghost of a smile flickering on his lips.

The silence stretches between us, heavy with accusation. A cow lows in the distance, sound echoing through the barn—lonely, hollow. How easy it would be for secrets to stay buried.

"The farmhand, Pete. What happened to him?" My voice is low, each word dripping with the intensity of a man on the edge. "I need answers, and I need them now."

Pete's eyes flicker, something unreadable crossing his face like a ripple. For a moment, I think I see a crack in his calm facade, a glimpse of something darker beneath. But it's gone as quickly as it came, leaving me wondering if it was ever there.

"Like I said... things go wrong out here. All the time." Pete responds, his words measured, revealing little. "Especially on a farm. You know that as well as anyone." Is there a confession buried in his words? His face stays impassive, but I sense guilt radiating from him. Or maybe it's my own, echoing back.

A tremor in his voice, faint but unmistakable, sets my nerves on edge. I've interrogated enough suspects to know when someone's hiding something. And Pete? His secrets run deeper than the roots of the old oak out front.

I step closer, my heart pounding. "This wasn't just an accident, was it, Pete?" I press, fighting the urge to grab his collar and shake the truth out of him. "What're you holding back?"

Pete's facade cracks, and something in him dulls. The red in his flannel washes to rust, his features flattening like old newsprint in the barn's stale light. He doesn't step into shadow so much as the color drains from him—as if he's always belonged to this place, always been part of its decay.

"I... I don't know for sure, Sheriff," he whispers, his voice barely audible over the rustle of hay and the distant lowing of cattle. "But there might've been... something."

Pete's admission hits like a punch to the gut. A firestorm of emotions ignites within me—rage, disappointment, a perverse sense of vindication. My fists clench, nails biting into my palms.

"Goddammit, Pete," I growl, fighting to keep my voice steady. "Why didn't you come to me sooner?"

He flinches at my tone, and I force a deep breath. The old itch creeps up my spine—the craving for something to dull the maelstrom threatening to overwhelm me.

"I was scared," Pete mumbles, eyes stuck to the floor. "Didn't know what to do. Thought maybe... if I kept quiet, it'd all just go away."

I bark a harsh laugh. "Nothing ever just 'goes away' in this town, kid. You should know that by now."

My mind races, years of law enforcement training clashing with the raw, primal anger surging through my veins. I want justice for the dead farmhand, but a darker part of me—the part I've spent years trying to bury—whispers for vengeance.

"Tell me everything," I demand, my voice low and menacing. "And God help you if I catch you lying again."

The tension in my body snaps like a frayed rope. Pete's words—his admission, his fear—are the final spark igniting the powder keg of my rage. His hand twitches—was it a move toward his belt? Or just a flinch? My brain hesitates. My body doesn't. I lunge, my hands seizing the collar of his worn flannel shirt.

"You miserable little—" I snarl, slamming him against the barn wall. The impact reverberates through us, and hay dust billows in a choking cloud. "People are dead because of your silence!"

Pete's eyes widen in terror. "Sheriff, please—" he gasps, but I'm beyond reason.

My fist connects with his jaw, a sickening crunch echoing the blow. The pain in my knuckles feels distant, drowned by the roaring in my ears. I know I should stop—this isn't justice, it's assault. But the adrenaline surges, the fury unwinds. Each punch is a question I don't want answered.

"I trusted you," I snarl, fists clenched. "This whole town trusted you. Look what we got."

The barn blurs into a storm of motion and violence. Pete's feeble attempts to defend himself, his protests vanish beneath the sound of flesh striking flesh. My vision narrows, locked on the target of my rage.

"Johnny, stop!" Pete's voice cuts through, thick with pain and desperation. "You don't understand—"

But I'm not after understanding. Not now. Each blow lands like a purge, a release, a filthy prayer. God help me, some part of me relishes this.

The red haze of rage fades, replaced by cold, stark clarity. Pete lies crumpled at my feet, barely recognizable.

Dying.

Blood. Swelling. Breath shallow and uneven.

I stand over him, chest heaving, hands scraped, knuckles raw. He looks broken.

"Christ," I whisper, the word escaping like a prayer or a curse. "What have I done?"

Pete's eyes flutter open, unfocused and glassy with pain. He groans softly, wincing, and presses two trembling fingers to the bridge of his nose—testing, maybe bracing. Blood trails down to his upper lip.

"Johnny," he croaks, his voice thick and nasal, "I never meant... I didn't kill anyone."

He wipes at his nose, blinking hard. His movements are slow, uncertain—shock, perhaps, or something worse.

He looks up, dazed, his lip trembling. Is that pity in his eyes? Or just pain??

Pete tries to speak but winces. Blood stains his face. Swelling distorts it. A mess I made.

My vision pulses at the edges. I can't tell what's real—and it doesn't matter.

I don't see Pete anymore. I see what's left of him. What I did.

Fists trembling, rage spent.

The realization crashes in, cold and merciless. My knees buckle. I stumble back, breath stuttering, gaze locked on the ruin I caused.

The barn's silence feels wrong now. Not heavy. Hollow. Empty.

"I'm... I'm sorry," I manage, the words woefully inadequate. "I shouldn't have—"

"You're right," Pete cuts in, his voice a hoarse whisper. "I should've fixed it when I had the chance, before everything rotted."

I shake my head, unable to process his words. My mind reels, replaying the violence in sickening detail. The righteousness I felt moments ago curdles into shame, leaving a bitter taste.

"I need to get you help," I mutter, more to myself than to Pete. I raise my hands, palms out, and back away. "I'm not going to hurt you again, Pete. I swear it."

My promise rings hollow, even to my own ears. The damage is done—to Pete, to my badge, to whatever fragile trust this town had in me. I stumble toward the barn door, legs unsteady beneath me.

"Where are you going?" Pete calls, a note of panic in his voice.

I pause at the threshold, the cool air outside cutting through the barn's stifling atmosphere. "To turn myself in," I reply, not daring to look back. "It's what I should've done long ago."

As I turn to leave, a glint of metal catches my eye in the dim light. The veterinary medicine cabinet, its glass door ajar, whispering promises I know better than to trust. And still, I go.

I've already let the town down. What's one more sin to carry?

"What are you doing?" Pete's voice wavers, thick with fear and confusion.

I don't answer. I can't. The vials swim before me, their labels blurred into meaningless symbols. My hands stay steady, but the floor shifts beneath me, like the world's trying to shrug me off.

Maybe this isn't the first time. Maybe I never stopped.

I move on instinct. My fingers find the bottle like they've done it a thousand times. No decision. No hesitation. Just need—the kind that hums beneath the skin, deeper than thought.

"Johnny, don't," Pete pleads, his voice distant, muffled by the roaring in my ears.

I draw the clear liquid with practiced ease. "I can't face it," I mutter, rolling up my sleeve. "Not again. Not sober."

The needle hovers over my skin, a harbinger of relief and damnation.

"You're better than this," Pete says, his voice soft now. "We can figure this out."

I laugh. Hollow. Unforgivable. "Better? Look at what I've done, Pete. I'm exactly who I've always been."

The needle pierces. The plunger slides. My badge, my duties, my sins—washed away in a heartbeat.

"I'm sorry," I whisper, unsure if it's to Pete, myself, or the ghosts.

The barn blurs, reality slipping like sand through my fingers.

In that moment, suspended between clarity and oblivion, I wonder if I'll ever claw my way back.

But as the drug answers first, I no longer care.

The shadows rise—not fingers now, but arms. Arms pulling me under.

My legs buckle. I catch myself on a weathered beam. Then I let go.

"Johnny, stay with me," Pete's voice echoes, distorted as if underwater. "What did you take?"

I try to focus on his face, but it blurs. "Doesn't matter," I slur. "Nothing matters anymore."

The world tilts, and I'm on my back, staring at the rafters. They writhe like serpents, and I can't tell if it's the drug or my guilt warping them.

"I see them, Pete," pointing toward phantom accusers. "All the people I've failed. They're here."

Pete's face swims into view, concern etched in every line. "There's no one here but us, Johnny. You're not well."

A bitter laugh escapes me. "I haven't been well for a long time."

The barn spins faster. I close my eyes, but the blackness behind my lids pulses with memories—the faces of those I couldn't save. Regret coils, slow and suffocating.

"Make it stop," I plead, unsure if I'm speaking aloud. "I can't... I can't bear it anymore."

As consciousness fades, Pete's voice grows distant. "Hold on, Johnny. I'm calling for help."

But in the haze between waking and oblivion, with their faces watching, I'm not sure I want to be saved.

12

Hospital Whispers

The world swims into focus, a hazy kaleidoscope of white and gray. Where am I? The question echoes in the hollow cavern of my skull, sharp and reverberating. I blink, trying to clear the blurriness from my vision, but it clings stubbornly, like cobwebs I can't sweep away.

A rhythmic beeping pierces the silence. Hospital. The word surfaces in my murky consciousness. But why?

Fragmented images flash through my mind—the glint of metal, a shout, the acrid tang of gunpowder. My heart races, the monitor's beeping quickening in tempo.

"Easy there, Johnny," a soft voice murmurs. Who...?

I try to turn my head, but pain lances through my temple. A groan escapes my cracked, dry lips.

"Here, sip some water."

Cool liquid soothes my parched mouth. I swallow greedily, coughing as it catches in my throat.

"Whoa, slow down, cowboy," the voice says again, achingly familiar yet just out of reach.

My eyelids, heavy as lead, fight to open. A blurry figure comes into view, backlit by harsh fluorescent lights.

"Liz?" I croak, my voice a faint echo of itself.

A pause. "No, Johnny. It's Ashley. Deputy Kowalski."

Of course. Liz is... gone.

The realization strikes like a physical blow. I try to sit up, to escape the suffocating weight of memory and regret, but my limbs are heavy, unresponsive. Plastic tubes snake across my body, tethering me to machines that hum and whir.

"Don't move," Ashley says, her hand gentle on my shoulder. "You've been through hell."

Hell. That sounds right. But which circle am I in now?

"What happened?" I rasp.

Ashley's face tightens, worry lines etching deeper into her skin. "You don't remember?"

Remember what? My mind buzzes with static, distorting every memory before I can grasp it. A chill courses down my spine, raising goosebumps across my skin.

"I..." My voice breaks, overcome with uncertainty. "It's all a blur."

She nods, her expression guarded. "That's to be expected. You took quite a dose."

But there's a flicker in her eyes—fear, perhaps? No, that can't be right. What could Ashley possibly fear?

Unless...

A creeping dread coils in the pit of my stomach as a thought takes hold: maybe it's not what happened that has her scared.

Maybe it's me.

The sterile hospital room sharpens into focus, a stark landscape of white and chrome. Beeping machines encircle me, their rhythmic pulses mocking life itself. Fluorescent lights cast a sickly pallor, turning even Ashley's warm features cold and unfamiliar.

I blink, trying to pierce the surreal haze. "How long have I been here?"

Ashley opens her mouth to respond, but a soft voice from the hallway interrupts. She turns, her curly red hair catching the harsh light.

"I should take this," she murmurs, stepping out of sight.

I strain to hear, catching snatches of her hushed conversation.

"...condition is stable, but..." A pause. "...concerns about long-term effects..."

My heart races, the monitor beside me betraying my rising panic. Long-term effects? What the hell happened to me?

"...keeping him for observation..." Ashley's voice fades in and out, like a poorly tuned radio. "...best to prepare for..."

Prepare for what? The words reverberate in my mind, each echo amplifying my fear. I try to call out to Ashley, to demand answers, but my voice falters. I'm trapped in this bed, in a body that feels alien, at the mercy of whispered half-truths and my fractured memories.

The room seems to close in, the walls pulsing with my ragged breaths. In this moment, I'm not Sheriff Johnny McCallister, protector of Stormy Valley. I'm just a man—broken, afraid, facing an uncertain future in a world grown terrifyingly unfamiliar. I sink into the pillow, my limbs heavy as lead. The ceiling blurs, white tiles dissolving into a hazy expanse. I'm falling, slipping through layers of consciousness, each breath pulling me deeper into a shadowy realm between waking and dreaming.

"This can't be happening," I whisper, my voice a rasp in the sterile air. "It's too soon. I'm not ready to..."

The thought trails off, unfinished. I blink, and suddenly I'm standing on Stormy Valley's main street. Familiar brick buildings loom, distorted and elongated. A cold mist swirls around my ankles.

"Johnny?" A voice calls, distant and echoing. Is it Ashley? Or someone else?

I try to respond, but my mouth feels stuffed with cotton. The world tilts, buildings stretching impossibly tall, their shadows reaching for me with grasping fingers.

"I'm here," I croak, though I'm uncertain where "here" is anymore. "I'm still..."

The sentence fades as I slip back into the hospital room, the beeping monitors a stark counterpoint to the eerie silence of my dreamscape. Reality and imagination blur, leaving me adrift in a sea of uncertainty.

Am I dying? Or am I already gone?

A soft glow materializes beside my bed, coalescing into a familiar silhouette. Detective Elizabeth Montgomery stands there, her dark hair neatly tied back, her eyes warm with concern.

"Johnny," Liz murmurs, her voice a soothing balm. "You look like hell."

I try to chuckle, but it emerges as a wheeze. "Feels worse than it looks, I'm sure."

Liz's hand finds mine, squeezing gently. "You've been through so much," she says. "But you're strong. You'll pull through."

Her words wash over me, a comforting tide. I close my eyes, letting this moment of solace anchor me. "Thanks, Liz. I'm not sure I—"

"Although," she interrupts, her tone sharpening, "maybe you don't deserve to."

My eyes snap open. Liz's face has hardened, her eyes now cold and accusing. "What?" I croak.

"How many people have suffered because of your failures, Johnny?" Her voice cuts like a razor. "How many lives ruined while you played sheriff?"

I try to pull my hand away, but her grip tightens painfully. "Liz, I don't—"

"Remember the Miller case?" she hisses. "An innocent man rotted in prison because you couldn't be bothered to dig deeper."

The memory strikes like a freight train. I'd been so sure... "That was different," I protest weakly. "The evidence—"

"Was circumstantial at best," Liz snarls. Her face flickers, shadows dancing across her features. "You saw what you wanted to see."

I struggle to sit up, to put distance between us, but my body refuses to obey. "Why are you saying this?" I plead, my voice breaking.

Liz leans closer, her breath cold against my cheek. "Because someone has to make you face the truth, Johnny. Before it's too late."

Her accusation hangs heavy, suffocating. I want to deny it, to shove her words back down where they came from—but they lodge deep, leaking poison into everything I am.

"I've always tried to do right," I mumble, more to myself than to Liz. "To protect this town."

She laughs—a harsh, grating sound that fills me with unease. "Protect? Is that what you call it?"

Her face shifts, features twisting into a grotesque caricature. One moment she's Liz, the next something unrecognizable. I blink hard, trying to clear my vision.

"What about Kayla Hart?" the figure demands. "Remember her, Johnny? The girl who came to you for help?"

My heart races, monitors beeping frantically. "I couldn't... there wasn't enough evidence," I stammer.

"Wasn't there?" Her voice rises, echoing off the sterile walls. "Or did you just choose not to see it?"

I press my hands to my ears, desperate to block her words, but they seep through like smoke. "Stop," I plead. "This isn't real. You're not real."

The guilt, the memories she's dredging up—these are real enough. Each accusation lands like a physical blow, stealing my breath.

"Face it, Johnny," she hisses, her face a nightmarish blur. "You're a failure. A fraud. And deep down, you know it."

"No!" I shout, my voice hoarse and raw. "I've made mistakes, but I've always tried to—"

"To what?" She looms over me, her presence suffocating. "Hide from the truth? Bury your sins under a badge? At the bottom of a bottle?"

"And while you were chasing ghosts at the Thompson farm," Liz hisses, "you were blind to the monster right next door. The one who poured septic tanks for a living and couldn't keep his eyes off a pretty girl. But you wouldn't have noticed that, would you, Johnny? You were too busy hiding in a bottle and feeling sorry for yourself to be a real cop!"

The room spins, reality fraying at the edges. I can't tell where the hallucination ends and my thoughts begin. Am I losing my mind? Or finally facing what I've spent years fleeing?

Something snaps inside me. With a guttural roar, I lunge at Liz's specter, my hands clawing at empty air. "Shut up!" I scream, swinging wildly. "You don't know me!"

My fists meet nothing, but I keep swinging, fueled by a primal rage I can't control. IV lines rip from my arms, warm blood trickling down my skin. The pain feels distant, drowned by the storm of emotions tearing through me.

"I did my best!" I shout, my voice breaking. "I saved who I could!"

The room dissolves into a chaotic whirl of motion. Machines topple, their alarms shrieking in protest. Sheets tangle around my legs as I thrash, battling an enemy only I can see.

"Johnny, look at you—so pathetic!" Liz's voice echoes, warped and inhuman, cackling as it fades. "You're only hurting yourself!"

For a moment, I catch my reflection in the IV stand—eyes wide, mouth bloodied, fists raw. I look like every suspect I've ever booked.

Am I? I can't tell anymore. My fists slam into the bedrail, the wall, anything solid. Each impact sends shockwaves of pain through my battered body, but I welcome it. It's real, something to cling to in this maelstrom of guilt and madness.

"I'm not a failure," I pant, my words slurring. "I'm not..."

But doubt gnaws at me even as I speak. The room spins faster, a dizzying kaleidoscope of white walls and flashing lights. I'm dimly aware of a warm wetness on my face—tears? Blood? Both?

My legs buckle, and I collapse to the cold floor, still swinging weakly at phantoms. "I tried," I whisper, my strength ebbing. "God help me, I tried..."

The chaos subsides, leaving an eerie silence in its wake.

The silence after is worse. Every breath feels stolen. The room smells of chemicals and blood—mine, I think, but I can't be sure anymore.

I blink, my vision clearing for a moment.

The room is a battlefield of my own making: overturned chairs, scattered medical equipment, torn sheets. In the corner, a dent in the wall marks where my fist struck.

"What have I done?" The words slip out, barely a whisper.

My hands tremble as I raise them, knuckles raw and bleeding. The gravity of my actions crashes over me like a tidal wave, threatening to pull me under. I've lost control. Again. Just like that night in Stormy Valley, when everything went to hell.

"I'm... I'm losing my mind," I murmur, a hysterical chuckle bubbling up. "Liz was right. I'm not fit to wear the badge."

A commotion erupts in the hallway, muffled voices growing louder. I catch snippets of urgent conversation:

"...Sheriff McCallister..."

"...violent episode..."

"...restrain if necessary..."

My heart races. They're coming for me. To lock me away, like those I've put behind bars. Is this justice? Or the universe's cruel joke? My thoughts spin, untethered.

"Johnny?" Ashley's voice cuts through the confusion, laced with concern. "We're coming in. Don't... don't do anything rash."

I want to reassure her, to say I'm okay. But the words lodge in my throat. I'm not okay. I haven't been for a long time.

The door creaks open, and I glimpse Ashley's wide eyes before the world begins to fade. My last coherent thought is a prayer—not for salvation, but for oblivion.

As darkness closes in, I cling to fragments of reality like a drowning man grasping driftwood. The sterile hospital room warps and twists, blending with memories of past crime scenes. Blood on my hands—is it mine, or someone else's?

"Johnny, can you hear me?" Ashley's voice echoes, distant and distorted.

I try to focus on her face, but it shifts. One moment, she's the concerned deputy I know; the next, she accuses me with Liz's piercing eyes.

"I… I don't know what's real anymore," I choke out, my voice a ragged whisper.

The room spins, and I'm back in Stormy Valley, standing over a body. No, not a body—a broken bicycle, its wheel still spinning. The jogger. The driver. The gun in my hand.

"It wasn't supposed to happen like this," I mumble, unsure if I'm speaking to Ashley or another hallucination.

"What wasn't, Johnny?" Ashley asks, her tone cautious. "Talk to me."

But how can I explain when I don't understand myself? The line between duty and obsession, justice and vengeance—it's all blurred now.

"I thought I could fix it," I say, my words slurring as exhaustion takes hold. "Fix the town. Fix myself. But I've only made things worse."

Straps tighten across my ankles and waist, a fitting punishment for the chaos I've unleashed. The orderlies move with practiced efficiency, their faces blank, as if securing violent patients is as routine as changing bedsheets. For them, it likely is. My muscles ache from my outburst, my knuckles raw and throbbing. But the shame—that cuts deeper, spreading through my chest like poison.

"That should hold him," one orderly mutters, giving a final tug on the restraint across my chest. "Call if he starts up again."

The orderlies retreat, leaving the acrid scent of sweat and disinfectant in their wake. My eyelids droop, heavy as iron gates, but I fight to keep them open. I deserve this—the aftermath, the consequences. The room swims in and out of focus, fluorescent lights pulsing like a heartbeat above.

Ashley steps into my field of vision, her face drawn and pale. Her presence triggers another wave of shame, so intense I look away.

"Johnny," she says, her voice soft but firm. "I know you can hear me."

Her words reach me from far away, muffled by clouds. I try to answer, but my mouth feels packed with cotton.

"I'm still here," she continues, edging closer to the bed. Her hand hovers near mine but doesn't touch. "I'm not going anywhere."

A bitter, raw laugh escapes me. "Why not?" The words scrape my throat. "Didn't you see what I did?"

Ashley's gaze flicks to the dented wall, the overturned equipment. "I saw someone who's sick and needs help."

"Sick." The word lingers between us. "Is that what they're calling it now?"

My vision blurs, and for a moment, Liz stands behind Ashley, her expression cold and accusing. I blink hard, and she vanishes. The hallucinations come faster now, slipping through reality like thieves.

"The doctor will help you, Johnny. Something's wrong, and they'll figure it out."

I turn my head away, unable to bear the hope in her voice. What's there to figure out? My mind is a house of cards, collapsing in slow motion.

"Pete," I mumble, the name clawing its way from a dark corner of my memory. "What did I do to Pete?"

Ashley pauses, a beat too long.

"Johnny, listen to me. Pete's alive. You didn't kill him. You couldn't have," she says, but a hesitation in her voice—a careful neutrality—twists my stomach.

"Don't lie to me." My voice cracks. "I remember… blood. His face. I hit him, didn't I? More than once."

The memory surges—Pete's shocked expression, my fist slamming into his jaw, the sickening crack of bone against bone. Did I kill him? The thought sends nausea rolling through me.

"Pete's alive," Ashley says firmly. "That's all you need to know right now. You need to rest."

But rest feels impossible. Every time I close my eyes, Liz's accusing face or Pete's blood on my hands haunts me. I strain against the restraints, not to escape but to feel their resistance, a reminder I'm contained, unable to hurt anyone else.

"I'm a danger," I whisper, more to myself than to Ashley. "I should be locked up."

"You're not thinking clearly," Ashley insists, leaning closer. "This isn't you, Johnny. Something's happening to you, and we'll find out what it is."

"Ashley," I manage, my tongue heavy as the sedative takes hold. "Tell Mike... tell him I'm sorry. For everything."

"You can tell him yourself," she says, her voice echoing strangely in my ears. "He'll be here soon."

The room dims, its edges softening like a watercolor left in the rain. Ashley's face hovers above me, a pale moon in a darkening sky.

"Johnny, listen to me," Ashley says, her words stretching and distorting. "Whatever you think you did, whatever you're seeing—it might not be real. Your mind is playing tricks."

I try to anchor myself to her voice, to hold fast against the current pulling me under. "How do I know what's real?" I slur, the question burning through me like a swallowed ember as consciousness slips away.

"Trust us," her fading voice replies. "Trust the people who care about you."

But trust feels like a luxury I can't afford. Not when my own mind has turned traitor. The darkness closes in, soft and insistent as a lover's embrace. I surrender, too exhausted to resist. As I drift, one thought lingers, a buoy in the black sea of unconsciousness: Pete is alive. Whatever sins I've committed, I haven't added murder to the list. The thought offers little comfort as I sink into restless sleep, where dreams wait with teeth and claws.

Something heavy presses against my feet, pulling me from the murky depths of sedated sleep. I crack open my eyelids, wincing at the hospital room's harsh fluorescence. Mike stands at the foot of my bed, his fingers resting on a manila folder across my blanket-covered feet. His bushy mustache twitches—a nervous tic I've noticed over two decades of friendship. The clock on the wall shows I've been out for just over an hour—long enough to sleep, not long enough to forget.

"Mornin', sunshine," Mike says, his attempt at casual cheer falling flat. His bloodshot eyes and the deep creases bracketing his mouth make him look a decade older since I last saw him.

"Not morning," I rasp, my throat dry as sandpaper.

Mike shifts his weight, uneasy. "Figure of speech." He lifts the manila folder, waving it slightly. "Brought you some reading material."

I tug at the restraints binding my wrists to the bed. They hold firm.

"Not sure how I'm supposed to turn pages," I mutter.

Mike's face falls, as if he'd forgotten my restrained state. "Right. Sorry." He pulls a chair to my bedside, its legs screeching against the linoleum, the sound drilling into my skull.

"I can read it to you," he offers, opening the folder. "It's the report on Pete Collins."

At Pete's name, my heart races, the monitor betraying my anxiety with its frantic beeping. Images surge—Pete's face twisted in fear, my fists striking soft tissue, blood spraying.

"Is he dead?" The question escapes, raw and desperate.

Mike's head snaps up, eyes wide with shock. "Dead? Jesus, Johnny, no." He leans forward, the folder forgotten in his lap. "Pete's fine. Well, not fine, exactly, but nowhere near dead."

I close my eyes, distrusting the relief flooding through me. "Don't lie, Mike. I know what I did."

"And what exactly do you think you did?" His voice is cautious, measured, like he's calming a spooked animal.

"I beat him," I say, each word dragging behind it more than I want to feel. "I remember his face... the blood. The sound of my fist hitting his jaw. I kept hitting him, even after he went down." I open my eyes, forcing myself to meet Mike's. "I saw him die, Mike."

Mike's expression shifts from concern to alarm. "Johnny, listen. Pete Collins has a black eye, a bloody nose, and some bruised ribs. He walked out of the ER on his own hours ago."

I shake my head, the motion sending splinters of pain through my skull. "That's not possible. I saw him. I saw what I did."

The memory washes over me in vivid detail—Pete's accusing eyes as I confronted him at the farm. Him backing away, hands raised. My rage, a living thing clawing out of me, unleashing violence I couldn't control. The sickening crunch as his head hit the ground. The stillness that followed.

"It was so real," I whisper, doubt creeping in. "I can still feel his blood on my hands."

Mike sighs, rubbing his face. "Johnny, you hit him a couple of times. He fell, got a nosebleed."

"He's telling the truth, Johnny," Ashley says, her voice soft but firm. "Pete's okay. He refused to press charges—he's worried about you."

I stare at her, searching for any hint of deception. Her fixed gaze holds mine, unflinching.

"I thought..." My voice falters. What had I thought? The certainty I clung to crumbles, leaving confusion in its wake.

"Your perception doesn't match reality," Ashley says, choosing her words carefully. "The doctors think it might be stress, or possibly—"

"Let's not get ahead of ourselves," Mike interrupts, shooting Ashley a warning glance. He turns to me, opening the folder. "Look, I brought photos from Pete's medical exam. See for yourself."

He holds up a glossy photograph. Pete's face stares back, one eye swollen and discolored, dried blood crusted beneath his nose. But he's undeniably alive, his expression more annoyed than traumatized.

I blink, struggling to reconcile this image with the one seared into my memory—Pete's face a ruined mess, eyes vacant and unseeing.

"This can't be right," I mutter. "I remember—"

"What you remember and what happened aren't the same," Mike says, his tone softer now. "Pete walked out of the hospital, Johnny. Black eye, sore ribs, wounded pride, but otherwise fine."

"He even joked about learning to duck faster next time," Ashley adds, a tentative smile flickering on her lips.

I close my eyes, exhaustion crashing over me. What's happening to me? How can my memories be so vivid, so detailed, yet utterly false? The thought sends a chill through me. If I can't trust my own mind, what can I trust?

"There's something wrong with me," I whisper, the admission cutting deeper than I care to admit.

Mike's hand rests on my shoulder, warm and reassuring. "We'll figure it out, Johnny. You're not alone."

I want to believe him—God, how I want to. But doubt has taken root, its tendrils weaving through every certainty I once held. What else have I imagined? What other horrors has my mind conjured as truth?

"How do I know you're real?" The question slips out, unbidden. "How do I know any of this is real?"

Mike's expression falters, pain flickering across his face. "I'm real, Johnny. As real as the ache in my knees and the coffee stain on my shirt." He points to a brownish spot I hadn't noticed before. "Spilled it rushing to see you."

Such a mundane detail, so specific. Could my broken mind invent something like that? I don't know anymore.

"Pete's fine," Mike repeats, tucking the photos back into the folder. "He doesn't want to pursue anything. Says it was just a misunderstanding."

A misunderstanding. The word feels inadequate for the violence I recall inflicting. But if Mike's telling the truth—if the photos aren't a deception—what did I actually do?

And more terrifying still: what else might I have done that I don't remember correctly?

Mike flips through the folder, revealing more photographs and medical forms. I squint, struggling to focus through the fog clinging to my consciousness. Each image shows Pete—alive, mobile, far from the bloody, lifeless body I recall creating. My reality unravels thread by thread, and I can't tell which strand to grasp.

"This is the ER admittance form," Mike says, holding up a document with Pete's name at the top. "Time of arrival: 3:42 PM. Presenting with facial contusion, suspected nasal fracture, minor lacerations, possible rib contusions." His finger traces the page. "Discharged at 5:17 PM with home-care instructions."

I stare at the form, its clinical language detailing injuries far less severe than the fatal wounds I remember inflicting. The document is crisp, official, stamped with the hospital's logo. Could my mind conjure such details?

"Here's the last photo," Mike continues, revealing another image. Pete stands at the ER entrance, one hand pressed against his side, the other clutching a small white pharmacy bag. His profile, though swollen, is unmistakable—alive.

"You took pictures of him leaving?" My voice sounded distant, hollow, like an echo in an empty room.

Mike shrugged, a faint flush of embarrassment crossing his face. "Had to document everything. Standard procedure when an officer's involved in a physical altercation."

Of course. The department would demand evidence, would need to build a case. Against me.

"Am I being charged?" The question rasped in my dry throat.

Mike and Ashley exchanged a fleeting glance.

"No charges," Mike said firmly. "Pete refused to press any. Said it was just a... misunderstanding. He was more relieved to know that you were still alive."

That word again. Misunderstanding. As if I'd merely stepped on his foot or spilled his coffee, not attacked him in a blind rage.

"He just walked out of the ER?" I pressed, still grappling to reconcile this new reality with my fractured memories. "After what I did to him, why would he care if I was alive?"

"He walked out under his own power," Mike confirmed. "The doc prescribed painkillers, told him to ice his ribs, and to return if breathing worsened. That was it."

I closed my eyes, struggling to piece together the fractured reality. The images in my mind burned vivid—Pete's body crumpled on the ground, blood pooling beneath his skull, his eyes vacant, unseeing, his stillness, the absence of breath. The bone-deep certainty that I had killed him. Yet here was evidence, tangible and bureaucratic, weaving a starkly different tale.

"I saw him die," I whispered, opening my eyes to meet Mike's—full of concern and something else I couldn't name. "I felt it, Mike. Under my hands. How could I be so wrong?"

Mike's face softened, a blend of pity and worry that made my stomach clench. "I don't know, Johnny. But the doctors are working on it. They'll figure out what's happening to you."

Something shifted in my periphery. I flinched. A shadow swelled in the corner—indistinct, but watching, its eyes gleaming.

"Do you see that?" I hissed, jerking my chin toward the shadow.

Mike and Ashley turned to look, their faces etched with puzzlement.

"See what?" Ashley asked, her eyes sweeping the empty corner.

The shadow rippled, its form swelling, edges bleeding into the surrounding wall. A faint whisper drifted from it, words indistinct but laced with accusation.

"Nothing," I muttered, squeezing my eyes shut. "Just a shadow."

When I opened them again, the corner stood empty. Another hallucination. Another betrayal from my fractured mind.

The door opened with a soft hiss, admitting a nurse I didn't recognize. Middle-aged, her dark hair pulled into a severe bun, she wore a professionally neutral expression.

"Time for your medication, Sheriff McCallister," she said, wheeling a small cart beside my bed. "Doctor's orders."

I eyed the syringe she prepared, apprehension tightening my chest. "More sedatives?"

She nodded, checking the dosage. "Dr. Patterson wants you to rest properly. It's critical for your recovery."

Recovery. As if I had a flu or a broken bone—something simple, mendable with time and medicine. Not a mind unraveling, splintering reality into jagged fragments.

"I don't want to sleep," I said, tension sharpening my voice more than I intended. "I need to understand what's happening to me."

The nurse's expression remained impassive. "The doctor will discuss your condition when you're more stable. For now, rest is the priority."

She approached my IV line, syringe poised. Panic surged in my chest as I strained against the restraints.

"Wait," I pleaded. "I need to talk to Mike more—about Pete, about what happened."

The nurse paused, glancing at Mike and Ashley. "I'm afraid visiting hours are nearly over. Sheriff McCallister needs uninterrupted rest."

Mike rose from his chair, reluctance etched in every slow movement. "We'll come back tomorrow, Johnny. When you're feeling more like yourself."

"This is myself," I said bitterly. "That's the problem."

The nurse cleared her throat. "I must ask you both to step out while I administer the medication. Hospital policy."

Ashley stepped closer, her hand briefly grazing mine. Our fingers brushed, sparking not static but a fleeting connection—a tether to the world beyond my fractured mind. It jolted me all the same.

"We'll be back first thing tomorrow," she promised, her eyes locking onto mine with a sincerity that stung. "Try to rest, Johnny. Let the medication help."

Help. Could anything tame the chaos in my mind? I wasn't sure anymore.

Mike tucked the folder under his arm. "Hang in there, partner. We'll get through this, like always."

The nurse gestured toward the door, her directive clear. As they moved to leave, a desperate thought seized me.

"Mike," I called, my voice raw and strained. "The file—leave it. Please. I need to see it again when I wake. To remind myself."

Mike hesitated, glancing at the nurse, who offered a slight nod.

"Alright," he said, setting the folder on the bedside table. "It'll be right here for you."

As they filed out, the nurse approached with the syringe. I watched the clear liquid flow into my IV line, resignation settling over me like a heavy shroud.

"It'll take effect quickly," she said, disposing of the syringe. "Try to relax."

Relax. As if I could, with my mind betraying me at every turn. I stared at the ceiling, counting tiles as the medication seeped into my system. One, two, three... The edges of my vision blurred, the harsh fluorescent light softening into a hazy halo.

The last thing I saw before oblivion claimed me was the manila folder on the table—my fragile link to a reality I could no longer trust. My fingers twitched against the restraints, aching to reach for it, to grasp something solid and true.

But the sedative dragged me under, and I surrendered to the abyss, hoping that when I resurfaced, the world might make sense again.

Somehow, I doubted it would.

Mike watched Ashley's slender figure vanish down the sterile hallway, her steps quickening as if fleeing the antiseptic stench and muffled suffering. Leaning against the wall outside Johnny's room, exhaustion settling into his bones like an old friend. The fluorescent lights buzzed overhead, casting a sickly pallor that made even the white walls look diseased.

"Deputy Langley?"

Mike turned to see a doctor approaching, clipboard in hand. Young, likely fresh from residency, with dark circles under his eyes mirroring Mike's own. His name tag read "Dr. Singh."

"That's me," Mike said, straightening out of habit. Twenty-five years in law enforcement had ingrained certain reflexes.

"I have Sheriff McCallister's preliminary evaluation." Dr. Singh extended a manila folder, his expression carefully neutral, the practiced mask of a medical professional delivering grim news. "Dr. Patterson thought you should know the findings, given your role as second-in-command."

Mike's fingers closed around the folder, its weight surprising for something so thin. "Appreciate it, Doc."

Dr. Singh hesitated, his professional mask slipping just enough to reveal a breath of compassion. "He'll need support. When he wakes, when he learns—" He cut himself off, nodded once, and continued down the corridor, his white coat trailing behind like a surrender flag.

Mike stood frozen, the folder clutched in his grip. He should open it, read the verdict within. But for one fleeting moment, he clung to the illusion that Johnny was just having a breakdown—something fixable with therapy and time. Something that wasn't—

He flipped open the folder.

The medical jargon swam before his eyes, but certain phrases leaped out with brutal clarity: "right temporal lobe lesion—suspected glioblastoma multiforme. Rapid progression noted. High probability of behavioral and perceptual distortion."

Mike's knees buckled. He slid down the wall, collapsing onto the cold linoleum, the folder trembling in his hands. A brain tumor. Not a psychological break, not PTSD, not the scars of years of stress, drugs, or tragedy. A tumor, growing inside Johnny's head, twisting his perception, unraveling his reality.

Mike forced himself to read on, each line striking like a physical blow. "Estimated size suggests development over 6-8 months... Positioned to affect memory, emotion regulation, and sensory processing... Hallucinations and personality changes consistent with frontal lobe involvement..."

And then, the sentence that stole his breath: "Prognosis: Poor. Estimated survival without intervention: 3-6 months. With aggressive treatment: 12-14 months."

His hands went numb, but a warmth flared in his chest—a searing grief he recognized all too well. His oldest friend, his partner through decades of small-town crimes and personal demons, was dying. And Johnny didn't even know.

Mike closed the folder, unable to continue. The wall's coolness pressed against his back as he tilted his head, staring at the flickering fluorescent light without seeing it. Suddenly, Johnny's behavior over the past few months made a terrible kind of sense—the mood swings, the bouts of confusion, the increasingly vivid "memories" of events that never happened.

The Pete Collins incident flashed through Mike's mind. Johnny had been so certain he'd killed the young farmhand, describing the murder in such visceral detail that, for a moment, Mike had nearly believed it himself. But Pete had walked away with only bruises and a nosebleed. Johnny's brain had woven the rest, conjuring a horror that existed solely in his mind.

How many other distortions had Johnny endured? How long had he been waging a silent battle against his own perception, struggling to separate reality from the lies his tumor fed him?

Mike hauled himself to his feet, legs unsteady. Through the small window in Johnny's door, he glimpsed his friend's silhouette—still, peaceful in drug-induced sleep, unaware that his body was betraying him in the most profound way.

The contrast between Johnny's fleeting tranquility and the storm Mike knew was coming felt obscene. Soon, Johnny would wake. Soon, doctors would explain that the visions, the false memories, the emotional outbursts weren't signs of madness but symptoms of something far more final.

Mike pressed his palm against the cool glass, watching Johnny's chest rise and fall. His own breath caught, each inhale and exhale now a counted treasure, their total diminishing with relentless certainty.

What would Johnny do when he learned the truth? Would he fight, pursuing aggressive treatments that might grant him a year? Or would he reject them, choosing to spend his remaining months with clarity rather than enduring the grueling side effects of therapies that could only delay, never prevent?

Mike wasn't sure what he'd choose in Johnny's place. The thought twisted his gut.

A flicker overhead sliced the light, plunging the corridor into dim shadow. In that fleeting darkness, Mike saw with brutal clarity what lay ahead—watching his friend fade day by day, guiding him through a world that would grow increasingly alien, and, inevitably, saying goodbye.

Mike stood frozen, dread pooling in his gut as he faced the unyielding truth. No miracle cure, no last-minute reprieve—just the cruel march of time, each day drawing Johnny closer to an end that felt both too distant and too near.

The light steadied, but doubts lingered in Mike's mind. He tucked the folder under his arm, its contents seared into his memory. Tomorrow, he would sit with Johnny. Tomorrow, they would confront this together, as they had every challenge in their long partnership.

But tonight, in the sterile hospital corridor with its antiseptic stench and merciless lights, Mike let the full weight of the truth settle over him. Johnny wasn't crazy. He was dying. And he didn't know it yet.

Mike pushed himself away from the door, legs heavy as he forced himself forward. Each step down the corridor felt like wading through deep water, resistance mounting with every yard. But he kept moving, because that's what Johnny would need in the days ahead—constant, relentless resolve, even when every instinct urged him to stop, to turn back, to deny this reality.

As he passed the nurses' station, a young nurse looked up, her expression softening at the grief etched across his face.

"Are you alright, sir?" the nurse asked.

Mike nodded mechanically, his voice untrustworthy. The folder under his arm felt not like paper but lead, its terrible knowledge anchoring him to the floor.

He paused at the elevator, finger hovering over the call button. In the polished metal doors, his reflection stared back—haggard, aged, a man who had glimpsed an unbearable future.

"No," he whispered to himself, answering the nurse's question honestly now that no one could hear. "I'm not alright at all."

He pressed the button, watching the numbers descend, each digit pulling him closer to a world forever altered by the folder's contents. A world where Johnny McCallister, sheriff of Stormy Valley, keeper of its secrets and guardian of its people, now counted days instead of cases, sunsets instead of arrests.

The elevator arrived with a chime that rang obscenely cheerful. As the doors slid open, Mike stepped inside, turning to face the corridor he'd just left. From here, he could just make out Johnny's room, a faint rectangle of light at the far end.

"I'll be back, partner," he vowed as the doors began to close. "You won't face this alone."

The elevator descended, carrying Mike away from Johnny but not from the truth that sat like stone in his chest. Johnny wasn't crazy. He was dying. And tomorrow, the hardest conversation of their decades-long friendship awaited them both.

13

Chaos in the Ward

The alarms tore through my skull like a banshee's shriek, yanking me from the depths of unconsciousness. My eyes flew open, but the world remained a hazy blur of white and gray. Where am I? What's happening? Panic clawed at my throat as I tried to piece together my surroundings.

The sterile smell of antiseptic assaulted my nostrils, mingling with the metallic tang of... blood? My God, was that blood I smelled? I tried to sit up, but my limbs felt leaden, unresponsive.

"What's going on?" I croaked, my voice barely audible over the wailing alarms. No one answered. The room spun as I turned my head, searching for a familiar face, anything to anchor me to reality. Something snagged in my peripheral vision—

A strip of nylon, torn and crusted with blood.

It dangled from the bed frame like a warning. I blinked, and it blurred. Maybe it had always been there. Maybe I'd imagined it.

I couldn't remember.

Shadows danced at the edges of my vision, taking on sinister shapes. Were they real, or were they products of my fractured mind? I couldn't trust my senses anymore. What I'd done pressed in from all sides, too monstrous to face, too real to escape. Each glance around the room threatened to shatter what remained of my sanity.

Suddenly, footsteps thundered down the hallway outside. I strained to make sense of the commotion, my heart pounding in time with the approaching stampede.

"Code Blue in Room 237!" a voice rang out, sharp with urgency. "All available staff, report immediately!"

Footfalls pounded closer, their frantic rhythm echoing through the halls. The tension seemed to seep through the walls, sinking into my bones. What horror lay beyond that door? And why did I feel the gnawing certainty that I was somehow to blame?

"Johnny?" My voice wavered, a faint plea for control. "Pull it together, man. You're the sheriff. You've got to take charge."

But dread coiled tighter, whispering that control was a fleeting illusion. As the chaos outside swelled, I retreated inward, seeking refuge in the shadowed corners of my mind—a familiar sanctuary from my darkest days of addiction.

Yet, as before, it offered no solace, only the stark realization that the most terrifying monsters are often the ones we forge ourselves.

The door burst open with a thunderous crash, shattering my thoughts, jolting me into the present. The scene before me was a nightmare given form.

Emma Martinez, the compassionate nurse who'd cared for me just hours ago, lay sprawled on the sterile linoleum. Her eyes, once warm and kind, now stared blankly at the ceiling. A crimson pool spread beneath her, stark against the pristine white floor.

There I was, straddling her lifeless form, my hands slick with her blood. I couldn't stop. My fists pounded, driven by a feral rage I couldn't comprehend.

"What have I done?" The thought, horrified. But my body refused to obey, as if I were a prisoner in my own skin.

"Oh God, Johnny! Stop!" A familiar voice sliced through the haze. Ashley Kowalski stood in the doorway, her young face etched with horror and disbelief.

I wanted to explain, to beg for help, but only guttural snarls broke free. Ashley hesitated, her slight frame trembling. I saw the struggle in her eyes—the deputy I'd mentored battling the terrified girl facing a monster.

"This isn't you," she whispered, more to herself than to me. Then, steeling herself, she stepped into the room. "I need backup in here, now!" Her voice cracked, betraying her fear.

As Ashley approached, a flicker of recognition stirred within me. But the darkness clouding my mind surged, drowning reason. My hands, once instruments of protection, now reached for her throat.

"Johnny, please," she pleaded, tears welling in her eyes. "Remember who you are."

But who was I? Sheriff or murderer? Protector or destroyer? As Ashley's trembling hands reached for me, I no longer knew.

The door burst open again, and Mike Langley's imposing frame filled the threshold. His presence cut through the chaos, a refreshing balm in the storm.

"Easy now, Johnny," Mike's gravelly voice rumbled, his eyes scanning the scene with practiced precision. "Let's take a breather, alright?"

I watched, detached, as Mike approached. His movements were slow, deliberate, as if he were nearing a wounded animal—which, I supposed, I was.

"Mike," I croaked, my voice a stranger's rasp. "I can't... I don't know what's happening."

He nodded, his eyes warm with understanding. "I know, old friend. We'll figure this out."

As Mike edged closer, movement flickered in my peripheral vision. Faces, pale and frightened, peered from neighboring rooms. Their wide eyes caught the stark fluorescent lights, casting an otherworldly glow over the scene.

"Christ," I thought, "what nightmare have I stumbled into?"

The sterile hospital corridor stretched before me, a grim backdrop to unthinkable horror. The scent of antiseptic clashed with the metallic tang of blood, a nauseating blend that churned my stomach.

"Johnny," Mike's voice pierced my spiraling thoughts. "Focus on me. Can you do that?"

I tried to nod, but my body felt unmoored, disconnected. The faces in the doorways blurred, morphing into a grotesque audience to my unraveling.

"This isn't real," I muttered. "It can't be."

But Mike's hand on my shoulder, gentle yet firm, anchored me to this harrowing reality.

Ashley's trembling hands reached for me, her freckled face set with determination edged with fear. I saw the struggle in her eyes—compassion warring with self-preservation.

"Sheriff, please," she pleaded, her voice quivering. "Let us help you."

I longed to reach back, to seize her offered lifeline, but my body betrayed me. My muscles tensed, poised to lash out at the slightest trigger. The world tilted, reality fraying at the edges.

"Stay back, Ashley," Mike warned, his voice steady but taut. "Johnny, it's me. Your old friend. Remember our times together—the good and the bad?"

Mike's words stirred memories of shared laughter and quiet understanding. But they also unearthed darker recollections—secrets buried deep, clawing toward the surface.

"Mike," I rasped, "something's wrong. I can't... I can't trust what I'm seeing."

He nodded, his mustache twitching with suppressed emotion. "I know, buddy. We'll get through this, like always."

In his eyes, I saw the weight of our shared history, a loyalty forged through countless storms. But there was something else—a flicker of doubt, of fear—mirroring my own uncertainty and amplifying the moment's horror.

"What if I can't come back from this?" I whispered, more to myself than to them.

The sterile walls seemed to close in, the air thick with unspoken dread. In that moment, caught between trust and terror, I realized the true nightmare wasn't just what I'd done—it was the fear that I might do it again.

Orderlies burst into the room, their white uniforms a stark contrast to the crimson stains marring the floor. Their arrival triggered something primal within me. My muscles tensed, adrenaline surging through my veins.

"No!" I roared, lashing out with a strength I didn't know I possessed. "Stay away!"

Bodies collided in a frenzied tangle, hands grappling with my flailing limbs. Mike's voice, taut with urgency, cut through the chaos, straining to reach me.

"Johnny, stand down! We're here to help!"

But his words drowned in the maelstrom of my mind. Every touch felt like an assault, every face a looming threat. I twisted and thrashed, my elbow striking something soft. A grunt of pain sliced through the air.

"Christ," I thought, "what am I doing?"

Yet I couldn't stop. My body moved of its own volition, driven by a nameless terror. The room spun, a kaleidoscope of fear and confusion. I caught glimpses of Ashley's wide eyes, Mike's clenched jaw, the orderlies' resolute faces.

In that moment, I wasn't Sheriff Johnny McCallister. I was a cornered beast, lashing out at shadows.

Then, as suddenly as it began, it ended. Multiple hands pinned me down, a needle pierced my arm, and the world began to fade. The last sound I heard before blackness claimed me was the abrupt silence as the alarms fell quiet.

When I awoke, dusk bleeding through the blinds, the silence was deafening. The only sound was the ragged breathing of those around me. I blinked, struggling to focus. The walls, once pristine, now bore witness to the violence that had unfolded. Splashes of red, stark against the white, told a story I wasn't sure I wanted to remember.

"What have I done?" I whispered, my words barely audible in the eerie stillness.

No one answered. The silence stretched on, heavy with unspoken horror and the lingering echoes of a nightmare I couldn't escape.

Ashley's freckled face came into focus, her green eyes wide with a mix of fear and concern. She looked so young, almost like a kid playing dress-up in her deputy's uniform. But there was nothing childish about the way she surveyed the scene, her gaze flitting from the blood on the walls to my restrained form.

"Sheriff?" Her voice trembled. "Can you hear me?"

I nodded, my throat too dry to speak. My mind raced, grasping at fragments of what had happened. Was this real? Or another cruel trick of my fractured psyche?

"Emma," I croaked. "Is she...?"

Ashley's face fell, confirming my worst fears before she could speak. "I'm sorry, Johnny. She didn't make it."

Those words crushed me, stealing what little breath I had left. I'd known Emma for years. Hell, she'd been there when I was fighting to get clean. And now...

Mike's gruff voice sliced through my spiraling thoughts. "We need to get him secured, Ash. Can't risk another... incident."

I turned my head, catching sight of my old friend. The lines on Mike's face seemed etched deeper than ever, his eyes haunted. He wouldn't meet my eyes.

"Mike," I pleaded, "you know me. This isn't... I wouldn't..."

He flinched, and I saw the struggle raging in his eyes—duty battling loyalty, present horrors clashing with shared history.

"I know, Johnny," he said softly.

As they prepared to move me, I glimpsed my reflection in a shattered mirror—blood-spattered, wild-eyed, barely recognizable. I wondered, not for the first time, if I was losing my grip on reality entirely.

The hospital corridor, once pristine white, now bore the scars of violence. Nurses huddled in corners, their hushed whispers a quiet contrast to the earlier chaos. Patients peered from behind half-closed doors, their eyes wide with fear and confusion.

I felt the bite of new restraints on my wrists and ankles—industrial-grade nylon, tight and unyielding. Not like the ones from yesterday, which I'd torn through like paper. The memory was hazy, but the damage I'd done was undeniable.

They're not taking chances this time.

I couldn't blame them. Not after this. Not after... everything. As they wheeled me down the hall, the gurney's wheels squeaked, unnaturally loud in the oppressive silence.

"What's going to happen to me?" I asked, my voice a faint whisper.

Ashley's eyes flicked to the blood-spattered blanket clinging to the gurney. Her grip tightened on the rail, though her voice remained soft. "We're moving you to a secure ward, Johnny. For your safety."

My own safety. The words echoed in my mind, mocking me. I'd been the one to... to...

"I can't remember," I admitted, the words tasting like ash. "Ashley, I swear, I don't know what happened."

She hesitated, glancing at Mike. "It's okay, Johnny. We'll figure this out."

But I saw the doubt in her eyes, the fear—a look I'd glimpsed in the mirror during my darkest days of addiction.

As we passed the nurses' station, I caught sight of a TV. The local news played, muted. My face flashed across the screen.

"Mike," I called, my heart pounding. "What are they saying about me?"

He sighed heavily. "Nothing good, Johnny. Nothing good."

The world tilted, spinning around me. What was real? What was in my head? The line between truth and delusion frayed, leaving me adrift in a sea of uncertainty.

As they wheeled me into the secure ward, I caught a final glimpse of the world outside. The sun was setting, painting the sky in hues of blood and ash—a grim omen of darker days to come.

The door closed behind us with a heavy, echoing click.

14

The Mind's Abyss

White light stabbed my eyelids like needles, then vanished. I tried to raise my arm to shield my face, but something held it fast—tight, unyielding. The ceiling above swam in and out of focus, its grid of acoustic tiles pulsing with my heartbeat. A machine beeped to my left, its steady rhythm a metronome ticking toward something I couldn't name.

My tongue felt swollen, alien in my mouth—a mix of cotton and chemicals. I tried to swallow but couldn't recall how. Plastic chafed my wrist when I moved—restraints. Why was I restrained?

The thought slipped away, like smoke through my fingers.

Voices murmured nearby, clinical and detached. Fragments drifted in: "...frontal lobe..." "...aggressive episode..." "...keep him under until..."

I wanted to shout that I was awake, that I could hear them discussing me like a specimen, not a person—not Sheriff Johnny McCallister. But my lips produced only a dry rasp, clawing at my throat.

The ceiling tiles blurred again, darkness seeping in from the edges of my vision. I fought it, but the weight was crushing. Somewhere distant, a door closed with a soft click.

When I opened my eyes again, the light had softened, tinged with orange. Evening, perhaps. Or morning. Time had no anchor.

The beeping persisted, joined now by a new sound—breathing, not my own. Someone sat beside me. I turned my head, pain lancing through my neck. A figure in scrubs checked the monitor, scribbling a note. Their face twisted and warped as I struggled to focus, features melting and reforming like wax.

"Pete," I rasped, unsure why his name spilled from my lips. "Pete Collins."

The nurse—I assumed they were a nurse—glanced at me with surprise, then something else. Fear? Pity?

"Try to rest, Sheriff," a woman's voice said, not from the nurse but from someone unseen in the room.

Pete's face flashed before me—eyes wide with terror, hands raised. Blood coated my hands, warm and sticky. The memory struck like a physical blow, and I jerked against the restraints.

"He's becoming agitated," the unseen voice noted. "Increase the dose."

"No," I tried to protest, but it emerged as a groan. "Need to... explain..."

Something cold surged through my veins, spreading up my arm like ice water. The restraints bit into my wrists as I strained against them, panic clawing at my chest.

"Pete," I said again, my voice steadier. "I didn't... he was..."

The words dissolved as the medication gripped me. The room tilted, then spun slowly, like a carousel. My eyelids grew impossibly heavy. A memory surfaced—Liz smiling across a table, her hair catching the sunlight. But no, not Liz. Elizabeth. My Lizzy died years ago. This was Detective Montgomery. Why couldn't I keep them straight? Their features blurred in my mind, merging and separating like oil in water.

"Vitals stable," a distant voice said. "Keep him on observation protocol. "

I wanted to ask what that meant, but my mouth refused to move. A dull pressure settled on my chest—not painful, but heavy, like grief made tangible. My hands were numb, yet a warmth bloomed in my chest, an uncomfortable heat I recognized as guilt.

The restraints seemed to tighten around my wrists and ankles, or perhaps my awareness of them sharpened briefly before dulling again. I grasped at why I was here, what had happened. Fragments flickered behind my eyelids—the jogging trail, a struggle, a gun. My gun? Pete's face again, twisted in fear or rage, I couldn't tell which.

"Sheriff McCallister," a new voice said, close to my ear. "Can you hear me?"

I managed a faint nod—or thought I did. Perhaps I only imagined moving.

"You're in the county behavioral health lockup. You're safe. Do you understand?"

Behavioral Health. Where we sent the ones who cracked—junkies, burnout cases, folks who'd slipped but still had one foot in the real world. A laugh welled in my throat but emerged as a choked gasp. They'd locked me away with the crazies. Me, the sheriff. What would Stormy Valley say? What would become of the town now?

The medication dragged me under before I could form a coherent thought. This time, the darkness was absolute—no dreams, no memories, just a blank void swallowing me whole.

In the fleeting moment before consciousness slipped away, a single thought crystallized with stark clarity: something was deeply wrong with my mind. And in some unclouded corner of my brain, I knew Pete Collins was dead—and I was responsible.

I woke to a room steeped in antiseptic and despair. Sunlight filtered through half-drawn blinds, casting prison-bar shadows across a floor too pristine to be anything but institutional. My throat felt scraped raw, my wrists throbbed where restraints had bitten—the skin chafed an angry red, whispering stories my mind couldn't fully grasp. A thin hospital gown clung to my back, damp with sweat that had dried and bloomed anew, marking time in a way the featureless clock on the wall couldn't.

The restraints were gone, but their bite lingered. I pushed myself upright, my head swimming with the effort. This wasn't the same room. Smaller. One window. A door with a narrow rectangular pane at eye level. Through it, I glimpsed a nurses' station, figures moving with practiced efficiency.

My mouth tasted of old pennies and fear. I ran my tongue over my teeth, struggling to muster enough moisture to swallow.

The door opened with a soft click that carried a finality. A young man entered—late twenties, perhaps, wearing scrubs the color of faded sky, a lanyard heavy with ID badges and swipe cards. A nurse stood behind him, her posture braced for trouble.

"Good morning, Sheriff McCallister," the young man said, eyes fixed on the tablet in his hands. His voice held the practiced neutrality of someone who'd learned to bury emotion. "I'm Dr. Patel, psychiatric resident. How are you feeling today?"

I tried to answer but managed only a dry croak. The nurse stepped forward, offering a small paper cup of water. I took it, my hands trembling. The water was tepid, tinged with chlorine.

"Where am I?" I rasped, though I knew. The asylum beyond the hills.

"You're in the observation unit at Lakeside Behavioral Health," Dr. Patel replied, fingers swiping across his tablet.

Of course. Lakeside. The asylum beyond the hills. Where we sent the dangerous ones. The ones who couldn't tell what was real anymore. The ones we didn't expect to come back.

"Do you know what day it is?"

I didn't. Days had slipped through my fingers like water.

"Tuesday? Wednesday?" I ventured, voice still rough.

"It's Friday," he said, jotting a note. "Can you tell me who the current president is?"

A cognitive test. They thought my mind was broken. The realization set-tled like ice in my gut.

"I know who the damn president is," I snapped. "What I don't know is why I'm here."

Dr. Patel's eyes flicked up briefly, then returned to his tablet. "Standard assessment questions, Sheriff. Bear with me." His pen clicked—a nervous tic. "Can you state your full name and occupation?"

"Johnathan McCallister. Sheriff of Stormy Valley." My patience frayed. "Listen, I need to know what happened. There was—" Blood on my hands flashed before me, and I faltered.

"We'll get to that," Dr. Patel said, jotting another note. "Any headaches? Visual disturbances?"

"You mean besides waking up strapped to a bed?" I tried to stand, but my legs buckled, unsteady as a newborn colt's. The nurse stepped forward, one hand raised in caution. I sank back onto the bed's edge. "I need to talk to my deputy. There's been a—I need to know about Pete Collins."

They exchanged the quiet glance of people who'd already decided what kind of patient I was. A cautionary tale. A cliché.

"Sheriff McCallister, you're here for observation and evaluation," Dr. Pa-tel said, his voice adopting the careful tone reserved for the unstable. "We need to complete the intake process before discussing other matters."

"Intake process," I echoed, the words scraping out like a bad joke—like I was something to be sorted, not heard. "Like I'm being processed. Cata-logued."

"It's procedure," he said, adjusting glasses that slid down his nose, too large for his boyish face. "Have you experienced unusual thoughts? Seen or heard things others don't?"

Liz's face flashed in my mind—not my late wife, but the detective with the same name. Or were they one and the same? The uncertainty sent a jolt of panic through me.

"What happened to Pete Collins?" I demanded, ignoring his question. "And Detective Montgomery—is she okay?"

Dr. Patel's expression remained carefully neutral. "I don't have that information, Sheriff. We're focused on your health right now."

"My health is fine," I said, the lie bitter on my tongue. My head had been pounding for weeks, maybe months. Tumor. The word surfaced from deep within, unbidden, though no one had spoken it to me. "I need to know what happened on that trail."

The doctor exchanged a glance with the nurse—the kind cops trade when the suspect just handed them more fuel. "Sheriff, try to stay calm. Dr. Chen will meet with you tomorrow to discuss your case in detail."

"I don't need details, I need answers now." My voice rose, reverberating off the bare walls. "Pete Collins. Is he dead? Did I—" My breath caught, the final word refusing to come. Did I kill him? I couldn't voice the question.

Fragments flickered in my mind—Pete's face twisted in anger, his hands reaching for me, the heft of my service weapon in my palm. The jogging trail. Detective Montgomery's voice, shouting something I couldn't grasp.

"Pete," I said again, my heart pounding. "He was coming at me. He had a—" Had he held a weapon? I couldn't recall. "He was going to—"

"Sheriff McCallister," Dr. Patel interrupted, stepping back. "I need you to calm down."

But the memories flooded back, distorted and terrifying. I stood again, this time steadying myself to remain upright.

"You don't understand," I insisted, my voice rising. "Pete Collins—he killed those women. He was going to kill Montgomery. I had to stop him!"

The nurse moved swiftly, slipping something from her pocket. Dr. Patel set his tablet down, hands raised in a soothing gesture.

"Sheriff, please sit," he urged, but I was beyond reason.

"I'm the sheriff, damn it! You can't keep me here! I need to know what happened to Pete!"

The nurse acted with practiced precision, the syringe in her hand glinting under the light. Before I could react, the needle pierced my arm.

"It's just a sedative," she said, her first words to me. "Dr. Chen will see you tomorrow."

The world thickened around me, sounds muffled, limbs turning to lead. Warmth coiled through my veins as my legs gave way. Hands guided me back onto the bed, firm and efficient, not gentle. The last thing I saw was Dr. Patel jotting another note on his tablet, his face a mask of clinical detachment.

Pete's bloodied, accusing face lingered at the edge of my vision, the only thing that stayed as the drug pulled everything else away.

I didn't know how many hours had passed—or days. Time dissolved in that place like sugar in hot coffee, leaving only the faint sweetness of lost moments. The restraints were gone, as was the paper-thin gown, replaced by pale blue scrubs that smelled of industrial detergent and resignation. I sat on the edge of the bed, bare feet pressed against cold linoleum, watching dust motes drift in the shaft of sunlight from the window. My head felt swathed in cotton, thoughts sluggish and heavy in the medication haze.

They'd taken my watch, my badge, my dignity. I flexed my wrists, the raw skin now fading to dull red bracelets—markers of my confinement. The room had stopped spinning, at least, though the edges of everything remained faintly blurred, as if I were seeing the world through a rain-streaked window.

The door opened without a knock, and I looked up, expecting another faceless resident with a tablet and rote questions. Instead, a woman entered alone—mid-fifties, perhaps, with steel-gray hair cut in a precise bob framing a face both kind and shrewd. She wore no white coat, only charcoal slacks and a navy blouse beneath a cardigan the color of autumn leaves. Her glasses hung from a beaded chain around her neck, and she carried a leather portfolio instead of a tablet.

"Sheriff McCallister," she said, her voice quiet and even-toned. "I'm Dr. Sarah Chen. I'd like to talk with you, if you're feeling up to it." No clipboard barriers, no clinical distance in her tone. She pulled a chair closer to the bed and sat, crossing her legs at the ankles. Her shoes were practical but worn at the heels, suggesting someone who spent long hours on her feet despite an office role. So this was the head shrink. No white coat, no stethoscope—just eyes that said she'd already seen inside me.

"Another shrink," I said, not hiding my bitterness. "Here to ask if I know who the president is?"

A faint smile touched her lips. "I think we can assume your general knowledge is intact, Sheriff. I'm more interested in what you recall about the events that brought you here."

I studied her face, searching for the barely concealed fear I'd seen in the resident's eyes or the nurse's clinical detachment. Instead, I found only calm interest, her dark eyes anchored on mine.

"No one will tell me anything," I said, frustration sharpening my voice. "I've been drugged, restrained, and questioned, but no one will say what happened to Pete Collins or Detective Montgomery."

Dr. Chen nodded, acknowledging my frustration without flinching. "That must be incredibly difficult," she said. "In my experience, uncertainty can be more distressing than even the hardest truths."

"Then tell me the truth," I demanded, leaning forward. "Did I kill Pete Collins?"

She didn't recoil at the question. Instead, she held my gaze with that same unshakeable calm. "What do you remember, Sheriff?"

I closed my eyes, trying to piece together the fragments swirling in my mind. "The jogging trail. Pete was there. He was... angry. There was a struggle." I pressed my fingers to my temples, as if I could force the memories into order. "My gun was drawn. I remember blood. Detective Montgomery was shouting."

When I opened my eyes, Dr. Chen was watching me with an expression I couldn't quite read—not pity, not judgment, but something deeper.

"And before that?" she asked. "What do you recall about the case you were working on with Detective Montgomery?"

The question caught me off guard. "The cold case. Women disappearing from Stormy Valley in the '90s. We reopened it because..." I trailed off, suddenly uncertain. "Because of new evidence. Pete Collins was a suspect."

"I see," Dr. Chen said, jotting a brief note in her portfolio. "And your relationship with Detective Montgomery—how would you describe it?"

My mind flashed to Liz—her face, her voice. But which Liz? My wife, dead over twenty years? Or Detective Montgomery? The two women blurred together in my memory, a chimera that made my head throb.

"Professional," I said at last. "We worked well together."

Dr. Chen nodded, her pen moving briefly across the page. "Sheriff, I want to be direct with you. You've been experiencing significant neurological and psychological symptoms. The episodes that led to your admission here are part of a larger pattern we need to address."

"Episodes," I repeated, spitting the word like a slur—I'd heard it too many times already. "You mean when I supposedly attacked Pete Collins?"

"I mean the periods when you've struggled to distinguish reality from what's in your mind," Dr. Chen replied, unfazed by my tone.

A chill spread through my chest. "Are you saying I'm crazy? That I imagined Pete attacking Detective Montgomery?"

"I'm saying your brain is under distress," she corrected gently. "And that distress is causing distortions in how you perceive and recall events."

I stood abruptly, ignoring the dizziness washing over me. "This is bullshit. I know what I saw. Pete Collins was going to hurt her, just like he hurt those other women. I did my job."

Dr. Chen remained seated, her composure steady. "Johnny," she said, using my name for the first time, "please sit. Getting agitated won't help us sort through this."

Her use of my name halted me. I sank back onto the bed, exhaustion overtaking me. "Just tell me if Montgomery is okay," I said, my voice rough. "Please."

Something flickered in Dr. Chen's eyes—compassion, perhaps, or concern. "Detective Elizabeth Montgomery is not a patient in this facility," she said carefully.

"That's not what I asked," I snapped.

"It's the answer I can give you today," Dr. Chen replied. "Johnny, I know this is frustrating. But we need to approach this methodically. You've experienced a traumatic event, compounded by serious medical issues we're still evaluating."

"Medical issues," I echoed. "You mean the tumor." The word slipped out before I could stop it, surprising even me. How did I know about a tumor?

Dr. Chen's expression shifted subtly—a slight widening of her eyes, a tightening around her mouth. "Yes," she said after a pause. "Among other things. That's why I'm here to help you navigate not just the events of the past few days, but the experiences you've been having for some time."

"What experiences?" I asked, though deep down, I already knew.

She leaned forward slightly, her voice gentle yet direct. "The times when you've seen or heard things others don't. The moments when memories shift or blur. The confusion between past and present."

My throat tightened. "Liz," I whispered.

Dr. Chen nodded, understanding in her eyes. "We're not here to punish you, Sheriff McCallister. We're here to help you separate what's real... from what isn't."

"Just—am I crazy or not?" I pleaded. "Please. Give me something straight."

Dr. Chen closed her portfolio with a soft snap. She didn't smile.

"No, Johnny. You're not crazy."

A beat, a moment to breathe, then—

"But your brain is lying to you. And we need to figure out why—together."

15

Shattered Perceptions

The familiar rumble of the cruiser's engine did little to ease my frayed nerves as we drove toward Johnny's house. Ashley sat beside me, her usual chatter stifled by the gravity of our discoveries. Three weeks had passed since we first noticed the cracks—misaligned timelines, missing witness statements, details that didn't add up. Ashley caught the first one in Johnny's old case reports. I'd brushed it off at the time. I didn't want to believe what I was seeing.

But the deeper we probed, the worse it got. Each discrepancy felt like a betrayal. I'd known Johnny for years—or so I thought. Now I wasn't sure I knew him at all.

The winding roads of Stormy Valley seemed darker than usual, the shadows of the pines stretching like accusing fingers across our path. My mind raced, memories of Johnny flashing like a grim slideshow. That easy smile of his—the one that always put folks at ease. The reassuring grip on my shoulder after last year's hellish standoff. The way he'd handled that road rage call with just a calm voice and unceasing presence. It was just how he did things, even when the rest of us were rattled.

But now, doubt seeped in like poison. Had it all been a facade? A carefully crafted illusion to conceal what, exactly?

"Deputy Langley?" Ashley's voice broke through my spiraling thoughts. "Do you think... I mean, is it possible Sheriff McCallister could have—"

"I don't know what to think anymore, Kowalski," I cut her off, harsher than intended. The guilt of my own hidden transgression weighed heavily, making me question my right to judge Johnny. "Let's just... see what we find."

As we rounded the final bend, Johnny's house loomed, a dark silhouette against the fading light. The porch steps creaked ominously under our feet, the sound echoing in the eerie stillness. Weeds choked the once-manicured lawn, reaching up like grasping hands.

I hesitated at the door, my hand hovering over the knob. A sense of dread crept through me, as if crossing this threshold would change everything irrevocably.

"You okay, sir?" Ashley asked, her voice barely above a whisper.

I nodded, not trusting myself to speak. With a deep breath, I pushed open the door, stepping into the remains of Johnny's sanctuary—and, perhaps, his sins.

The stench of stale alcohol and neglect hit me like a physical force. I stumbled over a stack of newspapers, my foot crunching on shattered glass. The sound echoed through the silent house, making Ashley flinch beside me.

"Jesus," I muttered, taking in the chaos. Empty bottles littered every surface, glinting dully in the dim light filtering through grimy windows. Papers, covered in Johnny's increasingly erratic handwriting, were strewn across the floor.

"It's like a tornado tore through here," Ashley whispered, her eyes wide as she carefully picked her way through the debris.

I nodded, my throat tight. This wasn't mere messiness; it was the physical manifestation of a mind unraveling. My heart ached for my old friend, even as a chill of apprehension crept up my spine.

We moved through the first floor, searching for clues to what Johnny might have been involved in. But the deeper we probed, the more it seemed he was drowning in his own turmoil. The once-elegant rooms were unrecognizable, consumed by piles of clutter. Papers, mail, and trash were heaped high, leaving only narrow paths to navigate. Grime stained the walls, and the windows were so filthy that little light could penetrate. Each room bore the scars Johnny's unraveling mind, leaving scant space for him to survive.

"Looks like unpaid bills and missed appointments," Ashley said, holding up a stack of mail. "Maybe he was grappling with something personal."

"Let's check the study," I said, leading the way down the narrow hallway. The floorboards creaked beneath our feet, each step feeling like an intrusion into Johnny's privacy.

The study door stood slightly ajar. I pushed it open, revealing a dimly lit room, papers and mail strewn across the floor. A single shaft of fading sunlight pierced the gloom, illuminating a framed photograph on the cluttered desk.

Ashley stepped closer, peering at the image. "Who's that with the sheriff?" she asked softly.

I swallowed hard, memories flooding back. "That's... Beth. Johnny's wife."

"I didn't know he was married," Ashley said, her voice tinged with surprise.

"Was," I quietly corrected. "She passed away over twenty years ago. Before you joined the force. Before... a lot of things."

The photograph seemed to stare back, Beth's kind eyes and gentle smile a stark contrast to the surrounding chaos. I recalled her laugh, her unwavering support for Johnny. Would she even recognize what he'd become?

"What happened to her?" Ashley asked, her curiosity tempered by respect.

I hesitated, old guilt gnawing at my gut. How much did she need to know? How much could I say without betraying Johnny's trust... or revealing my own role in the tragedy that might have set this all in motion?

"It's... complicated," I said, knowing it was a cop-out even as the words left my lips. "And not my story to tell."

Ashley's eyes narrowed with skepticism, but she didn't press further. Her sharp eyes scanned the room, though I could feel her unspoken questions lingering. I couldn't bear to meet her eyes—let alone look at Beth's photograph on the wall, its silent accusation piercing me.

Moving deeper into the room, my foot caught on something. A small, leather-bound notebook skittered across the floor, coming to rest in a patch of light. Johnny's journal. My hand trembled as I reached for it, knowing its pages might hold answers... and horrors I wasn't ready to face.

I reached for the journal, then stopped, suspended in doubt. The leather felt cool against my fingertips as I finally picked it up, its weight far heavier than its physical mass.

With a sigh, I turned my attention to the object in my hand. Its worn leather, frayed edges, and creased pages spoke of frequent use. I opened to the first page and began to read.

Johnny's handwriting was messy yet legible, each word carefully chosen and steeped in emotion. He wrote of his grief after Beth's death, how he'd thrown himself into work to cope. He detailed his struggles with addiction and his vow to stay clean after his promotion. But as I skimmed the entries, it became clear this wasn't merely a journal for venting—it also held observations about cases he was working on.

A pang of guilt washed over me as I realized Johnny had borne this weight alone. He'd poured his soul into these pages, revealing his deepest fears and uncertainties about cases that seemed unsolvable. But as I read on, my guilt turned to unease. There were mentions of unresolved cases—ones Johnny believed were connected. His handwriting grew more erratic with each entry from the past year or two.

"Mike," Ashley's voice was hushed, "what are these?"

My eyes scanned the documents, a chill creeping up my spine. "Medical records," I muttered, pulling out a thick manila folder. "Jesus, Johnny..."

The timeline of symptoms stretched back years, far longer than I'd imagined. Headaches, mood swings, other issues—all meticulously documented. How had I missed this?

"He's been struggling for so long," I whispered, more to myself than Ashley. "Why didn't he say anything?"

Ashley leaned in, her brow furrowed. "Look at the dates. Some of these go back... years."

My stomach churned. Had Johnny's condition influenced his recent cases? The thought was too horrifying to contemplate.

We left Johnny's house in silence, the truth dragging behind us like a chain. Each step heavier than the last. The overgrown lawn whispered secrets as we passed, the decrepit porch creaking a mournful farewell. Ashley's eyes brimmed with unspoken questions, but I couldn't meet her gaze.

"Mike," she ventured, her voice barely audible above the rustling pines, "what does this mean?"

I paused, hand on the car door. The truth was a razor's edge, and I feared we'd both bleed if I spoke it aloud. "I don't know, Ash," I said. "I just... don't know."

The drive back to the station was a symphony of silence, broken only by the rhythmic thump of tires on uneven asphalt. My mind raced, piecing together a puzzle I wasn't sure I wanted to solve. Johnny—my friend, my mentor—how much of the man I knew was real?

As we pulled into the station parking lot, Ashley cleared her throat. "Should we tell—"

"No," I cut her off, perhaps too sharply. "Not yet. We need... to be sure."

The office felt different now, shadows lurking in corners I'd never noticed before. On my desk, an envelope waited, its crisp white surface marred by a familiar insignia: Lakeside Behavioral Health. My heart stuttered, but my hands remained steady as I reached for it.

"What's that?" Ashley asked, hovering nearby.

I swallowed hard. "Nothing good," I murmured, tearing open the seal. "Nothing good at all."

The evaluation summary unfurled before me, each sterile phrase chipping away at the man I thought I knew. Foreign, clinical language landed like hammer blows, cracking the foundation of everything I believed.

"Frontotemporal meningioma," I whispered, the medical term foreign on my tongue. "Depression, anxiety, cognitive distortions..."

Ashley leaned in, her brow furrowed. "What does it mean, Mike?"

I reread the page, hoping the words would reshape into a less damning narrative. They didn't. "It means Johnny's sick, Ash. Very sick. His mind... it's turning against him."

The room tilted, the familiar confines of the sheriff's office warping like a funhouse mirror. I gripped the desk's edge, knuckles white.

"But how... how long has this been going on?" Ashley's voice seemed to echo from a distance.

I shook my head, trying to clear the vertigo. "The timeline here... it stretches back years. God, how did I not see it?"

My loyalty to Johnny, the bedrock of my career, began to crumble. Every shared moment—late-night patrols, quiet conversations over coffee—cast in a sickening new light.

"The road rage incidents," I muttered, more to myself than Ashley. "Sam Thompson... Christ, what if—"

"Mike?" Ashley's hand on my arm startled me. "You're shaking."

I looked down at my trembling hands, the evaluation report quivering like a leaf in the wind. "Yeah," I managed, my voice hoarse. "I guess I am."

The truth crashed over me like a tidal wave, leaving me gasping. Johnny's jovial smiles, his firm handshakes, the way he'd clap me on the back after a tough case—it was all a carefully constructed facade. A mask worn by a man I thought I knew better than anyone.

"He lied to us," I whispered, anger and sorrow warring in my chest. "All this time, he was... falling apart, and he never said a word."

Ashley's voice was soft, hesitant. "Maybe he didn't realize how bad it was."

I shook my head, memories flashing through my mind like a warped highlight reel. "No, he knew. The pills I'd catch him popping, the erratic mood swings, those moments when he'd just... zone out. He knew, and he hid it from all of us."

The betrayal seeped in slowly, heavy in all the wrong places. I slumped back in my chair, the old leather creaking under my weight.

"What do we do now?" Ashley asked, her eyes wide with uncertainty.

I had no answer. The ticking of the wall clock grew louder, each second hammering another nail into the coffin of my trust.

As dusk crept in through the blinds, Ashley gathered her things and left with a quiet, "Goodnight, Mike." I barely noticed her departure, lost in the labyrinth of my thoughts.

The office was silent now, save for the continual hum of the fluorescent lights overhead. I stared at Johnny's empty desk, grappling to make sense of it all.

Had I been willfully blind to his turmoil, or had I simply turned a blind eye, accepting his struggles with addiction but not these new behaviors? How could Johnny have been so steadfast in sharing one battle but so distant in another? He had confided in me about his fight against addiction, yet kept his health a secret. With his recent relapse, I couldn't help but wonder why I hadn't pushed harder to offer more support; perhaps there was a moment I could have intervened, a chance to change this outcome.

I shook my head, trying to dispel the doubt and confusion. But it lingered—an unwelcome echo reverberating through every thought, deepening my unease.

I needed answers. I needed to confront Johnny and demand an explanation for his actions. But how—how could I get answers from a man losing his grip on reality?

16

Cognition's Edge

The next morning—or so I assumed from the angled light filtering through the blinds of my room—Dr. Chen returned with a small paper cup balanced in her hand. Inside were two pills which looked innocuous, just ordinary capsules, one white, one blue. But I knew they signified something far greater: an admission that the problem lay within my mind. My hands trembled slightly as I took the cup from her—not from withdrawal this time, but from what accepting these pills meant.

"The white one is an antipsychotic," Dr. Chen explained, settling into the chair across from me. "It should help reduce hallucinations, helping your mind better distinguish between internal thoughts and external reality. The blue one addresses anxiety and agitation."

I stared at the pills, unmoving. They rattled in the paper cup like teeth—small, ordinary, yet heavy enough to tip a life. I stared too long. Dr. Chen waited in silence—not impatient, but composed. I used to be that way—steady—before I started doubting reality, before I started believing ghosts could speak. Not recovery. Not madness. Just the tipping point where the mind teetered, aware of its fracture, terrified of what lay ahead.

"And if I refuse?"

"That's your right," Dr. Chen said simply. "But these medications are tools, Sheriff. They can create a space to work through what's happened, free from neurological interference."

Neurological interference. Such a clinical phrase for seeing my dead wife or questioning whether the blood on my hands was real or imagined.

"Will they make the tumor go away?" I asked, already knowing the answer.

Dr. Chen's expression softened. "No, the medication won't affect the tumor itself, but it can help manage the symptoms it causes."

I swallowed the pills dry, their bitterness lingering on my tongue. "So, tell me about this tumor that's apparently making me crazy."

"Not crazy, Johnny," she corrected gently. "You have a frontotemporal meningioma, a growth in the membrane covering your brain, in the region that governs personality, decision-making, and the integration of memories and perceptions."

She paused, letting the information settle. "The pressure from this tumor disrupts how your brain processes information, causing hallucinations, muddling your memories, and sometimes making it hard to control impulses or accurately assess threats."

"And it's inoperable," I said flatly, the knowledge rising from somewhere deep in my mind.

Dr. Chen nodded, her eyes meeting mine. "Yes. Due to its location and integration with critical brain tissue, surgical removal would likely cause more harm than good."

I stood abruptly, pacing the cramped room. "I've had breakdowns before, Doctor. After my wife died—after the accident—I spiraled. Drank too much. Saw things that weren't there. But I got clean. I rebuilt my life."

"I know," she said, her voice calm. "Your history of addiction and depression is in your file. Those were psychological responses to trauma and substance abuse. What you're experiencing now is fundamentally different."

"How so?" I demanded, turning to face her. "I hallucinated before. I was paranoid before. How is this any different?"

"Because this time, a physical change in your brain is causing it," she replied. "The tumor is growing, Johnny, and as it grows, these symptoms will likely intensify."

Her words didn't just hang there—they reverberated inside my skull, louder than her voice had been, refusing to let me look away from what she'd said.

"How long?" I asked, my voice raw.

Dr. Chen hesitated, and in that pause, I knew the news was grim. "Based on the tumor's current growth rate and type, patients in your situation typically have about twelve months."

Twelve months. The words echoed in my head, hollow and final. "And then what? I just... die?"

"As the tumor grows, you'll likely experience worsening cognitive impairment, personality changes, and eventually, loss of motor function," Dr. Chen explained, her clinical words softened by the compassion in her eyes. "We can manage symptoms as they arise, but yes, eventually, the pressure on your brain will become incompatible with life."

I laughed—a harsh, broken sound. "Incompatible with life. That's one way to put it."

"I'm sorry, Johnny," she said softly. "I wish I had better news."

I sank back onto the bed, the reality of my situation crashing over me like a tidal wave. Twelve months. Less than a year to live. And not even with my mind intact.

"This can't be right," I said, desperation creeping into my voice. "I'm the sheriff. I solve cases. I protect people. How can I—" I broke off, a terrible thought striking me. "The case. Pete Collins. Did I really... did I kill him?"

Dr. Chen leaned forward, her expression grave. "Johnny, this is what we need to work through. Your condition has distorted your perception of recent events. Some of what you remember may be accurate, but other parts may be muddled or entirely fabricated by your mind."

"So I could be a murderer and not even know it?" An electric panic bloomed in me, tightening my breath. "Or I could be locked up here for something that never happened?"

"That's why we'll take this slowly," Dr. Chen assured me. "We'll work together to untangle fact from fiction, to understand what truly happened on that jogging trail and in the days leading up to it."

I pressed the heels of my hands against my eyes, trying to shut out the world, the truth crumbling like a rotted beam. "And Liz? Detective Montgomery? Is she real, or did I invent her?"

Dr. Chen's fingers brushed mine as she gently eased my hands from my face, the brief contact—charged with static from the dry air—snapping me back to reality. "Detective Elizabeth Montgomery isn't real, Johnny," she said softly. "She's likely a composite, a blend of a detective you once worked with and memories of your late wife."

Relief gave way to a deeper chasm of doubt. "Then who have I been seeing? Talking to?"

Her voice remained calm but firm. "Under extreme stress—whether from psychological trauma or your tumor—the mind can create such composites."

I recalled how Liz's face sometimes shifted subtly, her features blurring when I didn't look directly at her. How she'd speak of things only my wife could know. The realization spun through me, a dark spiral of horror.

"I'm losing my mind," I whispered.

"No," Dr. Chen said firmly. "Your mind is grappling with conflicting information under extreme duress. That's a sign of its resilience, not its failure."

I looked at her, desperate for something to cling to. "How do I know what's real? Right now, talking to you—how do I know this is real?"

"That's why we start with medication," she said. "To establish a clearer baseline. Then we work methodically through your memories and experiences, seeking external verification where possible."

"And if we can't verify?" I asked, already sensing the gaps, moments lost to the tumor's distortions.

"Then we accept the uncertainty," she replied candidly. "Part of this process is learning to live with not knowing everything, while trusting what we can confirm."

I nodded slowly, exhaustion settling over me like a heavy cloak. It wasn't the pills—not yet. But something about Dr. Chen, her steadiness, her refusal to flinch eased the panic clawing at my chest. I didn't want to trust her. I didn't want to need her. But in this moment, with the ground shifting beneath me and everything I thought I knew unraveling, her presence felt like the only solid thing left.

"I don't want to die not knowing what's real," I admitted, the words raw and painful to voice.

Dr. Chen's expression softened. "I know. And I'll do everything I can to help you find as much clarity as possible in the time we have. You don't have to face this alone, Johnny."

For the first time since waking in this place, I felt something beyond fear or anger—a faint flicker of gratitude for this woman's steady compassion. It wasn't hope, not exactly, but it was something to grasp in the uncertainty stretching before me.

Dr. Chen's office felt like a confessional wrapped in the trappings of modern psychology—all muted colors and soft edges, designed to soften the sharp truths. I sat in a chair too comfortable for the uncomfortable conversation ahead, my fingers tracing the arm's fabric—real, tangible, a texture I could trust. Three weeks of medication had cleared the fog from my mind, but in its place came a clarity that stung like antiseptic on an open wound. Liz was gone. Not dead—worse. She had never existed at all.

"How are you feeling today, Johnny?" Dr. Chen asked, settling into her chair across from me. No clipboard today, just her even gaze and hands folded loosely in her lap. A thin silver bracelet gleamed on her wrist, catching the light with each subtle movement.

"Empty," I said, the word slipping out before I could muster something more composed. "Like someone carved out a piece of me I didn't know was hollow to begin with."

She nodded, neither overly sympathetic nor coldly clinical—just present. "The medication is working, then. The hallucinations have stopped?"

"She's gone," I confirmed, my throat tightening. "Liz is—" I couldn't finish. How do you mourn someone who was never real? The grief felt obscene, illegitimate, yet it cut through me like a blade.

"That must be disorienting," Dr. Chen said, her voice calm but not unkind. "To have a presence that felt so real vanish so suddenly."

I laughed, a brittle sound that scraped my throat. "Disorienting. That's one way to put it. Another would be fucking terrifying."

The silence stretched between us, taut and elastic. Outside her window, rain pattered against the glass in an uneven rhythm. I focused on that sound, real and grounding.

"I want facts," I said finally, meeting her eyes. "Not observations or psychological jargon. Just tell me what I did. Who I hurt."

Dr. Chen studied me for a long moment. "Facts are complex when perception is compromised, but I understand your need for concrete answers."

"Pete Collins," I pressed. "Is he alive?"

"Yes," she said, and relief surged through me so fiercely I nearly doubled over. "Mr. Collins sustained a black eye and bruised ribs during your altercation, but he's recovering well."

My hands trembled slightly, and I clenched them into fists to quell the shaking. "I was so sure I'd killed him. I remember blood—so much blood."

"Memory can be like that—especially when affected by your condition. The brain fills gaps with details from other experiences, other moments."

I leaned forward, pressing my elbows into my knees. "What about the jogger? On the trail."

A subtle tension flickered in Dr. Chen's eyes. "That's more complex."

"Complex how?"

She shifted slightly, her movement deliberate, as if buying time to choose her words. "There was an incident on the Stormy Valley Jogging Trail. You were there, as was a man—a stranger. Witnesses reported an altercation between you."

My heart pounded against my ribs. "And?"

"He died, Johnny," she said. "The medical examiner ruled it an accidental death from head trauma sustained during a fall in the struggle."

The world tilted, then steadied. I tasted copper in my mouth, though I hadn't bitten my tongue. "I killed him."

"It was ruled accidental," Dr. Chen reiterated. "The investigation found you believed you were responding to a threat."

"A threat that wasn't real," I said flatly.

Dr. Chen's voice held firm. "You perceived a threat. Your brain tumor disrupts regions responsible for threat assessment and impulse control. Your actions were consistent with those neurological impairments."

"So I'm not responsible?" I asked, bitterness creeping into my tone. "Just blame it on the tumor eating my brain?"

"Responsibility isn't binary, Johnny. Your condition is a factor, not an absolution."

I stood abruptly, needing to move, to feel my body under my own control. The room felt both too vast and too confining. "What else? What else don't I remember correctly?"

Dr. Chen watched me pace, her calm a stark contrast to the storm raging inside me. "There was another incident—at the hospital."

I stopped, my back to her, fingers pressed against the cool window glass. Rain streaked down the outside, warping the world beyond. "What happened?"

"You had an episode—a violent outburst when you believed you were being threatened. A nurse was gravely injured trying to restrain you."

I turned slowly to face her. "How gravely?"

The silence lingered for three heartbeats. "She didn't survive, Johnny."

My legs buckled, and I sank back into the chair, my body suddenly heavy as lead. My hands were numb, but a searing guilt burned in my chest.

"I don't remember any of it," I whispered.

"That's not uncommon with traumatic events, even without neurological factors."

I pressed the heels of my hands against my eyes until colors burst behind my eyelids. "So I'm a murderer. Twice over."

"No," Dr. Chen said firmly. "You're a man with a serious medical condition that altered your perception and behavior. The legal system has accounted for your condition."

I dropped my hands, anger surging. "I don't care about legal definitions. I killed two people!"

"One accidentally, one in a neurologically compromised state," she corrected gently. "Neither makes you a murderer in the way you mean."

"Semantics won't bring them back."

"No," she agreed. "They won't."

We sat in silence, the rain's rhythm against the window the only sound. I tried to recall the hospital, the nurse, but there was nothing—just fragments that might be memory or illusion. The uncertainty was its own torment.

"I keep waiting for you to offer me some comfort," I said finally. "Some psychological trick to make this easier to bear."

Dr. Chen shook her head slightly. "Tricks or false comfort wouldn't serve you, Johnny. What you need is a framework to process what's happened and what's happening to you."

"And what is that framework, Doctor? How do I live with knowing I've taken lives because my brain is betraying me?"

"One day at a time," she said simply. "We acknowledge the pain—yours and that caused to others. We identify your triggers and warning signs. We develop strategies to protect you and those around you."

"And then I die," I said flatly.

"Eventually, yes. But how you live until then remains within your control, even if that control is imperfect."

I laughed again, the sound hollow even to my ears. "Imperfect? I'd settle for not endangering everyone around me."

"That's a starting point," Dr. Chen said, her voice softening. "And Johnny? The fact that you care, that you're devastated by what's happened—that matters. It doesn't change the outcome, but it reflects who you are at your core."

I looked away, unable to bear her gaze. Outside, the rain continued its steady rhythm, washing the world clean in a way I knew I could never be.

"I miss her," I admitted, the truth slipping out before I could take it back. "I know she wasn't real, but she felt real. She was the only thing that made sense when everything else was unraveling."

Dr. Chen nodded, understanding in her eyes. "Hallucinations often serve a purpose—they meet a need. Part of our work together will be uncovering that need and finding healthier ways to address it."

"How do you replace someone you loved?" I asked, knowing there was no answer.

"You don't," she said simply. "You learn to carry them differently."

I nodded, exhaustion washing over me. The medication, the revelations, the absence of Liz—it all pressed down with crushing weight. In less than a year, I would be gone, my mind unraveling long before my body. But first, I had to live with what I'd done, the lives I'd harmed. There was no escaping that, no matter how my diseased brain tried to rewrite reality.

There were still gaps—hours, maybe whole days—I couldn't reclaim. They told me I overdosed. That Pete found me. That the veterinary cabinet was empty when they arrived. I don't remember taking anything, don't remember deciding to give up.

It felt like something that had happened to someone else in my body. But the timeline made sense. I thought I killed Pete. I panicked. I tried to disappear.

And somehow, that act—the one I couldn't even recall—was the thing that finally got me help. Maybe the only reason I was still here.

"Same time tomorrow?" I asked, the fight draining from me.

Dr. Chen nodded. "Same time tomorrow, Johnny. We'll keep moving for-ward."

Forward. As if there were anywhere to go but deeper into the hollows of my own mind, where shadows already took root.

17

Town in Turmoil

The towering oaks loomed like silent sentinels as I stood before the weathered steps of Stormy Valley Town Hall. A chill wind whispered through their branches, carrying the scent of pine and damp earth. Dread churned in my stomach.

I adjusted my badge, its weight suddenly heavy on my chest. The brass felt cold, a stark reminder of my duty. Johnny's actions hung over us like a dark cloud, and now I had to face the storm. It had been three weeks since the town watched Sheriff McCallister crumble, and the dust hadn't settled.

"Evening, Mike," Old Man Jenkins said, nodding as he shuffled past. "Quite the turnout, eh?"

I forced a thin smile. "Looks that way, Hank."

My fingers trembled slightly as I reached for the door handle. Get it together, Langley. You've faced worse than this.

The moment I stepped inside, a hush fell over the crowd. Dozens of eyes turned to me—some accusatory, others pleading. The air felt thick with tension, pressing against me like invisible smoke.

"Deputy Langley," Mayor Hampton's voice cut through the silence. "We've been waiting."

I walked down the aisle, each step echoing in the cavernous hall. Familiar faces lined the pews, their expressions a mosaic of fear, anger, and confusion. Sarah from the diner clutched her purse tightly, while Bob the mechanic's usually jovial face was etched with worry.

"Sorry for the delay," I muttered, taking my seat near the front. "Had to finish some paperwork."

Mayor Hampton cleared his throat. "Now that we're all here, let's begin. Recent events have cast a shadow over our community..."

His words faded into a dull hum as my thoughts drifted. I remembered Johnny as he was years ago—strong, dependable, the embodiment of a small-town sheriff. Now? The man I saw in that hospital was a stranger, his eyes wild with paranoia and guilt.

A sharp elbow to my ribs jolted me back to reality. Marjorie Wilkins, head of the neighborhood watch, leaned in close. "This is all your fault, you know," she hissed. "You should've seen the signs."

I bit back a retort. If only she knew the half of it—the secrets I'd kept, the signs I'd overlooked. My own guilt weighed heavier than any accusation she could hurl.

The sharp crack of the gavel echoed through the room, jolting me out of my reverie. Mayor Hampton's voice boomed, "We will now hear testimony from Deputy Ashley Kowalski."

My stomach tightened. Ashley. So young, so determined to prove herself. I watched her rise, her petite frame commanding the space as she approached the podium. Her red curls caught the dim light, framing her freckled face like a fiery halo.

She cleared her throat, and when she spoke, her voice was poised, though I noticed a slight tremor in her hands as she gripped the podium's edges. "Good evening, everyone. I'm here to provide my account of the events leading to Sheriff McCallister's... current situation."

My mind raced. What would she reveal? How much did she know? The walls pressed in closer with every breath, each one thinner, tighter, until I could barely draw the next.

"I've worked alongside Sheriff McCallister for two years," Ashley continued. "In that time, I've known him as a dedicated officer and a good man."

A murmur rippled through the crowd, skepticism thick as the murkiness that often cloaked Stormy Valley.

Ashley's voice gained strength. "I understand there are questions about his recent actions. But I urge you to remember his years of service to Stormy Valley—the lives he's saved, the crimes he's solved."

As Ashley spoke, I found myself torn between admiration for her loyalty and dread of the truths that might surface. The weight of what I knew was a burden over my soul, threatening to engulf me.

"Sheriff McCallister has always prioritized the safety of this town, always treated me fairly. He... he was like a second father at times. Strict, sure, but he believed in me. He really did." Ashley declared, her red curls catching the dim light as she turned to face the crowd.

A low murmur of dissent stirred the room. To my left, old Mrs. Hanson shook her head, her wrinkled face etched with disapproval. To my right, Tom Baker nodded slowly, his weathered hands clasped tightly in his lap.

I closed my eyes, Johnny's face flashing behind my eyelids. Years of shared history flooded in, threatening to drown what little resolve remained.

"Deputy Kowalski," a voice rang out, sharp and accusatory. "How can you defend a man who's become a danger to our community?"

The tension in the room snapped like a rubber band stretched too far. Voices erupted, a cacophony of anger and fear echoing off the walls of the cramped town hall.

"He's unstable!" someone shouted from the back. "We can't have a madman with a badge!"

"Johnny's protected us for years," Tom Baker countered, his voice gruff but steady. "We owe him the benefit of the doubt."

I forced my features into calm, but my stomach roiled. Each word felt like a knife twisting in my gut. Ashley's words clung to me like burrs—part truth, part wishful thinking. Johnny's face swam before me, haunted and haggard. What had truly happened that day on the jogging trail?

"Order, please," I said at last, my voice carrying a weight I didn't feel. "We need to approach this calmly."

But calm was a luxury we couldn't afford. The air smelled of dust and sweat, the room a tinderbox where every shout was a spark from a town unwilling to see its sheriff as he really was.

"What about the evidence?" Mrs. Hanson piped up, her reedy voice trembling. "Surely that speaks for itself."

"Evidence can be misleading," I offered, more to myself than anyone else, remembering that empty evidence bag in Johnny's desk drawer.

As the meeting drew to a close, I stood, my joints creaking in protest. The crowd parted before me, a sea of familiar faces now etched with uncertainty and fear.

"Mike," Tom said, catching my arm as I passed. "You'll get to the bottom of this, won't you?"

I nodded, wishing I believed it myself. Not sure who I was trying to convince. "I'll do my best, Tom."

My mind was already miles away, fixed on the road that would lead me to Johnny. I had to uncover the truth, even if it buried us both.

Fog crept in, its tendrils curling around my tires as I navigated the winding roads of Stormy Valley. Each turn summoned an unbidden memory, sharp and unwelcome: Johnny and I, fresh-faced deputies, swapping stories over lukewarm coffee; the pride in his eyes when he made sheriff; the night everything changed.

"Damn it, Johnny," I muttered, knuckles white on the steering wheel. "What did you do?"

The road stretched before me, an endless ribbon of asphalt vanishing into the gloom. Trees loomed on either side, their gnarled branches reaching like skeletal fingers. In the rearview mirror, the town faded, swallowed by the mist.

My thoughts drifted to Ashley's testimony, her words resonating in the hollow of my chest. "Officer Kowalski saw what she saw," I told myself. But doubt gnawed at me, a relentless ache. What if she was mistaken? What if we all were?

The psychiatric facility emerged from the fog like a specter, its stark outline slicing through the surrounding gloom. I cut the engine, sitting in silence as raindrops pattered against the windshield.

"You don't have to do this," a voice whispered in my mind. But I did—for Johnny, for the town, for the secrets that bound us.

I stepped out, the damp air clinging to my skin. The building towered over me, its dark windows glaring like accusing eyes. Each step toward the entrance felt like wading through molasses, my feet heavy with dread.

At the door, I paused, my hand hovering over the handle. "You're just doing your job," I murmured, trying to convince myself. But the years between us, all the secrets and silences, pressed down like something I'd never be free of. I took a deep breath, bracing myself for what lay ahead. The truth waited inside, unrelenting. And no matter how much it might hurt, I had to confront it—for Stormy Valley, for Johnny, for my own damn peace of mind.

With a final flicker of hesitation, I pushed open the door and stepped into the fluorescent-lit lobby, leaving my last shred of certainty behind.

The antiseptic smell hit me like a slap, stinging my nostrils and coating my tongue. My footsteps echoed through the sterile corridors, each click of my boots against the linoleum a stark reminder of my solitude. The waiting room's walls, a sickly shade of green, seemed to press in around me.

"Just like old times, eh, Mike?" I muttered, a humorless chuckle escaping my lips. How many times had I walked these halls, visiting perps or victims? But never Johnny. Never my friend.

As I rounded a corner, a nurse's station came into view. The young woman behind the desk eyed me warily, her fingers hovering over a concealed button. I flashed my badge, watching her shoulders ease slightly. A low buzz sounded, the lock disengaging only after she'd looked me over.

"Deputy Langley," I said, my voice sounding hollow in the oppressive silence. "Here to see Johnathan McCallister."

She nodded, gesturing down the hall. "Room 237. End of the corridor."

With each step, memories flooded my mind: Johnny and I, fresh-faced rookies, vowing to uphold the law; late nights at the bar, drowning sorrows we couldn't name; the day I found him, trembling and broken, swearing he'd get clean.

I reached the door, my hand resting on the cold metal handle. Room 237 stared back, a number etched into my memory. My throat tightened, a maelstrom of emotions threatening to engulf me.

"You can still walk away," that traitorous voice in my mind whispered. But I couldn't. Too much history. Too many secrets. Every one of them bound me tighter to this place, to Johnny.

I closed my eyes, drawing a shaky breath. When I opened them, I saw not the stark white door but a barrier between past and present, between loyalty and duty. With a trembling hand, I turned the handle and stepped into the unknown.

The room's fluorescent light flickered, casting Johnny in a sickly pallor. He sat hunched on the edge of his bed, his once-commanding frame diminished, a shadow of the man I'd known. My heart constricted, a dull ache spreading through my chest.

"Mike," he rasped, his bloodshot eyes meeting mine. "You came."

I swallowed hard, forcing myself to approach. "Of course I did, Johnny. We're... we're partners, aren't we?"

A bitter laugh escaped his lips. "Partners? Is that what we are now?"

I pulled up a chair, its metal legs scraping against the linoleum. "I need to understand, Johnny. What happened out there?"

His eyes darted to the corners of the room, as if searching for unseen watchers. "You wouldn't believe me if I told you," he muttered.

"Try me," I urged, leaning forward. "We've been through hell together, Johnny. Whatever this is, we can face it."

He turned to me, his eyes suddenly sharp. "Can we, Mike? Can we really face what's coming?"

I froze. What did he know? What had he seen? I opened my mouth to respond, but Johnny cut me off.

"They're watching, Mike. Always watching. In the shadows, in the trees. They know what we did."

My breath caught in my throat. "Johnny, that was years ago. We... we did what we had to do."

He leaned closer, his voice a desperate whisper. "Did we? Or did we just tell ourselves that to sleep at night?"

I felt the walls of the room pressing in, our past filling the room like smoke. Johnny's words echoed in my mind, unearthing memories I'd fought to bury.

"Why the secrecy, Johnny?" I asked at last, taking a breath to ground myself. "Why keep what was going on in your head to yourself?" My voice was soft, threaded with grief.

He averted his gaze, staring at his trembling hands. "I... I didn't want to burden anyone. And who would believe me? A recovering addict seeing ghosts?"

He let out a humorless chuckle, a hollow sound reverberating in the room's stillness.

"I know it sounds crazy, Mike. Hell, I barely believe it myself. But the things I've seen... the things I've done... they're not just figments of my imagination."

He paused, summoning his courage.

"There's something wrong with me, Mike. Something inside my mind. It's like... my thoughts are playing tricks on me."

He looked up at me, his eyes pleading for understanding.

"I need your help, Mike. I need someone to believe me."

My heart ached for him. I knew too well the demons addiction could con-jure, the residue of it, clinging long after the last high. But this felt different.

"I believe you, Johnny," I said, reaching for his hand. "I'll get you the help you need."

For the first time in a long while, hope sparked in his eyes, a faint light in the darkness.

"Thank you, Mike," he whispered. "Thank you for believing me."

I squeezed his hand, a silent vow to stand by him, no matter what horrors his mind might conjure.

I hesitated, then added quietly, "After Kayla... I should've seen it coming."

Johnny's expression shifted, his jaw tightening.

"You weren't sleeping. You'd show up at the station looking like hell, disappearing in your own skin. I kept telling myself you just needed time."

I looked away, shame rising like bile. "I arranged your leave. Told every-one it was routine. But it wasn't. You were drowning, and I waited until you'd already gone under."

Johnny didn't speak, but his grip on my hand tightened—just enough to say *I remember.*

"I should've stepped in sooner," I said. "I thought I was protecting you. But maybe I was just protecting myself from what I didn't want to face."

I felt the words leave me like a confession, raw and half-formed. For a moment, neither of us spoke. There was too much between us now—regret, guilt, things left undone.

I closed my eyes, drew in a breath that didn't want to come. I couldn't change the past. God knows I'd tried. But I could try to hold the line now, even if I wasn't sure what that line was anymore.

"Right now, we focus on the present," I said, keeping my voice even, my throat burning with everything I wasn't saying. "The town needs answers, Johnny. They need to know you're okay."

A sorrowful expression clouded his features, his voice thick with despair. "Okay? I haven't truly felt okay in years, Mike. And the worst part is, I can't trust what's real anymore."

I couldn't bear that look. The knowing in it. The quiet accusation we'd never put into words.

He met my eyes, and for the first time, I saw it—not just fear, but recognition. Like he'd caught a glimpse of something in me I couldn't name, but feared all the same.

An uneasy silence settled over the room, broken only by the hum of the fluorescent lights. Johnny's words lingered, a reality I couldn't ignore.

I stood, my chair scraping hard against the floor. The sound was too sharp, too final, but I couldn't stay in that room another second. His words had cracked something open in me, and if I stayed, he'd see it all spill out.

A sinking realization hit me: the answers I sought might remain forever out of reach.

I stumbled into the hallway, my legs unsteady beneath me. The sterile corridor stretched ahead, fluorescent-lit and endless, a tunnel leading back to a world I no longer trusted. My footsteps echoed hollowly as I made for the exit, each one heavier than the last.

"You alright there, Deputy Langley?" The nurse's voice startled me.

I forced a smile, though it felt like a grimace. "Fine, just... tired."

She nodded, unconvinced. "It's never easy, seeing someone you know in here."

I couldn't bring myself to respond. How could I explain that the man in that room wasn't just someone I knew, but a mirror reflecting my own fears?

The automatic doors hissed open, and I stepped into the fog-shrouded evening. The mist clung to me, damp and oppressive, as if urging me back into the facility, my skin—cool, heavy, like grief made tangible. I fumbled for my car keys, my hands trembling.

As I slid behind the wheel, Johnny's words echoed in my mind: "They're watching, Mike. Always watching."

I gripped the steering wheel, my knuckles whitening. The weight of unspoken truths bore down, threatening to shatter what little resolve remained.

"Get it together, Mike," I muttered, starting the engine. But as I pulled out of the parking lot, I couldn't shake the feeling that I was driving not toward home but deeper into a darkness of my own making.

The roads twisted through the valley, familiar yet alien in the encroaching gloom. Shadows rose at every turn, like the land itself was watching.

Was this how it began for Johnny? The doubt. The creeping dread. The slow warping of truth?

I gripped the wheel tighter. I had to be the calm. The constant.

But as Stormy Valley came into view, shrouded in mist and secrets, I couldn't shake the sense that what waited in the dark wasn't just history.

It was coming for us all.

18

Tarnished Threads

Nearly a month had passed, but time seemed to thicken rather than flow. I sat in the records room, surrounded by cardboard boxes and manila folders, as dust motes danced in the late afternoon sun slanting through the blinds. Each file felt heavier than it should, weighted with more than paper and ink. The truth lay buried somewhere within, obscured by bureaucracy and human error. Johnny had known it. Now it fell to me to unearth what he couldn't.

"Deputy Kowalski," I called, not looking up from the stack of reports I was sorting. "Could you bring the Lawson files?"

Ashley's sneakers squeaked against the linoleum as she navigated the maze of boxes. Her shadow fell across my desk before she did, all efficiency and unspoken questions.

"These go back to '95," she said, setting a weathered box on the table. The cardboard sagged at the corners, stained with the fingerprints of officers long retired or gone. "I've marked the original statements with blue tabs. Follow-ups are in yellow."

I nodded, appreciating her thoroughness. In the weeks since Johnny's... ordeal, Ashley had stepped up. The rookie softness in her face had sharpened into determination, reminiscent of myself thirty years ago, before I learned justice was rarely clean or complete.

"What about the road rage case?" I asked, pushing aside a pile of loose photographs.

She gestured to another stack. "Over there. Witness statements contradict each other, as we remembered." Her voice lowered. "And I've pulled the Banks case too."

The jogger. My stomach tightened at the memory of that chaotic day. Johnny, in his unraveling state, had perceived a threat where none existed. In the ensuing struggle, the jogger was tragically killed—an innocent life extinguished by misplaced fear. By chance, we uncovered a shallow grave nearby, holding Sarah Lawson's remains—a discovery made too late to reach Johnny before his institutionalization. I pressed my palms against the table's cool surface, seeking solace in its grounding presence amid the turmoil swirling within me.

"Good," I said. "And the timeline?"

Ashley hesitated, then retrieved a rolled sheet of butcher paper from a cardboard tube in the corner. She cleared space on the adjacent table, securing the curling edges with a stapler and a hole punch.

"I've mapped it out," she said. "Starting three months before the first incident. Every public appearance, every call Johnny responded to, every personal day he took." Her finger traced a red line that grew increasingly jagged toward the end. "You can see where things started to... unravel."

I could. The orderly spacing of early events gave way to clusters, gaps, and overlapping actions that would have required Johnny to be in two places at once—a timeline of a mind unmooring from reality.

My hands were cold, but a warmth spread across my chest, an uncomfortable heat I recognized as guilt. I should have noticed sooner. We all should have.

"Let's start with Lawson," I said, reaching for the box Ashley had brought. The cardboard felt damp at the corners, as if it had absorbed decades of grief. "Johnny was fixated on her disappearance toward the end. Said we'd find her body at the Thompson place."

"But we didn't," Ashley said softly.

"No. Not until later, and not where he thought." I began sorting files, arranging them chronologically. "But he was right about one thing—she was murdered."

The methodical task of organizing the files consumed the next hour. Statements were separated from evidence logs, photographs from interview transcripts. We created piles, then sub-piles, building a paper altar to a girl we'd never met. The light outside shifted from amber to gray, and Ashley switched on the harsh fluorescents without prompting.

"You knew him a long time," she said suddenly, her voice breaking the mechanical rhythm we'd settled into.

I kept my eyes on the files. "Since he made deputy. Before the accident." Before the drinking. Before he clawed his way to sheriff, only to be dragged down by something none of us could fight.

"Do you think he knew? About the tumor, I mean. Before the diagnosis."

I paused; a sheet of paper suspended between my fingers. It was a question I'd wrestled with a hundred times over the past month.

"I think he sensed something was wrong," I said at last. "That's why he pushed so hard on these cases. He was racing against something he couldn't name."

Ashley nodded, taking it in. Her fingers continued their steady work, sifting wheat from chaff, signal from noise.

"This will take weeks," she said, her tone free of complaint.

"Then it takes weeks." I squared the edges of a stack of statements with more force than needed. "We owe him that."

The words lingered, their weight settling over the room like the dust we'd disturbed. We owed Johnny, yes, but also Sarah Lawson and every other victim whose case had been entangled in his unraveling mind.

I reached for another box; this one marked with a date from six months ago. Inside lay the beginning of the end—the first reports showing Johnny's perception fraying, reality and delusion bleeding into each other. I took a deep breath and lifted the lid.

"Ashley," I said, "better brew another pot of coffee. We're going to be here a while."

She nodded, understanding what I meant: we'd see this through, no matter what we uncovered.

The fluorescents buzzed overhead like dying insects. My eyes stung from hours of reading, but I couldn't stop now. Not with Johnny's journal before me, its leather cover worn smooth at the corners, its pages rippled from what I guessed were spilled coffee and perhaps tears. Ashley had hesitated before setting it on the table, as if it were a bomb rather than a book. In a way, it was both—an explosive glimpse into a mind unraveling and a timer counting down to a tragedy we'd failed to prevent.

"You sure you want to do this?" Ashley asked, her voice soft in the empty records room.

The wall clock read 9:17 p.m. Everyone else had gone home hours ago. I nodded, my voice untrustworthy. Reading it felt like trespassing, like pressing my ear to a confessional. But if we wanted answers, we'd have to breach Johnny's privacy once more. The journal didn't resemble a madman's manifesto. No frantic scribbles, no pages filled with repeated phrases. Just Johnny's regular handwriting, growing slightly more cramped and illegible toward the end, as if the words were squeezed out under pressure.

I flipped to the entries around the Sam Thompson incident. Johnny's account started methodically:

Thompson nervous during questioning. Kept glancing at the barn, avoiding my eyes. What's he hiding out there? Property records show the septic system was replaced in 1996—one year after Sarah disappeared.

"He was connecting dots that weren't there," I murmured, reaching for the Thompson case file. The interview transcript told a different story: Sam had been anxious, yes, but he'd explained it was due to a sick calf in the barn, even inviting Johnny to check on it.

The next entry tightened my stomach:

Saw Thompson burying something behind the barn tonight. Too dark to confront him alone. Will bring Liz tomorrow. Sarah's parents deserve closure.

But there had been no midnight burial. The next day, when Johnny went out, everything that could go wrong did.

Ashley leaned over my shoulder, her breath warm against my neck. "Look at the date on this one," she said, pointing to an entry from three months earlier.

Found something today at the old Thompson place. Small, under the bed in an abandoned bedroom. Sarah's locket. Has to be. The clasp is broken, just as her mother described. This is it. This is the break we've been waiting for.

I frowned. "We never recovered a locket. The place was clear."

"Because there wasn't one," Ashley said softly. "At least, not in evidence, just an empty bag."

My fingers traced the words on the page. The handwriting here was steady, even excited. This wasn't a delusion—or if it was, it was the seed from which all others grew.

I flipped forward, skimming until another entry caught my eye:

Crime scene tape still up at Thompson's place. County boys think they're being thorough, but they're missing the obvious. Sarah's not in the septic tank. She's under the floorboards. I can feel it.

"Jesus," I muttered. The septic tank repair had involved yellow caution tape, not police tape. Contractors had been replacing a pipe section, not conducting a search. In Johnny's faltering mind, the two had merged into something sinister.

As I read on, the entries grew more fragmented. Times and dates jumped erratically. People long dead appeared in Johnny's accounts of routine traffic stops. Through it all ran the thread of Sarah Lawson, a girl missing for nearly thirty years.

Saw her today by the trail. Just standing there in that blue dress from her prom photo. Didn't speak. Didn't need to. Her eyes said everything: 'Find me, Johnny.' I will. I promise.

"He was trying to hold it together," Ashley said, her finger tracing a line where Johnny's pen had pressed so hard it nearly tore the page. "Look how he tries to reason with himself here."

Need to focus. Facts only. Sarah disappeared May 15, 1995. Last seen at Dobbin's store buying a soda. Sam claims she left. No body found. No witnesses. But the locket... the locket changes everything. Must be certain before I act. Can't afford mistakes. Not with this.

The locket again. That phantom piece of evidence that had sent Johnny spiraling down this rabbit hole.

I flipped to the final entries, written just before Johnny's public break-down and the tragedy with Sam Thompson. The handwriting was differ-ent here—shaky, uncertain, each letter formed with the deliberateness of someone fighting to hold on to control.

Beth kept insisting I was mistaken about Thompson, claiming I saw things that weren't there. But she wasn't present when I found the locket. She couldn't grasp that some ghosts linger until justice is served.

Beth. His wife, gone for over twenty years. The woman he still spoke to when he thought no one was listening.

The final entry read simply: Today is the day. One way or another, it ends.

And it had ended—with questions no one could answer and truths John-ny might never reclaim.

I closed the journal, my fingers tracing its worn cover. Beside me, Ashley let out a trembling breath.

"He was right about Sarah's murder," she said. "Just wrong about who did it and where the body was."

"And about Sam Thompson's guilt," I added.

The journal rested between us, a roadmap of a good man's unraveling. Not the ravings of a madman, but the desperate struggle of someone cling-ing to reality as it slipped away. He'd been so close to the truth in some ways, yet tragically wrong in others.

"He was trying to do right," I said, my voice rough with emotion. "Even at the end, he sought justice for that girl."

Ashley nodded, her eyes glistening with unshed tears. "So we finish what he started," she said. "The right way."

I looked at the files strewn across the table, the timeline pinned to the wall, and Johnny's journal—its terrible, beautiful testament to a mind's collapse.

"The right way," I agreed.

I sat at Johnny's desk during lunch, a half-eaten sandwich forgotten at my elbow. Nothing in the office had been touched since they'd taken him away. The calendar still displayed last month, his coffee mug still bore the dried ring of his final cup, and his chair still creaked in the same spots when I shifted my weight. The manila envelope from Dr. Chen had arrived that morning—clinical, detached, as if the subject of her evaluation wasn't a man I'd known for twenty years but a specimen under glass.

The office door stayed shut, holding Ashley and the rest of the department at bay. This wasn't something I wanted an audience for.

Dr. Chen's report was typed in a crisp font, her signature an elegant flourish at the bottom. The language was precise, devoid of emotion:

Subject exhibits persistent confusion between objective reality and subjective delusion. Cognitive testing reveals significant impairment in short-term memory formation and recall. The tumor's location accounts for the subject's hallucinatory episodes and emotional dysregulation.

I skimmed past the medical jargon, looking for the name I knew would be there. I found it halfway down the second page:

Patient McCallister exhibits a pronounced fixation on the cold case
of Sarah Lawson (missing person, 1995). This case appears to serve
as an anchor for recurring delusional episodes, likely tied to
unresolved trauma from his wife's death in 1999. When discussing
the Lawson case, the patient displays heightened agitation and
a certainty inconsistent with documented evidence. He frequently
references a locket and an individual named "Liz," whose identity
remains unclear. Notably, these references often surface in emo-
tionally charged recollections involving both personal loss and
perceived investigative failure.

I'd seen what remained of him just weeks ago. The voice, the frame—still
Johnny, but buried beneath layers of fear and distortion. Yet this report still
managed to deepen the wound. Seeing it in ink made it indelible.

Liz. Detective Elizabeth Montgomery. The name Johnny called out to
empty rooms, believing she was there. The report offered little—just that
she appeared often, always during moments of heightened stress, always
unresolved.

Beth had been his wife. I hadn't let myself dwell on her in years—not
since the night Johnny got behind the wheel when he shouldn't have. Things
didn't explode after that—they just... faded. A slow unraveling. Less talk.
Less laughter. Until silence became the norm.

I remembered her laugh, her warmth. How young we all were. And how I
stood by him when perhaps I shouldn't have. If someone had drawn a harder
line back then—

I swallowed the thought.

The paper trembled in my hands. I set it down, the room now oppressive-
ly quiet. I suddenly needed to hear his voice, to find some proof he was still
in there somewhere. The phone sat heavy and black at the desk's corner. I
hadn't called the facility since that first week.

I'd seen what remained of him just weeks ago. The voice, the frame—still Johnny, but barely. The fluorescent lights had cast him as a ghost in his own story, and I'd left that day with more questions than answers. Now I needed to hear his voice again. Not as a deputy. Not even as a friend. But as someone desperate to make sense of this unraveling chaos. My fingers dialed before I could talk myself out of it.

"Lakeside Behavioral Health," a woman's voice answered, calm and professional.

"This is Deputy Michael Langley," I said, the formality tasting foreign. "I'd like to speak with Sheriff John... Johnathan McCallister, please."

"One moment."

The hold music was a tinny piano rendition of a classical piece. I stared at the water stain on Johnny's ceiling, counting the seconds. "Deputy?" The woman returned. "I can connect you, but Dr. Hansen asked me to inform you that Mr. McCallister is having what we call a 'mixed day.' He may not be fully present for your conversation."

"I understand." I didn't, not truly, but I needed this call regardless.

A series of clicks broke the silence, followed by the sound of breathing.

"Johnny?" I said. "It's Mike."

More silence, then: "Mike." His voice was thinner than I recalled, but unmistakably his. "You still keeping that mustache trimmed?"

Something eased in my chest. "You know it."

"Good man." A pause, then confusion crept into his voice. "Are you... here for the Henderson case?"

The Henderson case was fifteen years ago. I swallowed hard. "No, Johnny. Just checking in. Seeing how you're holding up."

"Fine, fine. They've put me on something new. Makes everything... slower." His words came cautiously, as if navigating thin ice. "Did you bring the files?"

"What files would those be?"

"The girl. The one in blue." His voice sharpened abruptly. "She was here again last night, standing at the foot of my bed. Didn't say a word, just watched me. Sometimes she looks like Beth. Or Liz. I can't always tell any-more."

My grip tightened on the receiver. "Johnny..."

"She's waiting for something," he pressed on, his words gaining urgency. "Waiting for me to remember. There was a locket, Mike. Did I tell you about the locket?"

"You did," I said gently. "In your journal."

"Journal?" His voice carried genuine confusion. "I don't... I haven't kept a journal since the academy."

I closed my eyes. "Johnny, the girl in blue. Do you mean Sarah Lawson?"

The line fell so silent I thought we'd lost the connection. Then, faintly: "Did we ever find her?"

The question cut through me. Simple, direct, unclouded by delusion. For that fleeting moment, he was my old friend again, asking the question that had haunted him long before his mind began to unravel.

"We're getting close," I said, and it wasn't a lie.

A sigh drifted through the line. "You always were better at the endings," Johnny said, his voice tinged with wistfulness. "I'd start us off, you'd bring us home."

Then came a clatter, as if the phone had slipped from his hand, followed by a distant voice: "Mr. McCallister, it's time for your medication."

"Johnny?" I called.

No response. Just faint background noise, then the line went dead.

I sat with the receiver pressed to my ear long after the dial tone returned, as if I might still hear him. The office felt colder now, emptier. The half-light of early afternoon cast long shadows across the desk where Johnny had worked for twenty years, striving to keep our small corner of the world safe.

Dr. Chen's report stared up at me, its clinical language a hollow echo of the man I'd just spoken to. Johnny wasn't merely a patient with delusions. He was a dedicated cop who'd seen something—or believed he had—that set him on a path from which he couldn't turn back. Now he was lost in the fragments of his own mind, grappling with the same question we all sought to answer: Did we ever find her?

I placed the receiver back in its cradle, the faint click resounding in the empty room. The sandwich lay untouched. In the outer office, I could hear Ashley moving about, preparing for our afternoon session with the files.

"We found her," I said to the empty chair across from me. "We'll solve this case, I promise you."

Morning arrived with the taste of burnt coffee and too little sleep. I'd spent most of the night staring at my ceiling, Johnny's voice echoing in my mind: You always were better at the endings. Now, as Ashley and I stood in the evidence room, fresh cups of coffee steaming between our palms, those words felt like both a burden and a blessing. My eyes were gritty, my shoulders stiff, but something had solidified in me during those dark hours. This was no longer just about clearing case files. It was about finishing the story Johnny had begun—the right way this time.

"You look like hell," Ashley said, her tone soft despite the blunt words. Her hair was pulled back tighter than usual, her uniform crisp despite the early hour. I could tell she'd been restless too.

"Spoke to Johnny yesterday," I said, setting my coffee beside a stack of witness statements. "He's in and out, but he asked about Sarah. Wanted to know if we'd found her."

Ashley's expression softened. "What did you tell him?"

"That we're getting close." I pulled out a chair, its metal legs scraping against the concrete floor.

We turned to the Thompson file first. It had been the catalyst for Johnny's final breakdown. For weeks, I'd avoided delving too deeply into it, dreading what I might find—confirmation of Johnny's madness, perhaps, or worse, evidence that I should've seen it coming.

"I've been thinking," Ashley said, spreading crime scene photos across the table. "Johnny was fixated on Thompson hiding something, right? What if we revisit the statements without that assumption?"

She was right. We'd been working from Johnny's conclusions, not his evidence. I picked up Mark Dobbin's original statement from his first interview:

WITNESS: Mark Dobbins   Case File: 173016
Date Taken: April 15, 1995
Time: 10:32pm
Method: Phone Interview

"Sarah arrived for her shift around 2:30 p.m. and finished around 7:00 p.m. She bought a soda before leaving and asked if Pete Collins had stopped by. I told her no. She headed east, toward the Collins farm. That's the last I saw of her."

RECEIVED
DATE: 4-15-95

Simple, straightforward. And the part about Collins—I'd missed that before.

"What about Sam Thompson's alibi for that night?" I asked.

Ashley pulled another sheet. "He was at the town council meeting until 7:00 p.m., then had dinner at Rosie's Diner. Three witnesses confirm he was there until at least 9:00 p.m."

"And Sarah was last seen around 7:00 p.m.," I said slowly.

"Which means..." Ashley met my eyes.

"Which means Thompson couldn't have done it." The realization settled like a stone. "Johnny was wrong."

I should've felt relief, but regret weighed heavier.

Ashley continued sorting through the evidence logs and supplemental files, her highlighter clicking rhythmically as she flipped pages. A loose clipping slipped from one of the older manila folders—thin newsprint, yellowed at the edges, its ink faded.

She passed it to me without a word.

Local Teen Missing; Boyfriend Last to Expect Her Arrival

STORMY VALLEY – April 17, 1995
Jeanette Malone, Staff Writer

Seventeen-year-old Sarah Lawson was reported missing Thursday night after failing to return home from her after-school job at Dobbins Grocery. Her parents last saw her leaving for the store around 2:00 p.m.

"She was supposed to meet her boyfriend for dinner at Rosie's Diner," said Linda Lawson, Sarah's mother. "She was excited. She loved their milkshakes."Samuel Thompson, 18, told authorities he waited for Sarah at the diner for over an hour. "She never showed," Thompson said. "I kept looking at the door, thinking she'd just be late. I even ordered her usual."

Waitstaff confirmed Thompson sat alone from approximately 7:15 p.m. to 9:00 p.m., appearing visibly distressed. One waitress remarked, "He didn't touch the milkshakes. Just stared at the door, like she'd walk in any second."

Deputy Johnny McCallister, handling early inquiries, stated that at this stage, "a voluntary runaway remains the most likely scenario," adding that the department was following leads from friends and coworkers.

When asked if Sarah had any reason to leave home, her father replied simply, "No. She was happy. Or she seemed to be."

Sarah Lawson, 17

I read the article twice. It hit differently now.

We'd written him off at the time—called him moody, dramatic, said maybe she'd run off after a teenage spat. Convenient conclusions for a town that couldn't face the truth.

He'd waited with two milkshakes and no answers, and we folded that into the narrative like it meant nothing. He wasn't a suspect. He wasn't a witness. He was a footnote in a headline.

He wasn't the killer. Yet he never stopped being punished like one.

Ashley glanced up. "What?"

I shook my head and refolded the clipping. "Nothing."

Just another kid the town never truly listened to.

We fell silent, both of us feeling the cost of what we now understood. Johnny had been so convinced, so certain. And in his deteriorating state, that certainty had turned deadly.

"It was the tumor," Ashley said quietly. "Dr. Chen's report made that clear. The paranoia, the hallucinations—he wasn't himself at the end."

"Doesn't bring them back," I said, my words heavy with resignation rather than bite.

"No. But it means Johnny wasn't corrupt or evil. Just sick. There's some dignity in that, at least."

She was right. It didn't absolve Johnny of responsibility, but it restored something of the man I'd known—a good cop who made a tragic mistake under the influence of a disease he couldn't control.

We worked through the morning, methodically revisiting statements, reconstructing timelines, and correcting the distortions Johnny's illness had introduced. It was nearing noon when Ashley made a sound—not quite a gasp, but sharp enough to cut through the quiet room.

"Mike," she said, her voice taut. "Look at this."

She slid a photograph across the table. It was from the original investigation, one of dozens taken at the Lawson house after Sarah's disappearance was reported. Grainy and slightly out of focus, it showed the front of the house with police cars parked along the street. But it was the edge of the frame that Ashley pointed to—a figure partially visible behind a tree, watching the scene.

"Is that...?" I squinted, then reached for the magnifying glass.

"Peter Collins Sr.," Ashley confirmed. "Look at the timestamp."

The photo was timestamped 8:17 p.m. on April 15, 1995. According to the case notes, Sarah's parents hadn't reported her missing until 7:30 p.m. that night.

"How did he know to be there?" I murmured. "They hadn't even put out a general alert yet."

"And look at this." Ashley slid another photo across the table, this one from a different angle. The same figure, clearer now, stood with a tense posture, his attention fixed on the front door of the Lawson house. "He's watching them—not like a concerned neighbor, but like someone monitoring the situation."

My mind raced back to Dobbin's statement: She asked if Pete Collins had been by. I told her no. She headed east, toward the Collins farm.

"Johnny almost had it," I said, the realization dawning. "In his journal, those last entries—he was starting to question his own theory about Thompson. He wrote that Beth kept saying he was wrong."

"Beth? His wife?" Ashley's brow furrowed in confusion.

"Or the hallucination of her," I clarified. "Either way, part of him knew something wasn't adding up. But by then, the delusions were too strong."

We spread more photos across the table, this time searching specifically for Collins. He appeared in three more—always at the periphery, always watching, never approaching the officers or offering help.

"There's more," Ashley said, pulling out a file I hadn't seen before. "I requested Peter Collins Sr.'s records last week, just to be thorough. Look at his work history."

Peter Collins Sr.'s employment record showed he worked for a septic tank installation company from 1990 to 1997.

"The same company that repaired the Thompson septic system," I said, connecting the dots.

The pieces were falling into place with terrible clarity. Johnny's delusions had tangled the truth, but the core of it had been there all along. Sarah Lawson had been murdered. She had been buried. Just not where Johnny thought, nor by whom he'd suspected.

I stared at the photo of Collins lurking at the edge of the crime scene, a cold certainty setting in. "He was right," I murmured. "Just not in the way he thought."

Ashley nodded, her eyes bright with purpose. "Let's finish what he couldn't."

The morning light had shifted to the harsh clarity of noon, illuminating the scattered photos, the timeline on the wall, and the truth we'd finally uncovered. There was still work to do—evidence to gather, a case to build—but for the first time in months, the path forward was clear.

Ten days later, we stood in a windowless room at the county courthouse, surrounded by the accumulated substance of our investigation. The fluorescent lights cast a sickly pallor over everything—the outdated wood-veneer table, the government-issue chairs with their frayed upholstery, the corkboard we'd filled with what we hoped was enough truth to finally lay Sarah Lawson to rest. The prosecutor was twenty minutes late, and each tick of the wall clock grated against my already raw nerves.

Ashley stood by the corkboard, making minute adjustments to the red strings connecting dates and locations. Her uniform was pressed to military precision, but dark circles shadowed her eyes. Neither of us had slept much over the past ten days.

"Stop fidgeting," I muttered, though my words carried no heat.

"Just making sure everything's clear," she replied without looking up. "Kirkland likes his presentations orderly."

County Prosecutor James Kirkland had a reputation for being methodical to the point of tedium. I'd worked with him on three cases over the years and knew he wouldn't proceed without ironclad evidence. That's why we'd spent every waking hour building this case—cross-referencing witness statements, cataloging photographic evidence, and reconstructing timelines that even Johnny's fractured mind had begun to piece together before the end.

The corkboard behind Ashley had transformed from a collection of hunches into something solid. Photographs of Peter Collins Sr. at the Lawson crime scene, enlarged and annotated. Maps showing the proximity of the Collins farm to where Sarah was last seen. Boot tread impressions from the original investigation, now matched to a style of work boot issued by the same company.

"You think it's enough?" Ashley asked, voicing the question that had kept us both awake.

Before I could respond, the door opened. James Kirkland entered, followed by a younger woman carrying a yellow legal pad. Kirkland looked exactly as I remembered—tall, lean, with the perpetually disappointed expression of someone who'd seen too many cases unravel due to technicalities.

"Deputy Langley," he said with a curt nod. "Deputy Kowalski."

"Prosecutor," I returned, rising to shake his hand. His grip was dry and firm, revealing nothing.

"My apologies for the delay. The Henderson appeal is proving... complicated." He gestured to the woman behind him. "This is Andrea Wells, my new assistant."

No one offered her a chair. She stood by the door, pen poised above her pad.

"I understand you've compiled evidence regarding the Lawson disappearance," Kirkland said, settling into a chair that creaked under his weight. "A case that's been classified as cold for twenty-nine years."

"Yes, sir," I replied, sliding a thick folder across the table. "The brief is comprehensive, but we thought a walkthrough might help contextualize the findings."

He nodded once, granting permission.

For the next forty minutes, I presented our work—every link we'd stitched together from the tangled mess Johnny left behind, every sickening misstep and overlooked detail. Ashley hovered at my shoulder, passing photographs and charts in the order we'd rehearsed. I began at the start: Sarah's final steps, the witnesses who'd seen her alive, the dead-end interviews that had rusted in the file for decades. Each fact was a knuckle rapping the table's wood: Sarah last seen at the market; Thompson's alibi airtight; the secondhand gossip that trickled in after midnight, all the voices in town suddenly recalling something vital.

Finally, I turned to motive. Collins' oldest daughter, Sue, had run off with a boy years earlier—a local scandal that lingered in the valley's gossip long after both had left town. The Lawsons had been the loudest in church about Sue's "fall from grace," and more than once, Collins had been overheard cursing their hypocrisy. None of it amounted to probable cause, but it was more than the case had ever started with.

I finished with the DNA match on the bone fragment. It wasn't a direct hit—Sarah's parents were both deceased, and she had no living relatives that we could locate. But mitochondrial analysis showed a maternal line consistent with the Lawsons, as close as we'd ever get.

I watched Kirkland set his pen down, his fingers interlocking as he studied the papers spread before him. The courthouse hummed with the relentless drone of the ventilation system, a sound that underscored the tension in the room. Andrea shifted her weight from one foot to the other, and the worn leather chair beneath her emitted a soft creak. Kirkland's gaze finally rose to meet mine, determination etched across his features. "We'll bring in Pete Sr.," he announced, his voice firm but laced with an undercurrent of doubt. "It's thin," he said at last. "But it's enough to ask questions he's never had to answer."

19

The Truth Unearthed

The next day was overcast, the kind of gray that seeped into your bones. I arrived early—too early—and spent much of the morning reviewing the case file again, not because I needed to, but because I couldn't sit still. The pages felt thinner than they had yesterday, or perhaps I just felt heavier.

We had the interrogation scheduled for one o'clock. I'd barely slept the night before, my mind chasing questions I'd already answered. Across the station, Ashley moved with quiet purpose, as she had during the worst of it. I could see it in her posture, the way she tucked her hair behind her ear as she prepped the file: she believed this would bring closure, perhaps even peace.

I wished I could share her optimism.

But as we approached the interrogation room, my anxiety mounted, a cold sweat breaking out across my brow. The ghosts of past mistakes whispered in my ear, urging me to turn back. Yet Ashley's steadfast presence beside me bolstered my resolve. Whatever awaited beyond that door, we would face it together.

The interrogation room door loomed before us, a portal to truths long buried. I paused, my hand trembling on the cold metal handle. Through the small window, I glimpsed Peter Collins Sr., his placid demeanor a mask I longed to tear away.

I entered. Fluorescent lights buzzed overhead, illuminating every wrinkle etched across Peter's weathered face. He sat unnaturally still, hands folded on the table, eyes fixed on some distant point. The air felt thick, oppressive, as if the walls themselves were closing in.

"Mr. Collins," I began, my voice steadier than I felt. "We have some questions about your whereabouts on the night Sarah Lawson disappeared."

Peter stared at me, his eyes dark pools betraying nothing. "I've told you everything I know, Deputy Langley," he said.

Deputy. The word hit like a taunt. All those years carrying the title, and what did it prove? I hadn't saved Sarah. I hadn't saved Johnny from himself, not after Kayla, not when the spiral was right in front of me. That badge was just a witness to everything I'd let slip through my fingers.

I swallowed the bile rising in my throat and forced the words out. "New evidence has come to light. We have reason to believe you were near the crime scene that night."

"Is that so?" Peter's voice was calm, almost amused. The corner of his mouth twitched, a gesture so subtle I might have imagined it.

As I laid out our findings, my mind raced. What secrets lurked behind that impassive facade? What had we missed all those years ago?

"Care to explain the muddy footprint matching your boots?" I asked, sliding a photograph across the table.

Peter glanced at it, his expression unchanged. "Lots of folks wear similar boots around here, Deputy. You know that."

His measured responses grated on my nerves, each word a carefully placed brick in a wall of denial. I leaned in, the scent of coffee on his breath mingling with the stale air.

"Cut the act, Peter". I almost never called him that. But in this room, I wanted the weight of formality for this criminal, not the man I used to know. "We both know you're hiding something."

For a moment, just a heartbeat, I thought I saw a flicker of something in his eyes—fear, perhaps, or anger. But it vanished as quickly as it appeared, leaving me to wonder if it had ever been there.

As I struggled to find a new angle, Ashley's soft voice cut through the tension. "Mr. Collins," she said, her tone gentle but firm, "we're not here to accuse you. We just want to understand what happened that night."

I watched, a mix of admiration and unease stirring within me, as Ashley leaned forward, her freckled face open and earnest. Her compassion, so at odds with my hardened approach, seemed to soften something in Peter's demeanor.

Peter's fingers curled into fists, his knuckles whitening. "I don't have to tell you anything. You've got no right to ask me this after what Johnny did to my boy."

I leaned in. "This ain't about Johnny or Pete Jr. This is about you and that night. What did you do?"

Silence stretched between us, thick and oppressive. Peter's gaze darted around the room, searching for an escape that wasn't there.

I pressed on, my voice low and insistent. "Come on, Pete. We've known each other a long time. Whatever it is, just say it."

Peter's jaw clenched, a vein pulsing at his temple. "You don't want to know. Trust me."

"I think we do," Ashley interjected, her tone gentle but firm. "Sarah deserves justice, Pete. Her family deserves answers."

A bitter laugh escaped Peter's lips. "Justice? There's no such thing. Not in this town."

I flipped open a folder and read aloud one of the old witness statements—unsigned, but clearly her mother's. The handwriting wavered near the bottom.

"*Sarah mentioned stopping by the Collins house. They'd asked her about babysitting Pete Jr. later that week. She said she'd just swing by after work to confirm. Wasn't planning to stay long, said Sam would be waiting at Rosie's.*"

I looked up from the page, letting the gravity of it settle in.

"She was just trying to help," I said. "Running a quick errand before her date. That's why she asked if you'd been by Dobbin's—just making sure she wasn't leaving anyone hanging."

Peter's hands twitched on the table, fingertips curling inward.

"Try us, Pete," I urged, fighting to keep my voice calm. "What happened that night?"

Peter's shoulders slumped, defeat etched into every line of his face. "I... I saw her walking. She always looked so pretty in that blue dress. Just like Heidi—before everything went to hell. I just... I couldn't help myself."

Ashley's face paled. I felt my own expression harden, jaw clenched against the rising tide of rage.

"What did you do to her?" I demanded, my voice low and sharp.

"I grabbed her, dragged her into the woods." Peter's words spilled out in a rush, as if a dam had broken. "She fought, screamed. But I was stronger. I... I forced myself on her. I was so pissed off at Heidi."

The confession hit like a physical blow. Ashley turned away, her hand covering her mouth. My fists clenched.

"You'd had a fight with your wife?!" I choked out. "You didn't plan it, did you? She just... showed up at the wrong time."

Peter nodded. Barely. "Yeah."

"And then?" I prompted, my rage barely concealed.

Peter lowered his eyes to the table. "She said she'd tell everyone. That I'd go to jail. I panicked. I... I put my hands around her throat and... squeezed until she stopped moving. Buried her right there in the woods."

Silence. Heavy. Final.

"You sick bastard. All these years, you've been walking around free while Sarah's family suffered." I couldn't contain the rage anymore, nearly spitting in Pete's face.

Peter's head snapped up, eyes blazing. "You think I haven't suffered? I've lived with this every day. It eats at me, consumes me."

"Good," Ashley snapped, her usual warmth replaced by cold fury. "You deserve to suffer for what you did."

I struggled to find words, my mind reeling from the revelation. "Why now, Pete? Why confess after all this time?"

Peter's shoulders sagged, the fight draining out of him. "I'm tired. Tired of carrying this secret, tired of pretending. Maybe... maybe it's time I paid for what I did."

Relief hit like a sudden wind. I turned to Ashley. She met my eyes, the same stunned disbelief mirrored back. We'd done it. We'd solved the case that had haunted this town for so long.

As Peter began to sob quietly, a chill crept up my spine. How many other secrets lay buried in this quiet town? What darkness still lurked, waiting to be uncovered?

The confession still echoed in my mind as I stepped out of the interrogation room, Ashley close behind. The fluorescent lights of the hallway felt harsh after the dim confines we'd just left.

"I can't believe we did it," Ashley whispered, her voice tinged with awe.

I nodded, unable to shake the melancholy that had settled in. "Yeah, we did."

As we walked, my thoughts drifted to the town I'd sworn to protect. Stormy Valley, with its quaint storefronts and friendly faces. How many smiles masked secrets as dark as Peter's?

"You okay, Mike?" Ashley's concerned voice cut through my brooding.

I forced a smile. "Just thinking."

"About?"

"This town," I sighed. "How we all pretend everything's perfect. But underneath..."

We pushed through the station doors, emerging into the late afternoon light, clouds finally breaking. The air was crisp, carrying the scent of pine and damp earth. It felt wrong, somehow—too peaceful.

Ashley's brow furrowed. "You don't think there are more... cases like Sarah's, do you?"

I didn't answer immediately, watching a group of teenagers laugh their way down the street. Their carefree voices seemed to mock the heaviness I couldn't shake.

"I hope not," I said finally. "But we can't be blind anymore. We have to look deeper."

The light outside was already shifting toward dusk, shadows stretching long across the pavement. A reluctant sense of purpose took root. We might not fix everything, but I'd damn well drag whatever was festering in this town into the open.

"Come on," I said. "We've got work to do."

Ashley touched my arm. "It's been a long day, you go home and relax. I'll stay and file the paperwork." She turned back inside, leaving me to keep walking.

I didn't go home after the interrogation. I couldn't. The station's lights burned too bright, the silence was deafening, like the calm after a storm you're not sure has passed. So I drove—past the town's outskirts, past where pavement turned to gravel and pine, where the cell signal faded and the questions I couldn't stop asking grew louder.

By the time I pulled into the parking lot of Lakeside, dusk had settled in, the last last scraps of daylight fading low in the sky. Visiting hours would end soon, but I'd called ahead. They knew who I was. Maybe they all did by now.

The nurse at the front desk offered a tight smile and handed me a visitor badge. "He's in the common room," she said. "A bit more alert today. Quiet, though."

Johnny sat by the far window, his silhouette framed by the amber haze of the fading day. He looked smaller than I remembered, worn down—not just by time, but by carrying what no one else bothered to see.

When he saw me, something flickered in his eyes—not quite recognition, but a kind of orientation. A thread snapping back into place.

"Langley," he said.

"That's me."

"Did I miss a meeting?" he asked, his frown fleeting, as if the thought had already slipped away.

I sat beside him. "No. I came to share some news."

He tilted his head. "Good news?"

"We got him, Johnny. Collins. Peter Sr."

For a moment, he just blinked. Then, softly, like it took effort, he said, "Sarah?"

I nodded. "He confessed. To everything."

He didn't quite smile, but he leaned back, closed his eyes, and let out a long breath, a sound of release.

"Told you something was wrong out there," he said. "Just couldn't find the thread."

"You did," I said. "We just followed it the rest of the way."

His hand, resting on the armrest, twitched once. Then he murmured, almost to himself, "Beth'll be glad."

We sat in silence after that, staring at nothing. Two old men who'd chased ghosts too long. But *this time*, one of them had a name.

20
Justice and Healing

Three months had passed since the interrogation—enough time for lawyers to posture, for the town's whispers to shift from disbelief to bitter consensus. Yet the uncertainty lingered.

The gavel fell like a thunderclap, shattering the courtroom's tense silence. Judge Harlow's voice, gravelly and solemn, echoed through the room.

"Peter Collins, having pleaded guilty to the rape and murder of Sarah Lawson, this court sentences you to life imprisonment without the possibility of parole."

A collective gasp rippled through the gallery. I felt it in my bones—a shudder of relief tangled with dread. Sarah's case, closed at last. But Johnny's loomed ahead, a yawning chasm.

Murmurs swelled around me, a tide of whispered reactions. Some faces shone with vindication; others twisted in anguish. The truth is rarely kind.

As the bailiff led Pete away, the fluorescent lights washed over his thinning, gray-flecked hair. For an instant, I remembered the man I'd first seen as a rookie—strong, unbroken, not yet haunted by what he'd done to Sarah.

The room emptied slowly, a trickle of bodies filing into the gray afternoon. I stayed, rooted to the hard wooden bench, my hands clasped so tightly my knuckles whitened. There was little time to rest—Johnny's trial was set for that afternoon. I wasn't sure I was ready, but the court didn't wait for feelings.

Johnny's trial. My testimony. The silence in between. All of it pressed closer, tight and unrelenting, fraying the last threads of my resolve.

I closed my eyes, trying to shut out the world, but memories flooded in. Johnny's steady hand on my shoulder after a grueling shift. The phantoms that haunted him, driving him deeper into madness.

"Mike?" A gentle voice broke through my reverie. It was Sarah's aunt, her eyes red-rimmed but clear. "Thank you. For everything."

I nodded, unable to speak past the lump in my throat. As she walked away, I wondered how she'd feel if she knew the whole truth—about Johnny, about me, about the secrets we'd kept buried for so long.

An hour later, the courtroom doors opened again, and a new wave of people filed in. Johnny's trial was about to begin. I took a deep breath, steeling myself for what lay ahead.

"You okay there, Mike?" Detective Holland slid onto the bench beside me.

"As okay as I can be," I muttered, forcing a wan smile.

He nodded, his eyes reflecting understanding. "It's never easy, is it? Testifying against a friend."

"No," I agreed, my voice barely a whisper. "It's not."

The room fell silent as the bailiff called for order. I straightened my back, trying to shake off the cloak of past decisions before my impending testimony, but it clung like a second skin, a relentless reminder of the choices that had led us here.

As the judge took his seat, I caught a glimpse of Johnny being led in. Our eyes met for a fleeting moment, and I saw a flicker of the man I once knew. But it vanished in an instant, replaced by the haunted, distant look that had become all too familiar.

The trial began, and with it, the unraveling of our shared past. I could only hope that somewhere in this tangle of truth and lies, justice would prevail—for Sarah, for Herb, for Emma, for all of us caught in Stormy Valley's web of secrets.

The judge's gavel cracked like a gunshot, silencing the whispers slithering through the courtroom. I flinched, my nerves raw and exposed. The air felt thick, oppressive, as if generations of silence and inaction had become too loud to ignore.

My eyes darted to Johnny, seated alone at the defense table. He was a shadow of the man I once knew, his face etched with defiance and vulnerability. For a moment, I glimpsed the old Johnny—the hero, the protector—but it was buried under years of silence, shame, and neglect.

"The prosecution calls Deputy Michael Langley to the stand."

The words struck like a physical blow. I rose, legs unsteady, feeling the burn of countless eyes on me. As I approached the witness stand, I caught Johnny's gaze. A plea lingered there, buried beneath layers of pain and accusation.

"Do you swear to tell the truth, the whole truth, and nothing but the truth, so help you God?"

I hesitated, my throat tightening. The truth—such a simple concept, yet so devastating in its reach. I thought of Sarah, of Herb, of the countless lives shattered by the secrets we'd kept.

"I do," I managed, the words tasting like ash in my mouth.

As I took my seat, I steeled myself for what lay ahead. The truth might set us free, but first, it would tear us apart.

The prosecutor's voice cut through the silence like a blade. "Deputy Langley, please describe Sheriff McCallister's character and service to Stormy Valley."

I swallowed hard, my mouth dry as dust. "Johnny was... is... a hero," I began, the words stumbling out. "He saved this town more times than I can count."

Memories flooded my mind, unbidden and relentless. Johnny, rushing into a burning farmhouse to save old Mrs. Peterson's grandchildren. Johnny, talking down a desperate man with a gun, his voice balanced and calm in the face of danger.

"He had a way of making people feel safe," I continued, the words quiet, reverent. "Like nothing could touch us as long as he was there."

But even as I spoke, darker images intruded. Johnny's eyes, wild and unfocused, as he ranted about shadows in the corners of his office. The sickening crunch of bone as his fist met a suspect's jaw, long after the man had surrendered.

"But something changed," I said, the words hanging like a death knell. "It was gradual at first—mood swings, paranoia. Then... violence."

I looked at Johnny, seeing both savior and sinner in his haunted eyes. Our gazes locked, and for a moment, I was back on the quiet streets of Stormy Valley, patrolling through countless nights, the weight of our shared secrets pressing down like a tangible force.

"He was my friend," I whispered, more to Johnny than the court. "My brother. But the man I knew... he's gone."

The courtroom faded, and all I saw was Johnny's face—a mosaic of light and dark, hero and monster. And I wondered, not for the first time, if I could have saved him from everything consuming him, or if we were both doomed from the start.

The defense attorney rose, a predatory gleam in her eyes. "Deputy Langley," she purred, her voice a silken noose. "You paint such a vivid picture of Sheriff McCallister. But I wonder, how clear is your own memory?"

I felt the trap closing but kept my face impassive. "Crystal clear, ma'am."

She paced before me, each click of her heels a metronome ticking toward an unseen detonation. "You testified about the sheriff's 'mood swings' and 'paranoia.' Yet isn't it true that you yourself have suffered from... lapses in judgment?"

My throat tightened, but I forced out a steady, "I'm not sure what you mean."

"No?" She raised an eyebrow. "Perhaps I can refresh your memory. The Parker Incident. You were there, weren't you?"

The courtroom blurred, replaced by flashes of that day. Johnny's face, twisted with rage. The sickening thud of flesh against metal. My own voice, pleading, "Johnny, stop!"

I blinked, banishing the memories. "Yes, I was there."

"And did you report the full extent of Sheriff McCallister's actions that day?"

The question hung like a guillotine. I felt Johnny's eyes boring into me, his unspoken plea almost palpable. But Sarah's face flashed before me—young, vibrant, gone too soon.

"No," I admitted, the word tasting like ash. "I didn't."

The truth hung heavy in the room. In that stillness, Sarah's face appeared—sweet Sarah, whose laughter once echoed through these hills. Her murder haunted us all—a festering wound beneath Stormy Valley's calm veneer.

The silence that followed was suffocating. No further questions.

"You may step down, Deputy Langley," Judge Hawthorne said at last. "Thank you for your testimony."

I rose on unsteady legs, the weight of everything unspoken pressing down harder than before.

The gavel's sharp crack split the air, and Judge Hawthorne's gravelly voice followed. "We'll take a fifteen-minute recess."

My legs felt like lead as I stepped down from the witness stand. The courtroom's oppressive silence gave way to a murmur of whispers and shuffling feet. I caught Johnny's eye as they led him away, and for a moment, I was back in simpler times—fishing trips and late-night patrols, laughter echoing across Stormy Valley's mist-shrouded hills.

But the Johnny before me now was a stranger, his eyes dark pools of accusation and fear. A silent exchange passed between us, charged with unspoken words. I wanted to say something, anything, but my throat tightened, choking back a torrent of explanations and apologies.

As I pushed through the courtroom's heavy oak doors, the chill autumn air hit me like a slap. I leaned against the weathered brick of the courthouse, my breath coming in ragged gasps.

"You okay there, Mike?" It was Donna from the diner, concern etched on her face.

I forced a weak smile. "Just needed some air."

She nodded, understanding in her eyes. "It can't be easy, testifying against Johnny like that."

"No," I murmured, "it ain't easy at all."

As Donna moved on, I was left alone with my turbulent thoughts. I'd spoken the truth, but at what cost? With every answer, the Johnny I remembered slipped further from reach, leaving only wreckage behind—deepening the cracks already etched in his legacy.

Herb Banks. His name echoed in my mind, a somber melody. I shut my eyes, picturing him—a man of routine, devoted to his daily jogs. Yet, unbidden, the vision shifted to his lifeless form, broken on the jogging trail. "I seek redemption for you, Herb," I whispered to the empty air. "I'm trying to make it right."

The courthouse bell tolled, calling me back inside. Fog gathered thick outside, a reminder of how close the past still clung. I squared my shoulders. The path to justice, I was learning, was paved with the bones of friendship and the ashes of loyalty.

The courtroom doors creaked open, the sound sharp in the silence. I slipped inside, my eyes drawn to Johnny. He sat still as stone, his face a mask of stoic resignation. The air felt thick, charged with unspoken tension.

Dr. Chen took the stand, her calm demeanor a stark contrast to the storm raging within me. Her voice, cool and clinical, sliced through the silence.

"Sheriff McCallister's condition is severe," she began, her words falling like leaden weights. "The frontotemporal meningioma has significantly impaired his cognitive function and emotional regulation."

I watched Johnny's face, desperate for any sign of emotion, but all I found was the stillness of someone already gone. Dr. Chen continued, her testimony painting a grim portrait of a mind unraveling.

"At the time of Mr. Banks' death, it's my professional opinion that Sheriff McCallister was experiencing acute psychosis, likely unable to distinguish reality from hallucination."

The courtroom held its breath. I felt every stare, every silent judgment tightening a noose of guilt and grief around my throat.

"And his prognosis?" The prosecutor's question hung in the air.

Dr. Chen's pause was fleeting, but in it, I heard the death knell of hope. "Poor. The tumor is inoperable. We can manage symptoms, but..."

She didn't finish. She didn't need to. The unspoken truth lingered, a silence louder than words.

As the judge adjourned court for the day, I caught Johnny's eye. For a moment, I glimpsed the man I once knew—brave, just, haunted. Then it vanished, swallowed by the abyss of his illness.

That night, sleep eluded me. The verdict loomed, a specter of finality. When dawn broke, gray and cheerless, I returned to the courthouse, my heart a leaden weight in my chest.

By midmorning, the gallery was full—neighbors, reporters, people I hadn't seen in years, all packed shoulder to shoulder, hungry for resolution. The air buzzed with whispers, then fell silent as the bailiff called us to rise.

The judge entered. Papers shuffled. A breath held across the room.

The judge's words blurred, a meaningless drone until—"Not guilty by reason of insanity. The defendant shall be remanded to the secure psychiatric ward at Lakeside Behavioral Health for the remainder of his natural life."

A beat of stunned silence—then the murmurs began. Whispers, gasps, a collective breath released like steam from a long-sealed valve. No one said his name, but everyone was thinking it.

Relief and despair warred within me. Johnny was spared prison, but condemned to a different cage. As the judge spoke of Johnny's "exemplary service," I saw flashes of our shared past—laughter, trust, brotherhood. All ashes now.

I watched as they led Johnny away, no longer a sheriff, no longer the friend I once knew, just a broken man, lost in the labyrinth of his mind. And I wondered if justice had truly been served or if we'd all fallen victim to the cruel machinations of fate in this godforsaken town.

The guards flanked Johnny like sentinels of his new prison, their faces impassive. I approached, my steps echoing in the now-empty courtroom, each one a reminder of the chasm between us.

"Johnny," I called softly, my voice rough with emotion.

He turned, his expression unreadable, eyes distant. For a moment, I wondered if he even recognized me.

"Mike?" he replied, his voice a hollow whisper of its former self.

I leaned in close, the scent of antiseptic clinging to him, a stark reminder of where he'd been—and where he was going.

"I've got news," I murmured, glancing at the guards. They stepped back, granting us a semblance of privacy. "About Sarah's case. It's over. Peter Collins Sr. confessed. He's been sentenced."

I watched Johnny's face, searching for a reaction. A flicker of something—gratitude? relief?—crossed his features, gone as quickly as it came.

"That's... good," he said, the words falling flat. "At least there's that."

But I saw only the faintest trace of the storm that once brewed behind his eyes—the war between acceptance and defiance reduced now to a dull calm. The Johnny I knew would have raged against this verdict, fought tooth and nail. This Johnny wasn't fighting—just adrift, as if the tide had already taken him.

"I'm sorry," I whispered, the words inadequate, tasting of ash. "I wish..."

But what did I wish? That things had been different? That I could have saved him? That I'd seen the signs before it was too late?

Johnny's eyes sharpened for a moment, focusing on me with startling clarity. "Don't," he said, his voice intense and purposeful. "You did what you had to. What I would've done."

Unspoken truths hung between us, years of shared secrets and burdens. I nodded, unable to speak past the lump in my throat.

As the guards led him away, a terrible thought struck me: Was this the last time I'd see Johnny as I knew him? Or was he already gone, lost to the storm that had started raging in his mind?

The echo of Johnny's footsteps faded, swallowed by the cavernous halls of justice. I stood rooted to the spot as the courtroom emptied around me. The air felt heavy with memories. Memories of late-night patrols, shared laughter, the weight of badges that once meant everything.

"You okay there, Mike?" Judge Harriet's voice was soft with concern.

I tried to smile, but it felt like my face might crack. "Fine, Your Honor. Just... processing."

She nodded, understanding in her eyes. "It's never easy, is it? Especially when it's one of our own."

"No, ma'am. It surely ain't."

As she walked away, I was left alone with my thoughts—a tangle of guilt and relief, shame and vindication. Had I done the right thing? Why did it feel like I'd betrayed everything I stood for, and my friend?

I made my way out of the courthouse, each step heavier than the last. The cold air hit me like a slap, and I welcomed it—real, tangible, unlike the murky waters of morality I'd been wading through.

I looked back at the imposing courthouse, its walls a silent witness to lives altered today. Justice served, they'd say. But at what cost?

"Time to face the music, old boy," I muttered, squaring my shoulders. Whatever came next, I'd meet it head-on. It's what Johnny would've done, once upon a time.

As I walked away, the events of the day settled over me, the cold weight of consequence pressing down. Yet a glimmer of something stirred within—hope, perhaps, or at least the strength to keep moving forward, one step at a time.

21

A Town Transformed

A month had passed since the verdict. The sheriff's badge still sat heavy on my chest, more burden than honor. They'd given it to me anyway—even after I confessed I hadn't always told the whole truth. Maybe because of it.

I stood in the silence of the sheriff's office, Johnny's legacy still looming large within. Faded photographs watched from the wall. The stale smell of coffee lingered, sharp with memory.

I ran my fingers over Johnny's desk, tracing grooves worn by years of service. How could I possibly fill the void he'd left behind? The thought returned with every piece of him still scattered around me. I made a mental note to try and clean up some of the more personal items, soon.

"You're not Johnny," I whispered to myself. "You'll never be Johnny."

The door creaked open, startling me from my reverie. Ashley Kowalski stepped inside, her red curls catching the dim light. Her eyes shone with an eagerness that twisted my gut.

"Good morning, Sheriff Langley," she said, her voice warm but edged with uncertainty.

I forced a smile, feeling it crack at the edges. "Morning, Deputy Kowalski. Ready for your first day?"

She nodded, her freckles dancing as she grinned. "Absolutely, sir. I can't wait to get started."

I watched her take in the office, her gaze lingering on Johnny's commendations. Did she see the lies lurking behind them? The secrets tangled in every corner?

"Well," I said, clearing my throat, "let's not waste time. We've got a lot to cover."

Ashley's enthusiasm was palpable as she pulled out a notepad. "I've been thinking about community outreach ideas, if you'd like to hear them."

I nodded, my mind drifting to darker places. How long before her eagerness turned to disillusionment? How long before she uncovered the rot beneath Stormy Valley's tranquil surface?

As Ashley spoke, her words fading into a distant hum, I found myself staring at the cruiser parked outside. Its faded paint gleamed dully in the morning light, a silent sentinel guarding its own terrible secrets.

"Sheriff? Are you alright?" Ashley's voice cut through my thoughts.

I blinked, forcing myself back to the present. "Sorry, just... thinking about all we need to do."

She smiled, oblivious to the storm behind my eyes. "We'll make a great team, sir. I know it."

I nodded, because it was easier than explaining what she hadn't learned yet. If only she knew the truth haunting these walls, the whispers echoing in the night. For now, I'd carry it, and let her keep that rookie shine a little longer.

The cruiser's shadow stretched across the cracked pavement, a reminder of the road ahead. I turned back to Ashley, her freckled face alight with determination.

"Transparency," I muttered, the word strange in my mouth. "That's what this town needs."

Ashley nodded eagerly. "Exactly. I was thinking weekly website updates, maybe even a community newsletter."

I leaned back in my chair, the leather creaking ominously. "Not a bad idea, Deputy. But words are cheap. We need action."

"What do you have in mind, Sheriff?"

The question hung in the air, thick as the fog clinging to Stormy Valley's hills. I closed my eyes, memories of Johnny's mistakes flickering behind my eyes like a movie I didn't want to see.

"Open house," I said at last. "Let the townsfolk see how we operate. No more closed doors, no more whispered secrets."

Ashley's pen scratched furiously across her notepad. "That's brilliant! We could even—"

A knock at the door cut her off. Deputy Hanmer poked her head in, her youth and enthusiasm mirroring Ashley's.

"Sorry to interrupt, but the town hall meeting's about to start."

I nodded, rising from my chair. Duty settled into my bones, snapping into place like a collar I couldn't loosen.

"Let's go face the music, shall we?"

The short walk to the town hall was quiet, our footsteps echoing off the brick facades. I went over the speech in my head while Ashley kept pace beside me. Fog clung low to the street, and curtains shifted as we passed—faces watching, waiting. As we rounded the corner to the hall, I saw more eyes peering from the windows, curiosity and fear mingling in their gaze.

Inside, the atmosphere hung thick with anticipation and lingering sorrow. Townsfolk filled the creaking wooden chairs, their faces a tapestry of conflicting emotions—hope battling despair, trust warring with suspicion.

As I made my way to the podium, I caught glimpses of familiar faces: Old Mrs. Henderson, her rheumy eyes brimming with tears; Tom from the hardware store, his jaw clenched tight. And there, in the back, a silhouette that looked eerily like Johnny.

I blinked, and it vanished—a ghost haunting the edges of my vision.

Taking a deep breath, I faced the crowd, ready to offer promises I wasn't sure I could keep.

I gripped the podium's edges, my knuckles whitening as I surveyed the sea of faces. The room fell into an uneasy silence, broken only by an occasional cough or whispered comment.

"Good evening, everyone," I begin, my voice composed despite the storm churning inside me. "I stand before you not only as your new sheriff but as a member of this community, sharing your pain and your hope." The words ring hollow in my mouth, yet I press on. "These past months have tested us all. The trust between law enforcement and our community has been... fractured." A murmur ripples through the crowd. I glimpse Ashley in the corner, her eyes urging me forward. "That's why we're introducing new transparency measures," I continue, infusing conviction into my tone. "Body cameras, civilian oversight committees, monthly public reports..." As I outline our plans, I can't escape the sense that Johnny's watching, weighing every word. Did he feel this same weight, standing here, making promises he couldn't keep?

"But more than any policy," I say, my voice dropping low, "I want you to know that we—that I—understand your pain, your anger, your fear." The admission lingers in the air, laden with unspoken truths. For a moment, I'm tempted to confess everything—the crushing guilt I carry, the secrets threatening to unravel me. But I swallow them, burying them deep where even I can't reach. "We can't change the past," I conclude, "but together, we can forge a safer, more transparent future. Thank you." As I step from the podium, the applause is tepid, hesitant. But it's a start. It has to be.

Fog rolls in as Ashley and I walk down Main Street, our footsteps echoing off the brick facades. The town's eerie stillness drapes around us, hushed and watchful. "You did well back there, Mike," Ashley says, her voice soft yet earnest. "I think they're starting to believe in us again."

I grunt, unconvinced. "Belief's a slippery thing—easy to lose, damn near impossible to regain." We pass the old hardware store, its windows dark and accusing. How many times had Johnny and I grabbed coffee there, mapping out our days? The memory cuts into my gut like a blade.

"But they're listening," Ashley presses. "Did you see Mrs. Thornton? She actually smiled when I mentioned the community outreach program."

"One smile doesn't erase years of distrust," I mutter, then pause. "But... you're right. It's something."

I push open the heavy door to the sheriff's office, the familiar scent of stale coffee and dusty files washing over me. Ashley follows, her footsteps light and eager. "Let's start with the Jameson case," I say, pulling a thick file from the cabinet. "Time we look at it through a new lens." Ashley nods, her eyes alight. "Mental health awareness could change everything."

We spread the files across my desk, a tapestry of tragedy and missed chances. As we pore over the details, a shift stirs between us. It's no longer just mentor and mentee—it's a partnership forged in shared purpose. "What if we'd known then what we know now?" Ashley muses, her finger tracing a line in the report. "About trauma... about triggers." I grunt, a familiar paranoia creeping at my mind's edge. "Knowledge is power, they say. But it's a burden, too."

Ashley looks up, concern etched across her freckled face. "Mike, are you—"

"I'm fine," I interrupt, my tone sharper than intended. But then she flashes a mischievous grin, her eyes glinting with playful defiance.

"You know what this case needs? Donuts. Stat."

A chuckle escapes me, the tension easing from my shoulders. "Careful, rookie. You're leaning into a dangerous stereotype there."

"Oh, please," she shoots back, already striding toward the door. "Like you can resist a maple bar."

As she vanishes, a faint smile lingers on my lips. Her lightness is a balm, holding the darkness at bay. Yet a treacherous voice murmurs: How long before she follows you down into the rot that festers beneath Stormy Valley's charm?

I shove the thought aside, focusing on the files spread before me. The names blur, each one a potential victim, each a stark reminder of my failures. In the depths of my mind, Johnny's laughter echoes faintly.

The school hallway hums with the patter of small feet and high-pitched chatter. I steel myself, adjusting my badge and forcing a smile that feels like a brittle mask. The classroom door looms ahead, a threshold to an innocence I'm not sure I deserve to enter.

"Welcome, Sheriff Langley!" Mrs. Hendricks beams, ushering me inside. Two dozen pairs of eyes lock onto me, a sea of curiosity brimming with barely contained energy.

"Mornin', kids," I say, my voice rougher than I'd like. A few nervous giggles ripple through the room.

As I scan their faces—rosy cheeks, gap-toothed grins, eyes alight with possibility—a lump rises in my throat. These are the futures I'm sworn to protect, the reason I haul myself out of bed each morning, carrying everything I can't forget.

"Who can tell me what mental health means?" I ask, leaning against the teacher's desk.

A freckled boy in the front row thrusts his hand up. "It's like... when your brain feels good?"

"That's part of it, son," I say, nodding, resisting the urge to ruffle his hair. "But sometimes our brains need help, just like our bodies do when we're sick."

A girl with pigtails furrows her brow. "Can you catch it? Like a cold?"

"No, sweetheart," I reply, my chest tightening. "But sometimes bad things happen that hurt us inside, where no one can see."

Their faces clouded with confusion. For a second, I thought about how fast innocence can crack once the real world gets ahold of it.

"Have any of you ever felt really sad or scared, even when everything seemed okay?" I ask, my voice soft.

A chorus of small voices responds, some eager, some tentative. As I listen to their simple fears—monsters under the bed, lost pets, spats with friends—a quiet ache stirs within me, envious of their unblemished world.

"It's okay to feel those things," I assure them, my voice trembling on the edge of breaking. "The important thing is to talk to someone you trust—a parent, a teacher, or even..." I tap my badge, "...someone like me."

A lanky boy in the back, all elbows and knees, raises his hand. "Have you ever been scared, Sheriff?"

The question lands like a sucker punch. For a fleeting moment, I'm back in that cruiser, the world spiraling, Johnny's accusations echoing in my ears. I swallow hard, shoving the memory down.

"Yeah, buddy," I admit, meeting his eyes. "I have. And that's okay. Being brave isn't about never being scared—it's about doing what's right even when you are."

As the words leave my lips, I wonder who I'm really trying to convince—the children or myself.

The fluorescent lights of the sheriff's office hum faintly as Ashley and I sink into our chairs. It had been a long day, and it showed. The scent of stale coffee lingered, a reminder of countless hours spent here, strategizing and second-guessing.

"How'd it go at the school?" Ashley asks, her eyes still bright despite the late hour.

I run a hand over my mustache, stalling for a moment. "It was... eye-opening," I finally say. "Those kids, Ash—so innocent, yet already carrying burdens we can't see."

She nods, understanding etched across her youthful face. "That's why we're doing this, right? To give them a shot at something better?"

"Yeah," I sigh, the word laden with unspoken doubts. "But sometimes I wonder if we're just fighting a losing battle."

Ashley leans forward, her tone leaving no room for argument. "Don't say that, Michael. You saw the community at the town hall. They're ready for change."

I want to believe her—God knows I do—but the past doesn't let go. It lingers, whispering every mistake I swore I'd never repeat.

"You're right," I concede, my conviction wavering. "So, what's our next move?"

As Ashley outlines her plans for community outreach, my thoughts drift. Johnny's face swims before me, his gaze accusing, tormented. I blink hard, anchoring myself to the present.

"...and maybe a support group for families touched by addiction?" Ashley says, her enthusiasm a tangible force.

I nod, clinging to her energy like a lifeline. "Solid idea. We'll start drafting a proposal tomorrow."

As Ashley gathers her things to leave, a pang of guilt gnaws at me. She deserves a mentor unburdened by the past, not a man barely holding his demons at bay.

"You did good today, kid," I say, meaning every word. "Get some rest."

The door clicks shut behind her, leaving me with the encroaching silence. I lean back in my chair, its familiar creak a hollow echo of human connection.

The evening's quiet wraps around me like a shroud. Outside, Stormy Valley slumbers, oblivious to the turmoil churning within its new protector. I close my eyes, but find no solace there.

Images flash unbidden—Johnny's blank stare, the children's trusting faces, Ashley's steady faith. It all sat heavy in my chest, a pressure I couldn't shake.

"You can do this," I mutter, the words ringing hollow in the empty room. "You have to."

But as the night deepens, my doubts grow heavier. The road ahead stretches long and shadowed, fraught with unseen perils and ghosts of past mistakes. Somewhere in the darkness, a reckoning looms.

I rise from my chair, joints creaking in protest. The floorboards murmur beneath my steps as I cross to the window, drawn by an unspoken urge.

Outside, Stormy Valley lies bathed in twilight's gentle embrace. The fading light paints the town in hues of lavender and gold, softening reality's harsh edges. For a fleeting moment, I see it as it could be—whole, healed, free from tragedy's burden.

"Ain't that a sight," I murmur, my breath misting the glass.

The soft glow of streetlamps flickers to life, like fireflies rising from the deepening dusk. In the distance, a dog barks, its sound muted and dreamlike. The air hums, carrying a sense that something might change.

I press my palm against the cool windowpane, half-expecting to feel the town's pulse thrumming beneath my fingers. "We'll make it right," I vow, uncertain to whom I speak. "Somehow."

A chill runs down my spine, a reminder of the challenges still lurking. Yet, for this fleeting moment, I felt hope pushing through the dark, fragile but real.

I turn from the window, my resolve fortified by the vision of what might be. I don't know if I'll ever be the man Johnny was—or even the man Ashley thinks I am. Hell, some days I don't know who I'm trying to be at all. But tonight, for the first time in weeks, the ground beneath me feels solid. I can see the spiral I've been in, the damage I've done. And I'm still here. Still breathing. Still willing to try. Tomorrow brings no guarantees—just another chance to carve a better path.

I gather my things, fingers brushing over the files on my desk—tragedy, maybe, but not failure. Not if we do better this time. As I step into the hall and close the door behind me, I let the quiet settle. Not the silence of guilt, but something simpler. Something closer to peace. For the first time in years, I find myself anticipating what the future might hold. And somewhere in that stillness, behind the walls of the psychiatric ward, I picture Johnny gazing into the dusk, searching for the peace that eluded him in daylight.

22

Final Days

Beth's smile stares back at me from the photograph, frozen in time, taken one ordinary morning before school. Her flannel shirt hung loose on her shoulders, her dark hair caught back in a scrunchie, gold hoops glinting as she smiled at me. Just Beth, young and alive, the way I wanted to remember her.

As evening shadows settle over Stormy Valley, my office seems to shrink around me, trapping me. Every decision, every transgression—carved into me like bone-deep scars.

I trace Beth's outline with a trembling finger. "I'm sorry," I whisper, my voice fracturing. The words linger in the stillness, unanswered.

Guilt gnaws at my core as I recall her laugh, her touch. How did it come to this?

The clock ticks, a relentless reminder of time slipping away. I should leave, but my legs refuse to move. Beth's eyes hold me captive, accusing yet forgiving in the same breath.

A knock at the door snaps me back to the present. Dr. Chen's voice drifts through, "Sheriff McCallister? It's time for our session."

I sigh, bracing myself. Another battle looms. The clinic is quiet now—not the soothing kind, but the sterile silence of observation windows, locked drawers, and daily medications.

The walk to Dr. Chen's office passes in a blur. I sink into the familiar leather chair, its creaks a fleeting reprieve from the storm raging in my mind.

Dr. Chen's steady voice pierces the silence. "How are you feeling today, Johnny?"

I focus on my hands, doing everything I can not to meet her eyes. "Fine," I mutter, the lie bitter on my tongue.

She waits, her patience maddening. I want to scream, to rage against the unfairness of it all. Instead, I stay silent, a war churning beneath my skin.

"You seem troubled," she probes gently. "Would you like to talk about what's on your mind?"

I nearly laugh. Where would I even begin? The words spill out before I can stop them. "I keep seeing her. Beth. She's everywhere."

Dr. Chen leans forward, her eyes softening. "That must be hard for you."

Hard? It's tearing me apart. But I can't say that. Can't show weakness. "It's nothing," I deflect, my jaw tightening.

"Johnny," she says, her voice a soothing balm, "it's okay to feel pain. To grieve."

I shake my head, memories threatening to engulf me. "You don't understand. It's my fault. All of it."

The confession lingers, damning and dense. Dr. Chen remains silent, waiting for me to continue. But I've said too much. The walls close in, and I can't breathe.

"I think we're done for today," I mutter, rising abruptly. Dr. Chen's protests fade as I flee, Beth's accusing gaze trailing me into the deepening darkness.

The sterile hallway of the clinic warps and twists as I stumble out, my heart hammering a frantic rhythm against my ribs. Beth's face flickers at the edges of my vision, her eyes accusing, her lips moving in silent reproach.

"Not real," I mutter, pressing my palms against my temples. "She's not real."

But the murmurs swell, a cacophony of guilt and regret threatening to drown me. I fumble for my car keys, desperate to escape.

The world lurches, and I'm thrust back to that cursed intersection, the screech of tires and shattering glass echoing in my ears. Beth's scream cuts through, a blade to my soul.

"No!" I gasp, stumbling backward. My back strikes something solid—my cruiser. The cold metal grounds me, if only for a moment.

"Sheriff? You okay?" Mike's gruff voice slices through the haze.

I blink, finding myself in the Sheriff's Office parking lot. How did I get here?

"Johnny?" Ashley's softer tone follows, concern etched across her freckled face.

I force a smile, but it twists into a grimace. "Fine," I lie, the word hollow even to me. "Just... lost in thought."

Mike's bushy mustache twitches, his eyes narrowing. "You look like hell, boss. Maybe take some time off."

"I'm fine," I snap, the words reflexive. Yet, even as they leave my lips, Beth's phantom fingers graze my cheek, her touch icy and accusing.

Ashley steps closer, her voice low. "We're worried about you, Johnny. You don't have to face this alone."

Their concern chokes me. I want to lash out, to shove them away. Instead, I nod stiffly. "Appreciate it. But I've got work to do."

As I brush past them, my reflection in the cruiser's window catches my eye. A stranger stares back, hollow-eyed and haunted.

Beth's whisper slithers into my ear. "Come home, Johnny. It's time."

I shudder, hastening my steps. The line between memory and madness blurs, and I no longer know which side I'm on.

My badge presses against my chest as I push open the office door, an anchor I can't shake. The familiar scent of stale coffee and old case files washes over me, anchoring me to the present. Amid the storm of my troubled thoughts, a sudden clarity pierces through—Sam Thompson. He stands before me, guilty of nothing but the ache of missing his high school sweetheart, Sarah Lawson, mourning her tragic death as I mourn Beth's.

I sink into my worn leather chair, its creaks a mournful melody underscoring my thoughts. I look at the dusty photo frame on my desk. Beth's flannel, that old scrunchie, the gold hoops—details I once found so ordinary—now feel like relics. Her smile is still radiant, frozen in time, but instead of comforting me it sharpens the ache of everything I've lost.

"Christ, Beth," I whisper, my voice fracturing. "What have I done?"

Memories flood back, vivid and sharp for the first time in years. Laughter echoing through our cramped first apartment. The sparkle in her eyes when I proposed by the lake. The pride in her voice when I became sheriff, a faith I failed to live up to.

And then... that night. Whiskey sour on my breath. The sickening crunch of metal.

"I should've been stronger," I mutter, tracing Beth's face with a trembling finger. "Should've put the damn bottle down."

The truth settles slowly, cold and tight around my chest. Every choice I made—every line I blurred, every rule I bent—it's all still here, coiled around me. Not justice. Just damage.

Beth's voice, a ghostly murmur: "You were always your own worst enemy, Johnny."

I close my eyes, fighting tears. "I know, sweetheart. I know."

When I open them, the photograph seems altered. Beth's smile now carries a trace of sorrow, her eyes accusing. The frame's edges blur, reality shifting like quicksand beneath me.

"I'm sorry," I choke out, guilt and grief threatening to engulf me. "God, I'm so sorry."

But apologies can't resurrect the dead. They can't undo the harm I've caused. As shadows lengthen in my office, I'm left alone with what I've done... and the inability to fix any of it.

A chill seeps through the air, raising goosebumps on my arms. Beth's photograph shimmers, and suddenly she's there, perched on the edge of my desk—not the Beth from the accident, broken and bloodied, but my Beth, radiant and alive.

"Johnny," she says, her voice a balm to my shattered soul. "You can't keep torturing yourself like this."

I reach out, desperate to touch her, but my hand passes through empty air. "I killed you, Beth. How can I forgive myself?"

She leans closer, her spectral presence filling the room with the scent of wildflowers. "It was an accident, love. You must let go."

"I can't," I whisper, shame searing my chest. "I don't deserve peace."

Beth's eyes, impossibly kind, pierce mine. "You do. And I forgive you."

Her words hit harder than anything I could bear. Tears blur my vision as the room shifts around me.

"Sheriff McCallister? Johnny, can you hear me?"

Dr. Chen's voice pulls me back to her office. The leather couch creaks as I shift, disoriented.

"You were miles away," she says softly. "Where did you go?"

I grunt, evading her searching gaze. "Nowhere important."

She leans forward, concern etched across her face. "Johnny, we've talked about this. Bottling things up isn't helping. You need to let it out."

A bitter laugh claws its way out. "Let it out? And say what? That I'm losing my damn mind? That I see my dead wife everywhere?"

"Is that what's happening?" Dr. Chen asks, her voice frustratingly composed.

I rise abruptly, pacing like a caged animal. "What does it matter? You can't fix me. No one can."

"I'm not trying to fix you, Johnny. I'm trying to help you heal."

But her words dissolve into static as Beth's apparition reappears, beckoning from the corner. I squeeze my eyes shut, willing her away, but she lingers—a beautiful, tormenting specter of all I've lost.

I stumble out of Dr. Chen's office, her concerned calls fading behind me. The world tilts and blurs, reality melting like wax under a flame. Suddenly, I'm back on that winding country road, headlights slicing through the dark. Beth's laughter echoes in my ears.

"Johnny, slow down!" she giggles, fear edging her voice.

I grip the steering wheel, knuckles white. "It's fine, Lizzy. I've got this."

But I don't. The road curves sharply, trees looming. Metal screams. Glass shatters.

"No!" I cry, jolted back to the present, clutching my head. Passersby stare, but I scarcely notice.

Beth's whisper brushes my ear: "It wasn't your fault."

"It was," I mutter. "I was drunk. I killed you."

Her ghostly hand grazes my cheek. "You've punished yourself enough."

I shake my head violently, trying to banish her soothing presence. It's a lie. A delusion. I don't deserve solace.

Somehow, I'm in my empty house. The silence deafens. Photos of Beth and me taunt me from every wall. I slump into my armchair, haunted not by Beth, but by the years without her—collapsing in on me like a wave I can't outrun.

"What am I doing?" I whisper into the void. "How did I end up here?"

No answer comes. Only the clock's relentless ticking, marking time I no longer feel entitled to.

The air shimmers, and Beth materializes, radiant as the day we met. Her eyes, once alive with spark, now hold an otherworldly wisdom.

"Johnny," she says softly, extending her hand. "It's time to come home."

My heart races. "Home?" I echo, my voice barely a whisper.

She nods, a gentle smile playing on her lips. "Where the pain ends. Where we can be together again."

I reach out, hand trembling. "But I don't deserve—"

"Hush," Beth interrupts, her touch impossibly warm for a hallucination. "You've carried this burden long enough."

Tears blur my vision. "I've made so many mistakes, Beth. I've hurt people."

"We all have," she says, pulling me to my feet. "But you've also protected this town and helped its people. It's time to forgive yourself."

I feel lighter, the crushing weight of guilt beginning to lift. "Will it hurt?" I ask, suddenly afraid.

Beth laughs—light and distant, like wind chimes. "No, my love. It's like falling asleep after a long, tiring day."

I look around my dim living room, seeing it as if for the last time—the faded curtains, the worn carpet, all the trappings of a life half-lived.

"What about the town?" I murmur. "They need a sheriff."

"They'll manage. They've got Mike and Ashley," Beth assures me. "You've done your part."

I take a deep breath, inhaling the lingering scent of pine and old leather that's always clung to me. Then look to Beth and nod, the fear fading.

"Okay," I whisper. "I'm ready."

As I embrace her, the world around us fades. The pain in my head vanishes, replaced by a profound sense of peace. Beth's arms are warm and real, and for the first time in years, I feel whole —a warmth that feels like coming home after a long, treacherous journey. The world dissolves into a soft, hazy light.

"I've missed you," I whisper, my voice thick with emotion. "Every day, every moment."

Beth's fingers intertwine with mine. "I know, Johnny. I've been waiting for you."

As we stand in this liminal space between worlds, memories flood my mind—not the dark, haunting ones that have plagued me for years, but moments of pure joy and love.

"Remember our first date?" I ask, a wistful smile tugging at my lips. "That picnic by Stormy Creek?"

Beth's laughter echoes around us. "You were so nervous, you spilled lemonade all over yourself."

"And you still kissed me," I muse, relishing the memory.

The light grows brighter, and I feel a gentle tugging sensation. "Is it time?" I ask, a ripple of unease whispering through my chest.

Beth nods, her eyes shining with unshed tears. "Are you afraid?"

I consider this for a moment. "No," I realize, surprised by my own certainty. "Not anymore."

As we drift toward the light, I cast one last glance behind me. The burdens I carried—guilt, sorrow, every hard-won scar—dissolve into the fading dusk.

"Thank you," I murmur, to Beth, to the town I protected, to the life I lived. "For everything."

The light envelops us completely, and a profound sense of peace washes over me. In this moment, I understand that love—imperfect, messy, and beautiful—was always the answer.

And so, hand in hand with Beth, I step forward into the unknown, leaving behind all my earthly burdens and embracing the promise of what lies ahead.

23
Legacy and Reflection

The fog clings to the tombstones, heavy as mourning itself, obscuring the edges of the cemetery. I stand apart, watching the somber procession file in. It has been nearly ten months since Johnny's breakdown, five since the trial, and one quiet week since the call came from Lakeside. He went quietly, the nurse said, like someone who'd already been halfway gone. Familiar faces emerge from the mist—Mayor Thompson's perpetual frown, old Mrs. Wilkins, damp handkerchief trembling in her grip. Ashley's stoic mask. They gather around the fresh-dug grave, a sea of black against the damp grass.

Johnny's casket gleams dully in the weak sunlight. I can almost hear his gruff voice: "Damn waste of good wood, if you ask me." The thought brings a wry smile to my lips, quickly hidden.

Reverend Holbrook's reedy voice cuts through the silence. "We are gathered here today to lay to rest Sheriff Johnathan McCallister..."

My mind drifts as the eulogy washes over me. Memories flicker like an old film reel—Johnny and I sharing a celebratory whiskey after closing a tough case, his rare belly laugh echoing through the office. Then darker images intrude—the wild look in his eyes as he ranted about conspiracies, the tremor in his hands as he reached for his gun.

"He was a good man," I mutter, more to convince myself than anyone else.

Ashley glances over, brow furrowed. "You okay, Mike?"

I nod, not trusting my voice. How can I explain the tangle of emotions choking me? Grief for the man I'd called friend, relief that his suffering had ended, guilt over the secrets I'd kept. And underneath it all, a gnawing fear—what if Johnny's demons weren't all just in his head?

I close my eyes, remembering the feel of Johnny's hand on my shoulder. "You're a good cop, Mike," he'd said. "Better than me, maybe. Don't let this town down." I'd promised I wouldn't. But standing here, the words I'd meant now tasting like failure, I wonder if I already have.

Lynn Miller's voice wavers as she concludes, "Johnny dedicated his life to protecting Stormy Valley. May his spirit watch over us all."

Scattered coughs, a muffled sob, the shuffle of shoes on damp grass—grief spilling unevenly through the crowd, each person carrying their own reasons for standing here. I draw a slow breath, the weight of it settling deep in my chest. If they only knew the truth...

"Time to move," Ashley murmurs, her small hand brushing my elbow.

We fall into step, leading the somber procession. The gravel crunches beneath our feet, each step a reminder of all we've lost and an echo of promises I'm not sure I'll be able to keep. I want to run, to confess, to scream into the eerie stillness of the pines. Instead, I walk on, unsure if I'm honoring him—or just wearing the badge and title he left behind.

"Remember that time Johnny talked down old man Granger?" Ashley asks, her voice barely above a whisper.

I nod, grateful for the distraction. "Twelve-hour standoff. Thought it'd never end."

"But Johnny, he just kept talking. So calm." Her eyes shimmer. "I hope I can be half the cop he was."

My chest tightens. If she only knew the doubts that plagued Johnny, the paranoia that ate away at his mind. But I can't shatter her illusions. Not yet. Maybe not ever.

"You will be," I say quietly, wishing I could believe it as fully as she does. "Johnny saw something special in you."

She smiles, a fragile thing in the gathering gloom. We walk on, guardians of a legacy built on shifting sands.

The casket settles into the earth, a stark punctuation mark on a story none of us were ready to end. My fingers twitch, longing for the familiar comfort of a cigarette—an addiction I buried long ago.

"Ashes to ashes," the preacher intones, his words carried away by the wind.

I close my eyes, memories flooding in unbidden: that night on the jogging trail, the metallic tang of blood, Johnny's wild eyes. My silence then, my silence now. The toll of it all surrounding me, threatening to crush me.

From the corner of my eye I notice a figure lingering just beyond the headstones—gaunt, shoulders stooped, face thinned to sharp planes by years of confinement. William Perry.

He doesn't approach the grave, doesn't speak. Just stands there, cap twisting in his hands, eyes fixed on Johnny's casket as if searching for absolution he'll never find.

The air seems to thin around him. A few townsfolk notice, their murmurs tightening into a hush. Someone mutters, "He's got some nerve," before steering their children away.

Ashley glances toward him, brows knit in confusion. "Who's that?"

I shake my head quickly. "No one you need to worry about."

"You okay, Mike?" Ashley's voice cuts through my spiraling thoughts.

I force a nod, my throat too tight for words. She doesn't push, bless her. Instead, she turns her gaze back to the grave, her red curls catching the light like dying embers.

"I keep thinking about what he taught me," she murmurs, almost to herself. "Not just the procedures, you know? But how to read people, how to de-escalate."

A laugh nearly escapes me. Johnny used to say de-escalation was ninety percent patience and ten percent luck—and he was always short on patience.

"He was... complicated," I manage, the understatement of the century.

Ashley nods, her eyes distant. "I want to make him proud. To be the kind of deputy he believed I could be."

The irony is stark. Here she is, aspiring to an ideal that never truly existed. And here I am, keeper of the truth, too cowardly to shatter her illusions.

As the first handfuls of dirt hit the casket, I wonder how long it will be before more shadows of Stormy Valley come calling, demanding their due.

My eyes drift to the adjacent headstone, and I freeze. Elizabeth McCallister. The name hits me like a punch to the gut.

"Beth..." Ashley whispers, her freckled face paling. "You don't think...?"

I nod slowly, the memory rushing back—a double date years ago, Johnny laughing, calling her Lizzy. No wonder the wires crossed. No wonder he couldn't separate the past from the hallucinations.

Our eyes meet, the truth dawning in silence. The pieces are falling into place, and the picture they're forming is both distressing and disheartening.

As the crowd begins to thin, I step back from the grave and let the breeze settle over my shoulders. I recognize most of the remaining faces—Ashley lingering by the headstone, Mayor Thompson talking too loudly to no one in particular.

But one figure stands apart from the rest, half in shadow. Jeanette Malone, editor of the Stormy Valley Sentinel, doesn't approach the casket or speak. She just watches, taking a piece of paper, folding it and carefully encasing it in an envelope. She waits until the last of the guests turn away. Then she steps forward, kneels beside the grave, and slips the envelope beneath a loose stone by the flowers.

I don't ask. I just nod as she passes. She nods back.

I turn toward Ashley, still standing by the headstone, arms crossed, eyes distant. The wind catches the hem of her coat, and for a moment, she looks smaller than usual—tired in a way that has nothing to do with sleep.

I cross to her slowly, careful not to intrude on whatever thoughts she's chasing.

"We should head to the square," I say gently, just loud enough for her to hear. "People will be gathering."

She glances up and nods. Her usual warmth is dimmed by everything that's taken place—too much, too fast, and few, if any, clear answers. As we fall into step together, I can practically hear the gears turning in her head. She's too smart for her own good sometimes.

The town square is a sea of muted colors and hushed voices when we arrive. Folks cluster in small groups, sharing stories about Johnny. Some laugh, some cry, but an undercurrent of unease runs through me, impossible to shake.

"Remember when he talked down that jumper on Miller's Bridge?" Harry chuckles, his eyes misty with memory.

"Or the time he organized that search party for little Timmy Jensen," Martha adds, clutching her handbag like a lifeline.

I nod along, playing my part in this collective myth-making. But my eyes keep scanning the crowd, searching for... what? A sign? A threat? I'm not even sure anymore.

I drift through the crowd like a ghost, my smile a mask that threatens to slip with every handshake, every murmured condolence. I carry my worries like smuggled contraband—tucked deep, fragile, dangerous. But today I carry it a little straighter. Maybe that's what leadership is: moving forward even when the truth is heavier than anyone knows.

"Mike, you alright?" Frank Peterson's voice cuts through my spiraling thoughts. "You're looking a mite pale."

I force a chuckle, but it sounds hollow even to my ears. "Just the strain of the day, Frank. You know how it is."

"Johnny was a good man," Frank says, his voice thick with truth—and maybe forgiveness.

I nod, the ache tightening behind my ribs. "Yeah."

Not perfect. Not unbroken. But he never stopped trying, even when the darkness closed in.

Across the square, I spot Ashley deep in conversation with Edna Wilkins, the town librarian. Even from here, I can see the determination etched on her young face, the set of her shoulders speaking of a resolve beyond her years.

"...and I promise you, Mrs. Wilkins, we'll do everything in our power to keep this town safe," Ashley's voice carries on the breeze. "Just like Johnny would've wanted."

The sincerity in her tone stirs a deep ache in me. She believes every word she's saying, and that makes it all the worse. Because I know the truth, and it's far uglier than she could ever imagine.

I turn away, unable to face the trust in her eyes—trust I haven't earned. The crowd blurs into a sea of expectation, all of it misplaced.

How long can I keep up this charade, alone, before it all comes crashing down around me?

The sun dips low, draping the town square in deep gold and gathering dusk. I slip away from the crowd, their murmurs fading as I find refuge behind the old oak tree at the edge of the cemetery. Its gnarled branches offer a semblance of privacy, a momentary reprieve from the crushing weight of expectation.

I lean against the rough bark, exhaling slowly. "What now, Johnny?" I whisper to the gathering twilight. "How am I supposed to keep this town together without you?"

The breeze whispers through the leaves, offering no answers. In the distance, a dog barks, its sound echoing off the hills that cradle our little town.

A twig snaps nearby, and I stiffen. "Sheriff Langley?" It's George Wilson, his voice tinged with concern. "You alright?"

I force a smile, stepping out from behind the tree. "Just needed a moment, George. It's been a long day."

He nods, understanding in his eyes. If only he knew.

As George ambles away, I look to the sheriff's office, a beacon in uncertainty surrounding us. Ashley's silhouette moves past the window as she starts her shift, and a pang of guilt, sharp enough to nearly double me over, strikes me.

She's out there now, patrolling our streets with a determination I remember from my younger days. It's not naivety—it's belief. I envy it, even if I can't share it yet.

I watch as Ashley's cruiser rolls slowly down Main Street, her watchful eyes scanning the sidewalks. The townsfolk wave as she passes, their faces a mix of sorrow and hope.

"Evening, Mrs. Patterson," Ashley calls out the window. "Everything okay at the diner tonight?"

"Just fine, Deputy," comes the reply. "You take care out there, you hear?"

Ashley's "Yes, ma'am" floats back on the night air, and my chest tightens. She's so damn earnest, so committed to upholding Johnny's legacy. If she only knew the whole truth about the man she idolized, about the darkness lurking beneath Stormy Valley's quaint facade.

As Ashley's cruiser disappears around the corner, I'm left alone with the encroaching night and my conscience. How long before the ghosts of my past—our town's past—demand their due?

The night creeps in, and I shiver, though not from the cold. Stormy Valley may seem peaceful now, but I know better. Storms are brewing on the horizon, inevitable as ever. I lean against the weathered facade of the general store, my eyes fixed on the spot where Ashley's cruiser vanished. The street swallows my feet in shadowy tendrils, as if the town itself is trying to pull me under.

Tom Wilkins emerges, eyes bleary but sharp. "Johnny would've been proud," he says at last. "She's good. Got hope in her still." He shuffles slowly away, swallowed by the fog.

Left alone, I draw a long breath of the chilled air and push off from the wall, my footsteps echoing in the empty street. Each step feels heavier than the last, as if the ground itself is trying to swallow me whole. The myth of Johnny, and everything the town expects me to live up to, bears down like armor I never agreed to wear.

"What am I doing?" I ask the empty streets. "Trying to be something better. For him. For her. For this town." Maybe that's the only answer that matters.

I pause at the corner, staring down the road that leads out of town. For a moment, I consider walking away from it all. But I know I can't. This town, these people—they're part of me now, for better or worse.

I glance at my reflection in the darkened window—a tired man, haunted but standing. "You've made your bed, Michael," I mutter. "Now you've got to lie in it."

The fog closes in as I walk on. Stormy Valley isn't healed yet—but it's still mine to guard. And maybe, just maybe, we're ready to face the dawn.

About the author

Ruthie Ambrose writes unsettling stories about fractured identities, haunted landscapes, and the quiet weight of things left unsaid. Her work unfolds across a multiverse jukebox of worlds—each track spinning with memory, mystery, and just enough madness to keep the ghosts talking.

When she's not writing, her feline editors remind her who's really in charge.

Stormy Valley is her debut novel.

Thanks for Reading Stormy Valley!

Bonus Story - The Ink's Secrets

If you're craving something stranger, something a little more surreal—your bonus story is ready.

The Ink's Secrets pulls back the veil on a different kind of reality, where memory distorts and truth doesn't sit still.

A Note Before You Begin: This story contains spoilers for Stormy Valley, proceed with caution.

Get your Copy today: https://dl.bookfunnel.com/td8epx81tg

This bonus novella is available free only until **December 31, 2025.** A digital release is planned for 2026.

The Ink's Secrets is part of that larger journey. It's a standalone tale, but it echoes with the same undercurrents you've just explored. Across worlds, Ande shifts from silent observer to reluctant participant, uncovering truths that bind—or unravel—the souls they encounter. Some entries lean surreal, some speculative, others intimate or philosophical—but they all explore what it means to exist across lives, and still remain... you.

The Ainsingly Chronicles is a multiversal narrative cycle.

The next entry, *Winter's Shadow*, is slated for release in Spring 2026.

www.ingramcontent.com/pod-product-compliance
Lightning Source LLC
Chambersburg PA
CBHW050325110726
47899CB00007B/2372